Should she...?

No. Ridiculous.

But he'd looked so sad, and she had to admit how edible his lips looked—

"Liam. Wait."

He paused and turned halfway to Kate, an eyebrow raised in silent question.

Yes. Try something new.

She rushed forward and rose high on her toes. His visor was cold against her forehead but his lips were so, so warm. And delicious. Like the kind of white candies that were supposed to spark when you chewed them in the dark. *Wintermint.*

Before she could pull away, a gloved hand cradled the back of her head and the kiss slowed, his mouth moving over hers as if he had all the time in the world and there wasn't a hockey game waiting for him. His tongue tangled with hers, and a rock-solid arm kept her from lowering to her heels.

Dear Reader,

A personal story before giving Kate and Liam the stage: At the same time the hockey lockout of 2004–05 left me with extra time on my hands, I read my first hockey romance. I fell in love with the subgenre and decided to write one of my own. That first manuscript remains in a figurative box under the bed, but putting my fingers to the keyboard in place of cheering on the Canucks was the beginning of my publication journey.

All this to say, hockey romance is one of my true loves, and I am thrilled to be writing my first for Harlequin Special Edition! Welcome to the world of the Denver Daggers, and the first Lucky Shot romance, where a kiss between the coach's daughter and a struggling star player lights up more than the goal lamp. Romance is the last thing on Liam Caldwell's mind, until Kate Sullivan skates into his life. Her job teaching minor-league hockey skills reminds him how much hockey is about community, something he's been missing while moving from team to team. Whether falling in love is enough to convince Liam to finally grow roots...read on!

To keep up-to-date on future Lucky Shot romances, my website laurelgreer.com has info, extras and a link to my newsletter. You can also find me on Facebook or Instagram. I'm @laurelgreerauthor on both, and would love to connect!

Happy reading!

Laurel

THEIR PLAYOFF ARRANGEMENT

LAUREL GREER

Recycling programs for this product may not exist in your area.

ISBN-13: 978-1-335-18041-4

Their Playoff Arrangement

For questions and comments about the quality of this book, please contact us at CustomerService@Harlequin.com.

Harlequin Enterprises ULC
22 Adelaide St. West, 41st Floor
Toronto, Ontario M5H 4E3, Canada
www.Harlequin.com

HarperCollins Publishers
Macken House, 39/40 Mayor Street Upper,
Dublin 1, D01 C9W8, Ireland
www.HarperCollins.com

Printed in Lithuania

USA TODAY bestselling author **Laurel Greer** loves writing about all the ways love can change people for the better, especially when messy families and charming small towns are involved. She lives outside Vancouver, BC, with her law-talking husband and two daughters, and is never far from a cup of tea, a good book or the ocean—preferably all three. Find her at laurelgreer.com.

Books by Laurel Greer

Montana Mavericks: The Tenacity Social Club

A Maverick Worth Waiting For

Harlequin Special Edition

A Lucky Shot Romance

Their Playoff Arrangement

Love at Hideaway Wharf

Diving into Forever
A Hideaway Wharf Holiday
Their Unexpected Forever
A Season of Second Chances

Visit the Author Profile page
at Harlequin.com for more titles.

To Ellie, my best bear forever—
happy sixteenth birthday. You have a book to
catch up on for each of those years. I hope you
enjoy every one, even though there are no dragons.

Chapter One

TWENTY-PLUS GOOSE-EGG GAMES FOR SHARP-SHOOTER CALDWELL
Was the midseason signing a bust for the playoff-cusp Denver Daggers?
Denver Star, March 30

Clang-g-g.

The sound—vulcanized rubber ringing off a cold metal goalpost—had featured in Liam Caldwell's nightmares for weeks.

"You hit the post eleven times."

The overly precise observation carried a wallop, even delivered in the voice of a child.

Liam spun on his blades to see who'd interrupted his solo ice time. A pint-size figure occupied the home team's bench, arms draped over the boards. If he had to guess, she was around ten. A long, black braid stuck out from her helmet and hung over one of her shoulders.

"Eleven posts?" he asked.

The kid nodded.

"I counted twelve," Liam said. He skated away from the place on the face-off circle where he'd been practicing hitting targets set up in the corners of the net. Pucks littered the spaces to the right and left of the net. Anywhere but *in* the net.

Didn't matter how long he stayed after his teammates left their game-day skate—it was like his wrist, the one he'd always thought of as his moneymaker, was detached from his body every time he was in a pressure situation.

Two psychologists, who billed a small fortune per hour, hadn't managed to get his head back in the game. Everyone seemed to have an opinion on what Liam needed to do to solve his slump. This kid was probably no different.

"It was definitely eleven," she said.

"I'll take your word for it."

His minor-league critic shouldn't be in this part of the facility. The Hollow Valley community used two ice sheets of the Denver Daggers' practice arena, but this one—as well as a gym, offices, lounge space and dressing rooms—was reserved for the NHL team's use.

The kid straightened and sidestepped toward the gate. She wore hockey gear similar to Liam's. Her jersey was even the Daggers' royal blue, though the logo on the front was a rodent of some kind, not a stylized blade. Even through her face cage, her confident chin tilt was obvious. She held a stick in one gloved hand. The other was braced in a fist on her hip, reminding him of his mother when she'd lectured him to pick his dirty socks off the living room floor as a teen.

"I'm here for practice, too," she announced.

"You're a bit small to be one of my teammates," he joked. "Maybe you could be a Dagger in ten years or so."

She giggled. "You're silly. I won't be a Dagger."

"You never know."

She shook her helmeted head. "I'll be on Team USA."

He nodded solemnly.

"But you can't be, because you're Canadian," she said.

"True story."

"And you haven't scored a goal in twenty-two games."

"Also true." But unlike his nationality, he hoped his goal scoring drought didn't become part of his identity. This kid was blunt, no question.

"What's your name, wise one?" he asked.

"Maude."

"Nice to meet you, Maude. I'm Liam."

Another ripple of laughter. "I *know.* Liam *Caldwell.*"

Her tone was more uh-yeah-obvious than anything approaching impressed-to-meet-an-NHL-player. He liked this girl's style.

But despite being the opposite of starstruck, she wasn't where she was supposed to be. "Remind me how you got in here?"

Her mouth screwed up for a second. "I'm supposed to wait for my coach."

"Here?"

She nodded. "On the bench. And no going on the ice without an adult."

Huh. Maybe he'd mixed up how the scheduling of the ice sheet worked.

He picked up a nearby puck and lobbed it toward the bench. "You want to show me how it's done?"

Her grin was brighter than the arena downlights. She hopped onto the ice and snagged the skidding puck.

Three power strides and a flick of her wrist, and the puck kissed the target in the top right corner.

Was it normal to be jealous of a 10U player?

"You have an excellent shot," he said.

"My uncle taught me." She skated around the net and started collecting the pucks he'd failed to bag, shooting them in his direction. One by one, he caught them and scooted them into a pile. Didn't have to stretch far to receive the passes—the kid was deadly accurate.

"Your uncle, eh?"

"He's a Dagger, like you. So's my grandpa."

"How can your grandpa be a—" *Oh, wait.* Only one family fit any semblance of that combination. His head coach and said coach's son, who happened to be the team's top-line center. The Sullivans were legends in the Dagger community, and a big part of the reason the practice arena was in the small, neighboring community of Hollow Valley rather than in a Denver suburb. And he guessed being the coach's granddaughter and the team captain's niece gave Maude free rein of the practice facility. "Is it one of them you're waiting for?"

She shook her helmeted head. "I have practice."

"Ah, right. Well, between your grandpa and your uncle, who gives better advice?"

"Don't tell Grandpa, but Uncle Connor."

"Your secret is safe with me."

"Maybe Uncle Connor would have good advice for you, too. On how to score. He scores all the time."

"He sure does." Liam cleared his throat. The captain *had* been mentoring Liam, in his taciturn way. "What tips has he given you?"

"He says if I want to shoot the puck harder, I need to bend my knees. A lot. And to pull the puck back farther."

He nudged a puck out of the pile and set up like she'd described. "Like this?"

"Yeah."

He bent his knees more, way too far. "How about this?"

She giggled again. "Too much."

He straightened, wound up and let off a shot. It veered right. Goddamn it. Didn't even hit the post. He'd have sworn, but for his young audience.

Even with their distance across the ice, Maude's frown was unmissable.

"My uncle says to try again, too," she advised.

"It's good advice. But it's not happening right now."

She skated closer. "Maybe try it out during your game tonight."

"I'd better try something."

The Daggers traded for him in hopes he'd fix their wounded locker room dynamic and add some much-needed scoring, and he was doing anything but.

"Maude?" A feminine call, quieted by distance, echoed from the tunnel leading to the home team dressing room.

"Uh-oh," the girl said.

"Someone you know?" he asked.

She nodded.

"Maude?" Louder, this time.

Another helmeted head appeared. Another dark braid, browner than Maude's black. Not a girl, though, a woman. A goddamn gorgeous woman, going off the soft angle of her jaw, the scattering of freckles across her peachy-pale skin and the curious glint in her gaze. She was probably close to his own thirty-one, give or take a couple years. Her gait indicated she wore skates, but she had on a royal blue athletic jacket instead of a jersey and hockey pads. She looked a bit familiar. No doubt he'd seen her around the rink a few times in passing, no matter how much he'd been keeping his head down since he arrived in Colorado.

She stopped behind the bench, her hands on her hips.

Ah. Maybe that's where Maude got it from.

"Hey, Coach," Maude said.

The woman's gaze flicked from the girl to Liam for a long pause.

"Wrong ice sheet. And practice doesn't start until twelve thirty."

"And here I thought I was all done practicing, Coach," Liam joked.

"Ha, ha," Maude's coach said. "No, I told my players not to come early today. This one, in particular. I didn't want any of them interfering with a Daggers game day."

Wouldn't be right to let the kid get in trouble when he was the one who'd suggested Maude join him.

He waved a glove. "She's been helping me out. I invited her on the ice."

"Against my strict instructions," she said. "You didn't know, but she did."

"You said I couldn't skate without an adult," Maude said, missing a bit of her earlier confidence.

Her coach narrowed her eyes at Maude. Liam skated over to the bench and leaned on the boards. "Seriously, we were just shooting the puck around a bit. I was enjoying myself. Real practice is long over."

"Do you try to sweet-talk your own coach like this?"

"Sweet-talking?" He pointed at his chest.

"Oh, yeah, I feel like it's your main mode of communication."

"Assuming you've got me all figured out when we've never met?"

"Which is honestly surprising. But yeah, your reputation preceded you long before you got traded here."

He lifted an eyebrow. "News to me."

He wasn't a saint, but he wasn't known for high-profile hijinks, either. Being a fixer meant calming the waves, not creating them. Especially not since he'd been traded from Carolina to the Daggers in November. He'd been too busy trying to score on the ice to worry about his off-ice chances.

"Professional hockey player." She fanned her fingers in a circle in the general direction of his face. "All I need to know."

"Oh, there's a story there," he said.

"Not one worth telling."

"I'll get it out of you," he vowed.

"Not today."

"Which isn't a no."

She made a face at him.

Up close, he could see her eyes. What a fascinating shade of brown. Almost like a deep honey—

"You're staring," she said.

"I am." No use denying it. He shot her a grin. "And I will convince you to tell me that story one day."

"We'll see. I'm sure we'll run into each other at some point."

"Because you want to see me again. I knew it." Teasing her was fun, a feeling he'd been short on lately. "You sure you wouldn't be willing to tell it to me over coffee, after your practice?"

"Oh, my God. I could not be surer, Liam Caldwell."

Christ, his name sounded good in her disdainful tone.

"I'm at a disadvantage. You know who I am, but I don't even know your name."

"Kate," she said curtly. "Maudie? Time to get off. We don't start for another half hour. The Zamboni driver is just waiting for Liam, here."

Maude, who was circling lazily around the net, pretending to poke a puck in, hung her head and skated toward the gate.

"Thanks for shooting the puck with me, Liam," she said.

"Let's do it again. I need all the help I can get," he said. "You saw my aim."

Maude looked some combination of hopeful and scheming, her gaze bouncing between him and her coach. "You know, when my dad went to play games, he always got a kiss for luck from my mom. He said it worked, every time."

The kid was a matchmaker? No way. Hilarious.

But her coach didn't seem to see the humor. Her face went as white as the scuffed-up ice. "How do you remember that? You were four."

Maude shrugged. "I don't know. I saw it a bunch of times, I guess."

Oh, shit. Maude was *that* granddaughter. His coach had a big family, four kids. *Had*, past tense. His oldest son, another member of the Sullivan NHL dynasty, had died close to six years ago. And Kate was clearly well informed about Maude's family history, as any caring, youth-hockey coach would be. Could also be from living in the same small town. Whatever the reason for Kate's familiarity, she and Maude were talking on a whole other level than the one Liam was on. Kate seemed more upset than Maude, whose expression was still matter of fact. He didn't like how Kate's eyes hinted at tears. He wanted to get some color back in her cheeks.

"Kid might have a point," he said, smirking.

She startled, and twin spots of pink marked her cheeks.

Excellent.

"Oh, good Lord, you have got to be kidding," she complained.

He shrugged. "You're right, I shouldn't have assumed you were free to throw around good luck kisses."

"She is," Maude announced, stepping off the ice and over the bench. "He's in a really bad slump, Coach."

"Really bad," he echoed with a wink.

"Slump or not, you wish."

He followed Maude off the ice and headed for the tunnel. "You know what, Coach Kate? I think I do."

She froze. "Let me assure you, you don't."

"How do you know?"

Her mouth pressed into a grim line.

The kind of face a guy could enjoy kissing off a woman, if she was willing. Kate obviously wasn't, and he was honestly kidding, but…

"I don't go around kissing random people, promise—but what am I missing here?"

"My last name, champ."

She walked down the tunnel, calling "Come on, Maude!" over her shoulder.

He didn't need to ask about her last name.

It was emblazoned across the bottom of the back of her jacket.

Sullivan.

Oh, hell.

If she told her dad he'd been flirting with her, he'd probably be benched for a week.

Then again, with his recent faulty play, he had more of a chance with his coach's daughter than he had with the puck. If he wanted to keep his place on the team—in the league—something needed to change.

Chapter Two

"Kate, where are you?"

Connor's voice neared a whine over the call system in her car. Two hours remained until puck drop. Her older brother did not need to be working himself into a lather over her hitting traffic on her way into Denver. Kate waved her dad's spare parking garage pass at the security checkpoint.

Driving under the open gate, she took a deep breath before replying, "Just went past parking security."

Her brother's sigh of relief was almost as strong as the jitters rippling along her skin.

"Thank you," he said. "I'm on too good a streak to risk the socks."

Connor's lucky Sunday socks occupied the passenger seat, ready to be switched for the Thursday socks he'd worn to the arena by accident. Hockey players. God, they were superstitious. And Kate couldn't even point fingers. When she'd played, she'd once used the same hair elastic for a year. Plus, she'd had a thing where she had to follow the exact same pattern around the face-off circles in warm-up. She'd always skated back to the bench feeling ready for the game ahead.

That was the opposite of how she felt about showing up at the Daggers game this evening, though she did have a plan. Get in, get out, long before puck drop and before she ran into anyone she knew.

More importantly, before she got out of the car she needed to stop her hands from shaking.

Slowing to scout for the closest spot to the team entrance into the arena, she said, "Yes, you owe me *big*, Conn. If I run into the wrong person, well… I'm done getting blamed for Daggers losing games."

He groaned. "They're over blaming you, I promise."

"It's still too soon to test that theory."

"Want me to meet you in the parking garage?" he asked.

"No. No need for you to go through security again. I'll meet you by the inside door," she said. "I see a spot. Just let me park."

"My hot streak thanks you."

"Yeah, yeah."

She hung up and parked, then grabbed the socks and darted for the entrance.

Her soft spot for her older brother knew no bounds. She knew it, he knew it, and so she'd bring him his damn socks, even though she might need to find a garbage can to puke in on the way to their rendezvous point.

She passed through security, glad she was the only person needing to go through the metal detector.

Talk about luck—if Kate had any on her side, traffic out of Denver would be light, and she'd make it back to Hollow Valley before puck drop. Maude and Sophie were expecting her.

Kate might not have watched the Daggers *at* the arena since her marriage went sideways, but she still caught every game.

She couldn't affect their season by watching the television broadcast. Then again, they weren't yet in a playoff spot.

Bad Luck Kate.

When opinionated fans looking for a reason to explain the Daggers' poor play had blamed Kate's divorce—primarily *Kate*—for the team's struggles, they'd saddled her with the nickname. It was the opposite of creative.

Ridiculous, too, how the team had bought into the accusation. The Daggers were a bunch of grown-ass men who could control their emotions and thoughts. They should have understood how Vincent, who'd never been the star winger he believed himself to be, had wanted out of Denver as much as she'd wanted to stay. She'd had nothing to do with the failed team dynamic, given she wasn't the one *on* the team.

A handful of Daggers still thought her the cause of their demise last season. She didn't particularly want to see them tonight.

And then there was the Dagger who'd blatantly ignored her reputation as a harbinger of doom. Or maybe, being new, he didn't understand the history.

Whatever his reasoning, Liam Caldwell had played along with her niece's suggestion of a *good luck* kiss. Could Maude have been more embarrassing?

The left winger was relatively new to town and to the team, and from what she'd heard from Connor, he hadn't quite gelled in the locker room yet. His goal drought couldn't be helping, given the Daggers had traded away two prospects for Caldwell, who was supposed to be a guaranteed points producer.

She hung her VIP access pass around her neck and entered the wide, high-ceilinged cement maze that curved under the seats and around the ice. The second she passed through the doorway, she ran into a cement wall.

No, wait.

Cement walls weren't warm.

They didn't wear fine wool suits.

They couldn't catch her by the arms with strong fingers.

Not to mention the chuckle. She'd heard that chuckle way too many times during their short conversation earlier today.

Well, maybe three times. But three times was too many.

She stepped back from Liam Caldwell's steady grip and tried not to get bowled over by the sum total of bespoke menswear hugging his hockey thighs and thick biceps topped off by a grin for the ages. She was willing to admit to herself how, earlier, she'd thought he was unbearably hot in his gear. The just-worked-out flush on his lightly tanned face and the few stubborn strands of brown hair curling out from under his helmet were like catnip.

Kate-nip.

She should have known she'd be done in by a subtle plaid

print and casually styled waves that could only look better if they had her fingers in them.

She backed up another step.

Distance did not lessen the effect. She clutched her brother's socks instead of reaching out and testing the softness of the strands falling across Liam's forehead.

He was still grinning at her. "Twice in one day. Are you here about my good luck kiss?"

He couldn't be serious.

"I know you're new here, but I don't kiss hockey players," she said.

Or at least she didn't *anymore.* Was he the exact physical type she usually flocked to? Obviously. But said type screamed heartbreak.

She held up the socks. "Kate Sullivan's family delivery service—present and accounted for."

"Sister Mary Kate. Answer to my prayers," a loud voice called from down the hall.

Her brother rushed in their direction.

"*Wait,*" Liam repeated, holding up a hand. "*Mary* Kate?"

"Mary Katherine, technically, but Mary was my mom," she explained. "Also, the Olsen twin. Just awkward. So, we keep the 'Mary' part quiet."

"Mary Katherine," he mused. His eyes lit up, and he pointed a finger at her. "Like the—"

"If you value your life, you will not make a *Saturday Night Live* reference right now."

"Okay." His mouth twitched. "Superstar."

He refrained from mimicking Mary Katherine Gallagher's trademark arms-up-full-lunge pose. She supposed she'd let him live. For now.

Being the only girl in a family of boys had taught her the best way to stop the teasing was to ignore it. The glint in Liam's too-green eyes egged her on, though.

"This is why I don't tell people," she said.

"Even me? I'm hurt." Liam said.

Connor halted beside them, hand outstretched in universal *gimme*. "Why would you be special, Weller?"

"Oh, I don't know. I think Kate likes me."

"Don't say shit like that around the others," Connor hissed. "Kate doesn't need you refueling the fires Vince lit."

She clenched the socks.

Liam shook his head. "It's a rule of mine not to pay much attention to team scuttlebutt. And when we first ran into each other, I thought she was only a hockey coach."

She didn't cross paths with most of the Daggers when coaching or teaching power skating, a measure of her *very* strict awareness of the Daggers' use of the practice arena. Only a handful of players with school-age kids sent their children to Kate's classes. Hopefully, they'd support her plans to expand into a full hockey academy, with a special focus on classes for girls.

"Kate isn't *only* anything," Connor said.

"Something I figured out but quick," Liam shot back.

He dealt Kate a mischievous look.

God, why did she feel it all the way to her core?

Liam fixed his attention on Connor. "I experienced quite the mind warp when I learned she was my coach's daughter."

"When it suits him," she said.

Damn. Should have saved the complaint for her inside voice.

From Connor's warning look, he agreed. "Kate's the middle sibling."

She blinked at him. It didn't matter how much time had passed since they lost Toby—she'd never get used to no longer sharing being in the middle with Connor. Not that Connor had ever shared Kate's experience of being overshadowed by talented older and younger brothers. He'd been a powerhouse since the moment he put on skates.

"Being an only child, it's *another* mind warp to imagine having any siblings, let alone a bunch." Liam's gaze traveled between her and her brother faster than a puck being passed back and forth on a power play.

"No frame of reference," she said, mocking sadness.

"Lucky ass," Connor said longingly.

She elbowed him right above the point of his tie.

He feigned doubling over.

She passed him the socks.

Connor took them with a sigh of relief. He rushed to toe out of his shoes and stood with his ankle over his knee, scrambling to change from his pizza pair to his taco pair.

Liam arched a brow. "New habit or old?"

"New-ish." He hopped back on his one foot to steady himself as he slid on the second sock. "A few years back, Maude gave me seven pairs of socks for Christmas, labeled by days of the week. The first day I wore one of the pairs, I scored a hat-trick. You know how these things go. Now I have to get a week's worth of socks from Maude every Christmas, and she has to designate them by day."

"I get it," Liam said. "I have to follow the exact same routine before every game, or I feel like I'm setting myself up for failure." His smile faltered. "Then again, it hasn't worked for me lately. Maybe I should try something new."

Connor inhaled sharply.

"I know, I know. What am I saying, right? I'm already messing things up." Liam checked his watch. "Usually, I'm taping my sticks by now. See ya."

He rushed off before she could even say goodbye.

Connor shook his head, the picture of faux solemnity. "You have got to stop scaring my teammates. Especially Weller. Guy needs to score."

"He was practicing with Maude today," she said.

"And trying to impress you," he said. "Until he figured out you're my sister."

She'd have rolled her eyes, but Liam *had* seemed thrown when he learned her last name. She gave Connor a quick hug, then backed away. "I'd better leave if I want to make it to Sophie's for dinner."

He caught her elbow. "Wait. You're already here. Why don't you stay?"

She shook her head.

"Come on… I donated my seats to the charity pool tonight, but we can sneak you into an empty seat somewhere."

The thought of settling in a few rows behind the Denver bench left her queasy. "I promised Maude I'd watch the game with her and Sophie."

"I miss doing fist bumps with you in the tunnel," he pressed.

They'd shared the routine for weekend home games. Started after Toby died, with the intent of putting on a united "the Sullivans are fine" face. He hadn't played for the Daggers, but he'd been well loved around the league. She and Connor had stood together many a game as the players passed them to go into the tunnel. But to give her ex space, she'd stopped doing it once she'd filed for divorce. She hadn't resumed when he signed with a different team last summer.

"I can't."

He sighed. "So, leave after you bump us in. Seriously—it'd be good luck. And then you can head home and catch the last two periods with Maude."

Luck. It was a theme today. The hockey gods had decided she'd be the Daggers' rabbit foot one way or another.

"Some of your teammates still think I'm the human equivalent of walking under a ladder."

"Yeah, well, I'm their captain. And I think it's about damn time for anyone who still thinks last year's losses had anything to do with you to get their head out of their ass. Our poor play was on Vince, and on me as a captain and us as a team. Not you."

"Conn," she murmured.

"I'm not saying we have to go back to you being here every weekend. But let's break the pattern, Kate. For your sake—I know it still weighs on you."

He had a point.

"I have a point."

Her jaw clenched. "Get out of my head."

"Gladly, so long as you show up in the tunnel. I'll let everyone know. They *will* go along with it."

Her stubborn insistence wobbled and crashed. She wasn't going to say "what could it hurt?" because it could. Embarrassment, rejection, messing up the Daggers' heads... *Or,* the opposite. Maybe her being there would help the team, and she'd slough off the "bad luck" moniker once and for all. The more positive energy she had to propel her forward into getting her school up and running by the fall, the better. Once she met her summer enrolment targets, she'd be able to secure ice time for the fall and winter season, which would give the academy a fighting chance of becoming the place Kate dreamed it could be.

A place where Kate could protect Maude from facing the same barriers Kate had struggled to climb over.

A place for herself in the hockey world, too, one that was more about being Kate and less about being a Sullivan.

The possibility of the positive was worth facing the chance of the negative.

"Fine. I'll stay. But I'm laying low until the team leaves the dressing room."

She left her grinning brother and hung out in their dad's empty office until she heard the Daggers' theme song throbbing through the arena.

Here goes nothing.

Her stomach disagreed, flipping one way, then the other.

She made her way to the tunnel right as her brother was coming out of the dressing room. She held out her fist, but instead of knocking his glove against it, he stood at her side and raised his hand, too. Something about his clenched fingers and severe scowl made her laugh.

She nudged him with her elbow. “You’re making me look like the way better option.”

“Not new.”

The Daggers filed past, lumbering out of the dressing room in a stream of royal blue and black.

Bump.

Bump.

Bump.

Serious nods from a few guys who she used to have over for summer barbecues.

Her stomach turned again, and she forced a smile.

Bump.

Bump.

A grin from the team’s equivalent of a class clown. She should’ve known Jonesy wouldn’t hold anything against her.

Five more flat expressions.

A hell of a scowl from one of Vincent’s best friends, third-pairing defenseman Brian Boyle.

And then, Lars. Pink rose up his pale face, flagging his cheeks and tense jaw.

Her heart ached. Oskar Larsen hadn’t deserved all the things her ex said about him any more than Kate had deserved the accusations that went along with it.

“Hey, Kate,” he said quietly, giving her the barest tap. “Good to see you.”

“You, too, Lars.”

Crap, she hadn’t expected to get choked up.

He moved along, and she cleared her throat, but God, the lump there ached.

More players filed past, dutifully following what had to be strict instructions from their captain. A few newer guys looked more curious than anything, unfamiliar with her, the tradition *and* the tension.

And the last half dozen players were an absolute *relief,* all smiles and cheery greetings.

Holy mother. Not *every* reception had been positive, but she was surviving. She hated to concede Connor a point, but the choking lump left from the low of Brian and the high of Lars was dissolving. Victory bubbled in her veins, energetic and heady.

Three more to go.

She kept expecting Liam to be next, but even the hulking, ungainly goaltenders came before him. He was last. Was that usual?

She glanced at Connor, who seemed unfazed.

Jerking her attention back to Liam, she offered him the kindest smile she could muster. The guy needed good vibes going into the game, for sure.

His face twisted, and he held up his fist for a cursory bump before trundling down the hall.

Oh, no.

Pained defeat was *not* the right mindset going into the first period. Nor was she going to even entertain the idea that his outlook had anything to do with finding out she was his coach's daughter. His goal drought *had* to be the issue.

She held in a wince. She didn't want him to keep struggling. For his sake, for the Daggers' playoff chances. And if she was honest, for her sake, too. If the media caught wind of her being in the tunnel before the game, and then the Daggers lost, some enterprising writer in need of a catchy headline might drag "Bad Luck Kate" back into the spotlight again. And fat chance getting her enrolment up if that happened.

How could she make the game work for her for a change? Create some good luck before someone else got the chance to twist the situation.

When my dad went to play games, he always got a kiss for luck from my mom.

Earlier, Kate had sloughed off Maude's silly suggestion.

But how silly was it, really? Should she…?

No. Ridiculous.

Though he'd looked beyond sad, and he was the one who'd mentioned trying something new—

"Liam. Wait."

He hadn't yet made it to the part of the tunnel visible to the people in the stands. He paused and turned halfway to Kate, an eyebrow raised in silent question.

Yes. Try something new.

She rushed forward and rose high on her toes. His visor was cold against her forehead.

His lips were so, so warm.

And delicious. Like white Lifesavers, the kind that were supposed to spark when you chewed them in the dark.

He let out a murmur of surprise, opening his mouth.

She traced the gap with her tongue, a quick taste. *Wintermint.*

A spark of pleasure tripped through her.

Before she could pull away, a gloved hand cradled the back of her head and the kiss slowed, his mouth moving over hers as if he had all the time in the world. His tongue tangled with hers, and a rock-solid arm kept her from lowering to her heels.

"Hey, Caldwell! What the hell?" her dad barked from a few yards behind her.

She stumbled back. Blood rushed up her neck, no doubt matching her already hot cheeks.

Liam blinked like he was adjusting after a hard check to the boards. Still shaken. A cocky smile spread across his face.

"Sorry, Coach. Just for luck, you know." He winked at her like it wasn't an utterly lecherous move—and it wasn't, not when he did it.

"Get lucky on the ice. Not with my daughter."

Liam saluted her dad, but then stroked her cheek with the thumb of his glove. "Thanks, Katie."

Katie.

No one had called her that since she was a kid.

But the hot look he was giving her was anything but juvenile. Her ears were scalding as she walked away from the sexy winger.

Her dad had taken her place in the hallway and between him and Connor, there wasn't much room left for her. She angled sideways to scoot between the two men, who were both staring at her like she'd gotten the Daggers' logo tattooed across her face.

Her dad was a silent wall at her back.

Connor's jaw ticked. "That was not a fist bump."

"Nope," she said, pausing to catch his gaze. "But hopefully, it wins you the game."

Chapter Three

"Here he is. Man of the hour."

Connor's declaration followed Liam as he ran the gauntlet of his teammates as they filed into the bar. Their good-natured shoulder nudges and backslaps propelled him toward the long table they'd snagged in the back corner of Sullivan's. Trying to be subtle while actually being desperate to learn more about Kate, he'd gleaned a quick history of the Hollow Valley institution. Apparently, Kate and Connor's grandfather had owned the place, and now their sister-in-law ran it.

"Someone pull up the replay on their phone," Jonesy crowed.

They were all making way too much of a deal over one goal. Hell, he usually got thirty to forty of them a season. Getting his twelfth today shouldn't merit celebratory drinks after a Sunday night game.

But the guys were excited by Liam's game-winner. The only goal of the game, no less.

He *had* been the only one to get a good luck kiss from Kate.

Something had jarred loose in his brain when Kate Sullivan's lips had touched his, her eyes sparkling with a heavy dose of throwing-caution-to-the-wind.

In the locker room, after the postgame media scrum, Connor had announced he got to pick where they were going for drinks. After all, he'd set Liam up to score.

It figured the captain would choose his family's joint. Connor had claimed it was easier for the guys with kids who lived in the small town—besides Connor and the coach, a half dozen Daggers called the place home. But Liam suspected family loyalty played a role, too.

Up until now, Liam had only gone out for drinks after the game when the crew had chosen a place in Denver. Sullivan's had none of the glamor of the dimly lit, vintage-inspired places he'd been dragged to on previous nights out.

The bar did have the nostalgia angle covered, though. Memorabilia plastered the walls, from black-and-white prints of the original six team arenas to signed pictures and sticks and enough 1970s and 80s Daggers' paraphernalia to fill a collectibles shop. From the back wall, right over the table where his teammates were filing in, all the way around the side wall, were framed jerseys from all three generations of Sullivans. A slightly smaller one hung near the front door, in University of Minnesota maroon and gold. Kate's, maybe?

Right before he could take a seat at the end of the table, Connor nudged him. "Go get the first round, Weller. My sister-in-law's bottom line needs padding. And make sure to tip the bartender extra, too, for putting up with your shenanigans."

"Shenanigans?" What on earth could he have done to cause trouble for the bartender in the few minutes since they'd arrived? And he wasn't planning on having more than two beers, let alone getting trashed. He glanced to the side, where a long, wood-topped bar polished by thousands of shirtsleeves backed most of the wide room.

A dark head bent over the long line of craft beer taps, focusing on pulling a beer into a bulb-shaped glass. A plush lower lip tugged between straight, white teeth.

He'd tasted that lip a few hours ago.

A lip in no small way responsible for the success he and his teammates had come out to celebrate.

"Ah," he said, "*shenanigans.*"

"Yeah." Connor's eyes narrowed. "Whatever you did to convince her to kiss you, jackass."

I wish I knew.

But he wasn't going to make excuses. Even if it had been Kate's idea, Liam had enjoyed every second of it.

A singular kiss.

"It was my irresistible charm," he told Connor.

The claim earned him the ticking jaw he'd hoped for. If his captain was going to be overprotective and meddlesome, Liam wasn't going to make it easy on him.

"No need to frown, man. *Linemate.* I feel we gelled on the ice today. You and me, that is. Not Kate and me. I skated with your niece, not your sister. I mean, *Maude* and I gelled, too. Maybe I naturally work well with Sullivans—"

"Don't change the subject."

Fair. Liam had been babbling something fierce.

"She surprised me," he said honestly.

Yikes. If Connor had had the ability to use The Force, Liam would be up against Mick Sullivan's framed 1960s era Bruins jersey, an invisible hand at his throat, choking.

"Kate wouldn't kiss you on a whim."

"You can't have seen what you saw and thought it was my idea," Liam said.

The initiative in the tunnel had been *all* Kate. He hadn't minded, of course. Had essentially planted the seed himself hours prior.

Her presence had thrown off his pregame routine, too. Connor wasn't the only one who had superstitions. And now, Kate had gone and tossed a new element into the mix. One with a stellar result.

Hmmm.

"You're not taking this as seriously as you should," Connor bit out. "This kind of thing screws up a dressing room dynamic. You should know that. *Kate* should know that. After she split with her ex, the team's chemistry…" Connor raked a hand through his hair. "I'm not blaming her. She was devastated, humiliated. Vince acted like a world-class dick. I was tempted to toss him off the bluff behind my house. But a lot of the team was loyal to him, and it took time to show them they were wrong. So, wield your *charm* on someone who isn't my sister."

"Heard, Captain. She's safe with me, I promise," Liam slapped Connor on the shoulder and made his way toward the bar.

Maybe if he played his cards right, she'd admit why she'd blessed him with the sweetest kiss he'd shared since he was a starry-eyed rookie.

Maybe she'd be up for a lucky second one.

Booths ran down either side of the room, and the wide area in the center was crammed with tables. Mostly full. He wouldn't have thought a sleepy town like Hollow Valley would have a packed bar this late on a Sunday night.

A few folks shot congratulations his way as he passed the tables. But other than seeming invested in the Daggers' victory, the patrons—even the ones in royal blue jerseys—appeared unfazed by the company of a bunch of hockey players.

Had Connor chosen somewhere in the city, they'd have attracted way more attention.

His appreciation for his captain's choice doubled.

Quadrupled, as his gaze landed on Kate again. He knew he shouldn't look. Shouldn't do more than appreciate. But he couldn't keep his eyes off her.

When he'd seen her at the arena, she'd been wearing a plain gray hoodie. She'd shed it at some point, and her T-shirt showed off her strong arms. Her hair was in a ponytail now, not a braid, and it swayed hypnotically as she moved. Her eyes were mesmerizing, too. The amber color shifted from dark to light, like shining a beam through the bourbon and whiskey bottles lined up behind her.

The stools were taken, so he squeezed into the space next to the small swinging door that provided entry behind the bar.

He leaned an elbow along the railing. "We keep meeting."

Her head jerked up, eyes widening as she took him in.

"You came," she said. "You never come when the guys pick Sullivan's."

"New leaf, new bar," he said. "Maybe I'd have come sooner if I knew you were the drink master."

A pretty flush crept up from the neckline of her navy T-shirt. "I work four nights a week. Wasn't scheduled for tonight, but one of the other bartenders came down with the flu, so I came to help as soon as I got back from the city."

She was right up against the bar on her side, leaning in toward him a little. He did the same. Something about her just drew him in. In the minutes following that bombshell of a kiss, he'd been certain gravity had disappeared. Kate Sullivan's perfect mouth had left him floating at least a meter off the rubber flooring. He could feel himself drifting again. Toward his *coach's daughter.*

Taking a deep breath, he straightened, trying to get away from her Creamsicle scent. He tore his gaze away from the temptation to count her freckles. Behind her, two televisions were mounted, one over each end of the bar. Basketball highlights played on both. In between the screens was a narrow, waist-high counter displaying the typical lineup of premium and well liquors. Above that was a mirror in need of resilvering with shelves built on top of it, lined with vintage beer bottles.

"Who's the antique bottle aficionado? Your sister-in-law?"

Kate's curious smile faltered. "No. My mom, of all people. Toby hung on to her collection after she died. Breast cancer. And now he's gone, too..."

His throat pulsed, a quick ache of regret. "Oh, damn, I—"

"He never got much of a chance to enjoy this place," she finished, exhaling forcefully enough to puff out her lips. "Bought it from Grandpa as a retirement plan."

"Did Toby play for Detroit his whole career?" Toby Sullivan's story—his tragic death after a routine surgery—had played on the news for weeks. Everyone had known him and loved him.

She nodded. "Sophie and Maude didn't move here full-time until...after. Hollow Valley was always their summer home."

He had no clue what to say. How did one properly acknowledge the sorrow of someone so young never getting the chance to put their plans in motion?

He let out a long breath. “Community matters a lot when a person is grieving.”

She worried the side of her lip with her teeth, then matched his exhale. “Personal experience?”

“Of a sort. Not like losing a brother, but…”

Dementia meant he was actively losing his dad. A piece at a time. There was a mental anguish that came with not knowing what would disappear next, which essential part of the man who’d made Liam who he was would be gone forever. It might be something simple, like the memory of hugging on the ice after his Stanley Cup victory, or something more foundational, like his dad’s ability to understand things most people took for granted. The purpose of a refrigerator. How to comb his hair. The progression would always be a painful mystery.

“But?” she prodded.

Christ, this was not what he’d intended when he’d come over here. And as much as bartenders were the stereotypical audience for confessions of all kinds, he wasn’t going to burden Kate with his troubles.

“People must tell you the wildest stuff,” he said instead. “Do you like slinging drinks?”

Her hands gripped the edge of the bar, close enough together for him to cover them both by stretching out his fingers, were he to reach for her. She studied him, as if deciding whether to call him on the subject change or not.

“Toby was always so supportive of my eventual plans to open a hockey school. Bartending for Sophie is the least I can do.” She smiled stiffly and picked up another pint glass, putting it under one of the taps. “Plus, Sullivans aren’t very good at relaxing.”

“I’ve noticed that.” He held out his credit card. “Can you start a tab for the table? Cap them off at a grand or two, though.”

She blinked at him, then swiped it into the system before

handing it back. "That much? It's Sunday. The drinks we serve here aren't that high end, Liam."

He waved her off. "We're in the mood to celebrate. Well, they are. I need to drive back to Denver tonight. But yeah. It was a big win. Thanks, in part, to you."

She cleared her throat. "Should I apologize?"

"For what?"

"Kissing you."

"Given it led to that, I won't accept an apology." He pointed at one of the television screens playing highlights from tonight's game. Mainly saves, considering the Daggers' shutout.

She peeked over her shoulder. Her eyes darted with the puck, from a near-goal by Lars. She stilled when the clip of Connor and Liam began.

"So much faster than it felt in real time," he said. On the screen, he and Connor barreled toward the Seattle net on an odd-man rush. Connor had the puck. "I wasn't sure your brother would trust me enough to pass to me."

He hadn't wanted to be caught off guard if the puck sailed his way.

Not like he'd been caught off guard by Kate's shocker of a kiss and—

Even on the replay, the puck was a bullet, hitting his waiting blade right in the sweet spot, and he wristed it toward the net.

The lamp lit.

"Your brother is a hell of a passer."

"And you're a hell of a goal scorer," she murmured, watching a slowed-down version of the play from a different angle, this one catching Liam's dumbfounded expression as the goalie whiffed on the save.

If only he could bottle the relief he'd felt. Just…lightness.

And that's when I spaced out for half a second, trying to remember how you tasted.

Enough to make him want to kiss her again before the next game. Would it have the same effect?

He cleared his throat. “I don’t even think I registered that I was shooting it.”

“But it went in.”

The angle changed again, to the post-goal celebration. Kate chuckled as she watched Connor crash into him. Then Larsen. When Jonesy and Tiimonen, the defensive pair, joined in, it was an official dogpile.

“Bit of an absurd celly, considering we’re still four points back from moving into a playoffs wild card position,” he said.

“Don’t give me that. Look at your face. You were loving life.”

“I was.” Snapping his goalless streak hadn’t lifted the weight of responsibility entirely, but it was half the mass it had been before the game.

“I was hoping I’d bring you luck,” she said softly.

“You were serious about that?”

Her shrug bordered on sheepish.

Well then.

With the TV volume off, he couldn’t hear what the commentators were saying. It must have been something about his goal drought because the clip played long enough to follow him back to the bench for more congratulations, including a thump to the shoulder from Coach Sullivan’s meaty hand.

“I was expecting him to throttle me instead of giving me a pat on the back,” Liam admitted, fixing his gaze back on her.

Kate winced. “See, I *do* owe you an apology. This is going to blow back on you.”

“How could it? Only your dad and brother saw.”

A chuckle came from Liam’s right, along with an elbow nudge. “Isn’t that the two of you?”

Liam glanced at the person who’d interrupted.

A gnarled-looking man wearing a cowboy hat and a Daggers’

jersey occupied the stool at Liam's elbow. He tipped the neck of his beer bottle to the screen.

Kate and Liam both followed his motion.

There, on the televisions—the two behind the bar *and* the eight evenly spaced around the rest of the place—was a slowed-down video of Kate pressing her lips to his. Of him, deepening it.

Liam froze, taking in as much as he could of the grainy, weird-angle video before the broadcast switched to a commercial. Someone seated next to the tunnel must have hung their arm, phone in hand, over the guardrail to get that shot—

The noise in the bar trickled to whispers.

"Get it, Kate"

Goddamn Jonesy.

Without looking at the table of Daggers, she lifted a finger in their direction.

Liam would have laughed at the perfectly timed gesture, but for the panic lighting her eyes. Her throat bobbed, and she scanned the quieting patrons around the bar. Her gaze finally landed on Liam.

A few wolf whistles sounded behind him before the chatter started back up, this time with the hum of a crowd with gossip on the menu.

"Sit down," she ordered.

He glanced to either side of him to look for a stool and came up empty.

"Not *here.* Jesus. With *them.*" She jerked her head toward the back corner.

"Katie," he said in as low a voice as he could while still being heard. "I don't think me scurrying away from here is going to look any less suspicious than the two of us continuing to have a conversation."

"So don't scurry. Saunter with that cocky, *I'm packing a stick blade behind my fly* strut that's in every professional player's repertoire. Just make sure it's far away from me." He wouldn't have thought it possible for her to turn redder, but somehow, she managed. "Your strut needs to be far away, not whatever's in your pants."

"Oh, you *want* a close-up on that, Katie? It's a little fast, but I wouldn't be—"

"*Liam.* No! That isn't even an option. It is not what I meant."

"Ah, but it's what you said, so it's clearly on your mind."

Before she could toss a full beer in his face, he strolled away, as instructed.

"Drinks are on me," he announced to his teammates, taking the last remaining seat.

"Order the good stuff, gentlemen," Jonesy announced from partway down the table, his smile turning downright gleeful. "Weller's celebrating. Screw getting a goal—he bagged the coach's daughter."

Connor cursed under his breath. "Jonesy, I swear to all that is holy—"

Liam held up an "I've got this" hand and turned to the defenseman, reaching past Lars to jam a finger into the big mouth's sternum. "Talk about her like that again, and I will end your career. Regardless of what's going on between her and me, she deserves your damn respect."

Jonesy lifted his hands, leaning back from Liam's finger. "S-sorry, man."

Liam glanced at Connor, who looked like he couldn't decide between praise and murder.

Whether the captain intended to murder Jonesy or Liam was also unclear.

"Fix this, Weller," he demanded.

Liam sneaked a peek of Kate. Her cheeks were still flushed, and she was pulling beer taps like they'd stolen her childhood diary and broadcast *that* on the news.

"Something tells me I should keep my distance," Liam mused.

"No kidding. Do it in *private*, jerkwad."

The overprotective routine was getting under Liam's skin, enough he wanted to irritate Connor.

"What's her number, Sully? I'll text her."

Connor morphed into a stone sentry for a good few seconds before standing up, nearly sending his chair toppling backward with the speed of it. "I'll check with her first."

The captain stormed over to the part of the bar where Liam had been standing. He angled in close to talk to his sister.

"How is his mood less attention-grabbing than me talking to Katie?" Liam mused to Oskar Larsen.

Lars tugged on the string of his tea bag—peppermint, by the smell of it—his expression serious and opaque as always. He'd earned the nickname "Oskar the Grouch" over the years, by fans, media and apparently around the clubhouse, too. Liam didn't think it was accurate, though. The Norwegian wasn't grumpy. He was just impossible to read, and as best Liam could tell, remarkably shy. He was fast becoming Liam's favorite person to sit next to on the team plane. Quiet and private topped brash and chaotic any day.

Lars had also been playing for the Daggers for years, so maybe he was friends with Kate.

"You don't happen to have her number, do you?" Liam asked.

"Certainly."

Pulling his phone out, Liam sighed in relief. "Great, I'll—"

"Put it away, Weller." Serious blue eyes peered at him over the edge of the plain, white mug. "If Kate wants you to have it, she'll tell Connor."

Connor, who approached the table.

Connor, whose mouth curved into a hint of triumph.

Liam set his jaw.

The captain sat, spreading his massive arms along the back of the wall bench.

"She didn't give me the go-ahead," he announced.

"Did you actually ask?" Liam bit out.

Connor lifted a shoulder.

Growling, Liam rose to go over himself.

"Fine, I didn't ask. But she said to stay here," Connor warned. "She's serious. She'll come find you after practice tomorrow."

Liam sat back in his chair. "By that time, PR will probably be on my ass. Not to mention your dad."

"Come now, Liam. There's nothing my dad loves more than a good romance disrupting his locker room. *Especially* when it involves my sister."

"Sully," Lars warned.

"After practice tomorrow?" Liam repeated.

"She'll be there," Connor said. "You can trust her."

"Tell her to run the bill on the card I gave her." He stood. No point staying and inviting more chatter. "As soon as she's willing to talk, I'll fix this for her. She can trust me, too."

Fewer congratulations on the game greeted him on his way out. More gazes bore curiosity, flicking between him and Kate behind the bar. As he pushed through the door to leave, he tossed her a glance, as much of an "it'll be okay" as he could manage.

He didn't believe it, necessarily. There were few ways to make kissing your coach's daughter look good.

He didn't want her to worry, though. The thought of that mouth curved in any direction but up hurt something deep inside him.

Jamming his hands into his pockets, he hunched his shoulders against the cool night air. Hollow Valley was the same elevation as Denver, but the surrounding peaks made it seem cooler. He made his way to his car, which he'd tucked into angle parking a block away, in between a beige, aging sedan and a shiny dually.

"Wait!" Feet stomped after him. "Liam, stop!"

What was it about that voice that made him want to bend his knee and pledge fealty?

He turned.

She was still in her T-shirt, and crossed her arms over her chest, her elbows tightening close to her body with a little shiver.

He shrugged out of his jacket and slung it over her shoulders. With his hands gripping the unzipped fronts closed, they were less than a foot apart from each other. She licked her lower lip, a nervous habit, no doubt, going off the wary tilt of her eyes.

It only made him want to test how good a second kiss would be.

He stepped back as far as he could without making it weird.

She clutched the two sides of the jacket together. "I *will* be there after practice tomorrow. But I need some time to process this. And to see what the reactions are before we decide what to do."

He nodded. "That's fine, Katie. Best to have all the information."

"Thanks. I—I should get back to the bar."

He watched her walk away, long, shapely legs shown off by her jeans.

A groan threatened to escape. God, she was gorgeous.

It took until he was halfway back to Denver to realize he'd been so enchanted by her face and the sway of her hips, she'd walked off with his jacket.

He grinned as he passed a slow-moving truck on the freeway. If she changed her mind and decided *not* to show up after practice tomorrow, getting his jacket back was the perfect excuse to chase after her himself.

Chapter Four

CALDWELL SLIPS ONE PAST A STRUGGLING SEATTLE DEFENSIVE SQUAD
Did he have a good luck charm waiting in the wings?
Denver Star, March 31

Mondays, especially the mornings, were Kate's day to get stuff done. No 6:00 a.m. practices or lessons, no shift at Sullivan's.

No too-superstitious-for-their-own-good hockey players leaning on her bar, wielding that ludicrous smile. Liam Caldwell could charm the stripes off a zebra if he put his mind to it. She had half a thought to check if she still had all her freckles on her cheeks.

Kate groaned into her pillow. She normally slept in a little on days she didn't have morning practice and was coming off a closing shift at Sullivan's. Today, though, there was no need for her alarm. She'd woken up, mind racing in the silence of her bedroom.

Last night, she'd evaded texts from her dad and Sophie before hitting the hay. Hadn't known what to say, not to Sophie's wild curiosity nor her dad's none-too-thinly-veiled hints about having to drag the Daggers' PR team into what he deemed "her mess." She would come up with a solution, would wrest back control of this. She just wasn't sure how yet. So last night, after sending them each the equivalent of a cheery All is well! Stay tuned, she'd set her phone to Do Not Disturb.

Not that it had resulted in a sound sleep.

Her mind was *still* pinging around like a ball in a squash court.

Liam's lips on hers. How easy it had been to forget where they were, kissing in the tunnel *and* bantering at Sullivan's. The spring-growth green of his eyes as the bar had gone silent, and how they'd widened at the too-loud buzzing afterward. The luxurious smell of his jacket, whatever hundred-dollar-a-bar soap he used after his game clinging to the collar…

The melted pool of something way too close to yearning, swooping around her stomach like mercury on a tipping plate.

Equally poisonous, too.

She was not built to entertain anything like *yearning* with Liam Caldwell.

Whether or not her kissing him had been the catalyst for his goal was impossible to know. And with the Daggers' win, she had, as hoped, avoided being seen as their bad luck charm. But she hadn't intended for their kiss to go public. Not at all. How would it impact the school?

The last time she'd made the news with an NHL player, her reputation took a devastating hit. What would fans think of this? Would her academy's potential clientele love it, or see her in the same negative light as they had during her divorce? If only there was a way to control what they thought, somehow…

And what would Liam think?

He *had* been patient last night, understanding that she needed to evaluate what the problem *was* before deciding how to address it…

Ugh. Why should he get credit for the bare minimum?

She couldn't deal with this alone. Now that she'd had the chance to mull things over, she needed to bring in Sophie.

Sophie Sullivan was and would always be staunchly on Kate's side. *Bestie* would never encompass the entirety of what she meant to Kate. *Ride or die* came close but fell short somehow. With Sophie being widowed and Kate's marriage having imploded, it was like they'd each lost a leg and were keeping the other propped up.

And Kate was feeling hellaciously wobbly this morning.

So, before she went to the rink to find Liam post-practice, she needed a state of the union with Sophie to recalibrate. Conveniently, they always met up on Monday mornings to set a plan for the hockey academy for the week, holed up at the table closest to the window in Page + Bean, Hollow Valley's bookstore and coffee shop.

She had a feeling they might get sidetracked today.

Sophie was going to demand a full rundown of what happened, and Kate only had half the story, so far. She'd have to fill her friend in on the meeting with Liam, too, after she survived it. Sophie managed the academy's social media accounts, and this had the potential to complicate her task.

Kate kept her phone off while getting ready. She was already distracted by her thoughts and didn't need other people's interference to delay her further.

Figuring out something to wear seemed a bridge too far. Something that would work for coffee with Sophie, but also for meeting up with Liam in the Daggers' half of the arena. She should put on something nicer than sweats.

Good grief. She didn't need to wear anything special. She yanked a clean pair of jeans and a simple sweater out of her dresser.

Maybe a bit of extra mascara and eyeliner.

And her nicer peacoat. It did get cold at the rink, after all.

Once she was ready, she grabbed Liam's jacket off her kitchen table, where she'd carefully folded it the night before. Wait, though, was she going to walk into the arena carrying it, for any Hollow Valley hockey mom to see? No, thanks. She put the jacket in her messenger bag along with her wallet and keys, and walked out her front door into her dad's cultivated paradise.

Even in early spring, his backyard, from the pool to the garden, was a sight to behold with sprays of pale green buds, bushy ferns and carpets of heather and phlox. Any minute he didn't spend with the Daggers or with Maude, he spent with his hands in the dirt.

It was also a sight that reminded Kate, multiple times a day, of how she'd moved into his pool house after the divorce last year and hadn't quite managed to move out yet. With building a business, she couldn't beat the rent, and it was a ten-minute walk into town, or fifteen minutes to the arena.

She made her way toward Hollow Valley Avenue, rushing a bit to make up for the time it had taken to put on, mess up, and then reapply her eyeliner.

By the time she rounded the corner onto the main drag, she was regretting the warm coat she'd picked. She sped past the drugstore, and then the Italian café. The table on the sidewalk, one where she regularly enjoyed a cannoli, was occupied by a pair of retired gentlemen who were regulars at Sullivan's on nights when the Daggers were playing. They'd been there last night, in fact.

"Guess you enjoyed that goal of Caldwell's last night, eh, Katherine?" one of the men called to her.

She caught her toe on a crack in the sidewalk and barely caught herself from landing on her face. *Crap.* They'd caught the highlight reel, then.

"Oh, sure, always love to see the Daggers score!" she replied.

They laughed, a little too hard in Kate's opinion, considering she hadn't been joking. But—her words replayed in her head. *Oh, no.*

They couldn't think she'd meant—

Her face felt like she was standing three inches away from a blazing campfire.

She waved at them, then rushed down the half block to Page + Bean.

Focus. What's done is done.

And what was kissed was kissed. One time only.

The video of her and Liam wasn't that interesting. Surely it would blow over. This wasn't nearly as salacious as Vince accusing her of sleeping with Lars.

Though that hadn't blown over at all.

More like blew through her life like a cyclone.

Stop.

She couldn't let that memory win anymore. She'd moved past the ugly headlines, Vince's accusations of her relationship with Lars being more than friendship. Past the thousands of comments blaming her for the Daggers not making the playoffs and for Vince asking for a trade. She'd managed to fill three academy classes for her current spring session, and her summer session was half-full.

With Sophie's help, she could assess the fallout and make a plan. Kate limited her social media to one private account. Sophie would be able to use her own accounts, as well as the academy's, to get a read on what people were saying online.

Even with her quick pace, she was late. Guilt rose, remnants of hockey practices past. At least Sophie wouldn't stick Kate with a bag skate as punishment.

A gust of wind blew at her back as she pushed through the door, only to be pummeled by the moist warmth of the café side of the business. The morning coffee rush, plus proofing pastries, always jacked up the humidity.

She spotted Sophie's ink-black hair in the far corner, facing away from the front door.

Kate passed the line of people waiting to put in their order. It felt as under-the-microscope as when she'd fist-bumped the Daggers last night. A few cheerful "Kate!" greetings reached her, alongside a bit of side-eye.

Hmmm. Curiosity with a mild undercurrent of judgy.

She rushed past them.

"Oh my God," her friend said, almost conspiratorially. "I thought you'd never get here. Why have you been ignoring my texts? I was two seconds from driving to your place to check on you."

Kate's cheeks burned. "I left my phone off."

She pulled it out of the front pocket on her bag and turned it on.

It started vibrating.

She groaned.

"I'll save you time with mine," Sophie said. "Essentially—Kate, Kate, Kate… Pick up, Kate… You better have a good reason for ignoring me… Holy crap, he didn't stay over, did he—?"

"Shh!" She waved a hand at her friend, slung her bag over the back of her chair and sat. "No, he didn't *stay over*. We barely kissed."

"Mmm-hmm. Sure, Jan." Despite Sophie's black hair and olive skin, she somehow managed to look exactly like the side-eyeing meme of the blonde actress who played Marcia on *The Brady Bunch*. "What is it with you and bagging hot hockey players? You said you were on permanent hiatus with anyone even hockey adjacent."

Kate's jaw dropped. "Okay. One—you take that back, because that violates the best friend agreement concerning positive comments and ex-husbands. Two—you can't exactly point fingers. Toby was my brother, so I didn't keep count, but I know he made a 'hottest NHL players' list more than once."

"Dozens of times." Sophie's smile softened. In the years since Toby's death, she had been open about progressing from the achy sort of grief to the kind where she more often preferred to celebrate the good times.

"It feels like there's a 'three,'" Sophie said.

"Um, yeah… I didn't *bag* Liam. The kiss was impulsive. I was worried about being seen as the Daggers' jinx again. He needed a goal, and I could tell he was in his head about it, and…"

"And you thought you'd get him out of his head." Sophie took a sip of her coffee.

"More or less." Kate pointed at her friend's half-empty, jumbo mug. "I'll get the next one."

"If I have any more caffeine, I'll be sprouting wings," Sophie said, clearing her throat. "Feel like guessing why the visits to our website jumped by 375 percent this morning?"

"I'm sorry, what?" She only half succeeded in keeping her voice from screeching.

"I know."

"Did the traffic get us more enrolments?" Kate asked.

Sophie nodded. "Three. And twenty inquiry forms."

A thrill ran through Kate. She wanted to run a full slate of academy-style intensives this summer, but to do that, she needed kids in skates on the ice. And three still left a lot of space, but it was a hell of a lot more than they'd usually get on a Monday morning. "Since yesterday?"

"Yes."

"Oh, wow." People were intrigued enough by the kiss to look up her and her school, and some had even registered. This hadn't been her plan, but she'd work with it. "We should be celebrating with doughnuts. They're on me. And I *am* getting you another coffee. Decaf."

She stood, but had to wait for Estelle Zvarych, the facilities manager at the arena, to pass by.

"If it isn't the famous Kate Sullivan," the older woman said, eyes twinkling.

"Would we call me famous?" Famous-adjacent was more accurate. She'd played college hockey in Minnesota but just missed making the national team. With more leagues and opportunities open to men in hockey, her brothers had accomplished far more.

"You certainly have been at the arena this morning. Every parent there to tie skates was yammering on about you and that boy."

Kate arched a brow. "There's nothing boyish about Liam."

"*Ohhh.* He's 'Liam' already. Not Caldwell. What a hottie *he* is." Estelle winked. "But then, you know that. As does the entirety of the hockey community in Hollow Valley. The figure skaters, too."

Kate cursed under her breath. She needed to tread lightly if she wanted to maintain respect with the people who entrusted her to teach and coach their kids.

"Hockey parents," she murmured. "They gossip like middle school students."

"It's all over my socials. Even a new angle from the one that made the news last night." Estelle put her drink down on Sophie and Kate's table and pulled her phone out of her jacket pocket. A few scrolls, and she turned her screen toward Kate. Sophie leaned across the table, making her coffee cup clink against the saucer.

"Easy, killer," Kate muttered.

"You're getting cozy with hockey players, single-handedly boosting our enrolment, and telling me to go *easy*?"

The new video was clearer than the one she'd seen last night. A lower angle, too, someone sitting down in the fourth or fifth row. Impossible to miss how carefully he'd cupped her head with his glove. Why had that felt beyond heaven? And then when he'd nearly lifted her off her toes with one damn arm. *Thank you, free weight training.*

Sophie's jaw was almost on the table.

"Good catch, Katherine, dear," Estelle said, winking as she took her coffee and walked off to the cream and sugar stand.

Sophie waited until she was out of earshot before saying, "That was not a man who was *being kissed.* He was into it."

"It was like, five seconds."

"Five seconds of something you swore you were going to stay far away from."

Kate buried her face in her hands. "Why do I get drawn in by the exact wrong type?"

"Because that type is magnetic and flashy and sexy? And under it, hardworking and community minded and cinnamon-rolly?"

"And they come with jobs that take priority over everything.

Look at Liam. He knows he's a temporary fix for the Daggers. Everyone's calling him a rental player. He'll be gone at twelve-oh-one Eastern time on July first."

"So don't fall in love with him."

"You're right. I need to stay far away. He's my dad's player. The coach's daughter can't have a casual fling with a player. Especially not when the fans still see me as the reason why Vince left Denver. And after my divorce, it's hard, uh…hard to want to risk something real again, you know?"

Sophie glowered. "Vince wanting a trade was part of *why* your marriage collapsed. He took his inability to work with your dad out on you. And then used your unhappiness at not being able to establish roots somewhere as an excuse to avoid how you grew apart. You got together before either of you knew who you were."

"I know that, and I'm glad you've always been able to see it, but that's not what the fans thought. Or the team. If anyone thinks I'm playing around with Liam, and so close to playoffs…"

Sophie winced. "Not that I'm telling you to read the comment sections—that's my job—but yeah."

"You can't tell someone not to read the comments and expect them to listen," Kate said. "I should have known it wasn't so simple as universal approval."

"Well…" Sophie reached over and squeezed Kate's forearm. "A lot of them like it. Coach's daughter and the new guy. So romantic."

Kate rolled her eyes. Romance, with Liam Caldwell? *Ha.* "What about the people who *don't* like it, Sophie?"

Sophie made a face. "They don't count."

Except they did. Her name, connected to a different hockey player this time, was an invitation for people to speculate and slander. Jesus, why did people have nothing better to do with their time than crap on other people on the internet?

"Give me the sketch outline, then," she said. "If I'm going to make a plan, I need to know what I'm dealing with."

Sophie scowled at her phone. "They're wondering if Caldwell's cold streak has anything to do with you. Saying you should know better. How much your relationship impacted the Daggers last year."

Sophie paused, wincing.

"What?" Kate asked.

"There's one ugly one. Wondering if the rumors about you and Lars were true after all."

Kate took a deep breath, waiting for the devastation to swamp her. The months of cruel speculation when her marriage ended had picked away at her until she felt like a vulture-pecked carcass bleaching in the sun.

Now, though… Sadness didn't slither up from the depths. Her gut was hot and sticky with anger. "I won't let people drag me down with baseless assumptions. Not again."

Sophie's smile tilted when she finally looked Kate's way. "Maybe they won't. For now, the attention is having a good effect on the school."

"Until someone decides to drag that through the mud, too," Kate ground out. "Loudmouths behind a keyboard cannot ruin this for us."

And she was going to need Liam Caldwell's help to control the narrative, and with it, to give her school a chance to get off the ground.

Chapter Five

Something about finishing practice with the coach's tractor-beam glare fixed on Liam had him on the verge of losing his lunch. That glare was worse than the threat of sprints up and down the spectator stairs, which Coach Sullivan had promised to assign the team if he heard one word of gossip about his daughter during practice.

He'd followed it up with a message to Liam—his ass, with PR, immediately after practice.

Apparently, if Kate did show up to talk to him, they were going to have company.

Liam went as hard as he could during drills. Even managed to jam a puck in the net on a wraparound. Maybe he needed to start doing that more—give up on wrist shots and slap shots and go for something ugly.

His goal during the game yesterday was a beauty, but any attempt to replicate the shot during practice had been wildly inaccurate.

Coach Sullivan eyed Liam from the other side of the red line, where he was running drills with the defense pairings. His mouth formed a hard line. Easy to assume the coach was mad, but in the months Liam had been a Dagger, he'd learned the older man's facial expressions. Ecstatic? Flat mouth. Contemplative? Flat mouth. Pissed off? Flat mouth. What changed was his eyes, and Liam was too far away to gauge the heat in them.

Was he like that as a dad? God, Liam couldn't imagine always having to guess what a parent was thinking. Even when his mom had been deployed with the Canadian military in Afghanistan, she'd done her best to communicate with Liam every chance she got. And his dad had filled in every gaping hole that came with having a parent serving overseas.

Money might have been tight around the Caldwell home, but not love.

Still wasn't, even though home as he knew it was disappearing, especially because of his dad's decline.

"Caldwell! Let's go!"

Liam startled to attention. Connor was his drill partner. They cycled the puck back and forth before shooting it toward the net.

Into Borisov's glove, to be specific—the goalie had Liam's number. Spectacular timing, given the practice was open to the media. Then again, if they were talking about Liam missing practice shots, maybe they wouldn't be talking about Kate laying a kiss on him.

"Weller." Connor came close and tapped Liam's chest with a fisted glove. "Block out the noise, man. You had it during the game last night. Compartmentalize, meditate, whatever the hell it is that brings out the sharpshooter."

Liam laughed. "It wasn't meditating that got my head on straight before the game last night."

Connor's face went as hard as his dad's.

Liam clapped his captain's shoulder. "Two more. Let's go."

Connor got the next shot by Borisov, and jealousy burned through Liam. The heat channeled into his next shot and he put way too much behind it, managing to almost pitch it over the glass in the corner. If it wasn't for the plexi, he'd have taken out the lone spectator lurking next to the stands—*Kate.* She was early.

Looking downright…bookish. Damn, that was sexy. A gray wool coat, jeans, a messenger bag. And God, he was weak in the face of a woman with glasses. Hers were blue acetate, and her hands were on her hips again. He wanted to be closer to her, right in front of her, to see what shade of honey-brown her eyes were today.

She pointed in his direction.

Connor caught the motion and straightened.

"Me? We've got ten minutes left, Kate," he shouted.

She shook her head and pointed again. "No, Caldwell. Obviously."

"Katherine!" A voice called from down the ice. "You're interrupting my practice."

"Sorry, Dad." Even through the glass, Liam could see her face turn red.

Not to mention a few media personality heads turning.

Kate glanced to her right, her gaze landing on the audience in the stands. She stiffened.

Liam propped his stick on the ice and spread the fingers of his gloves into as wide of a ten as he could make. He didn't want to be late to meet with PR, but he couldn't let Kate think he was blowing her off, either.

She was still standing there when practice ended. He knocked on the corner gate instead of following his teammates to the dressing room.

She opened it and let him through.

Man, he towered over her when he was in skates. She must have yanked him down to meet her lips yesterday in the tunnel, because there was no other way she could've closed the foot of distance between them. That moment was such a blur; he didn't remember the specifics. Made him want to try it again, to determine the logistics.

And to determine if my goal was a coincidence.

She had talked a lot about luck. And going off practice today, he still needed a hell of a lot of that if he wanted a contract offer anywhere near what he needed it to be.

Even so, he didn't think she'd agree to a repeat kiss here. Not with a few of the defensemen dawdling on the ice in conversation with her dad. And her brother was leaning against the boards, pretending to focus on the Daggers' home-broadcast color commentary guy, but actually giving Liam a death glare.

Liam wouldn't touch her. He wouldn't.

He wanted to.

No. I can't.

Not without her okaying it.

"And here I thought you were going to be subtle about our meeting, Katie."

Her cheeks flushed, like they always did when he used that nickname, which obviously meant he'd use it for the rest of their lives.

They would be eighty-five and playing with great-grandchildren and he would still be trying to get her to blush.

Or, I've detached from reality but good.

"We're going to have to be quick about this," he said. "Sounds like PR has some serious words for me."

"This won't necessarily mean bad press," Kate said. "You'll probably be dealing with Natalie. She's a friend of mine. Lives here in Hollow Valley—her nan is the facilities manager of this rink."

"Estelle? I haven't even been here a whole season, and I already know she's iconic."

"She is. And Natalie learned from her legendary example."

He blew out a breath. "I've been causing her no end of headaches since I arrived. Fan base loves to tear down a loser."

Fury bloomed in her eyes. "You are not a loser."

"You're right, I'm not," he said quietly. He did good work on the ice. He just never stuck around to become part of a team's long-range plan. Every time he'd been up for contract renewal, more money for a shorter term had been available, provided he'd been willing to move teams. And to meet his parents' needs, for the sake of his *own* long-range plan, he'd been willing to sacrifice the ties that formed from becoming a keystone player for one organization.

She grimaced. "I guess your phone is in your locker?"

"Yeah, why?"

"There's another angle of us last night, and I only have the screenshot my sister-in-law texted me."

"At the game, or at the bar?"

She blanched. "People were taking pictures at the bar?"

"Not that I saw, but who knows?"

She held up her phone, the screen filled with a still shot of them. It caught their side profiles, mouths fused, her hands clutching his shoulders, his glove making a mess of the back of her hair. They looked…hot.

But the social media icon in the corner made his stomach lurch.

"Guess a few folks thought our little encounter was interesting, eh?"

"Apparently the comments are mixed," she said.

"Apparently?"

"Sophie told me not to look."

"Well, all that does is make me want to look more," he said. "Pull it up. Rip off the Band-Aid."

She shook her head. "Yeah, I, uh, don't have much social media anymore. One account for photo sharing, and it's private. But I know what the comments and captions say, without having to look. No one likes when the coach's daughter creates chaos."

She looked so miserable. He stroked his gloved thumb along her cheek. "Is that what this is, Katie? Chaos?"

"I don't want it to be. But if the chatter gets too loud about what we were doing together, it could get there. And the recent launch of my hockey academy can't afford me getting dragged through the mud."

"I hear you. I know how much damage trolls can do, and women usually bear the brunt of it. And this might not be a crisis yet, but I understand the importance of staying in front of PR issues."

"I need to be seen as trustworthy, Liam."

"Right. I'll be honest, I'm concerned about the image I'm projecting, too. With being stymied for goals, I need to be seen as reliable and serious ahead of free agency. And being perceived as fooling around with the coach's daughter isn't that."

"Especially one who's already known for disrupting locker room chemistry."

He arched an eyebrow at her. "Known for? Sounds like you agree with it."

"I'd like to think I'm not responsible for the choices of over two dozen grown men. Others would disagree with me. And some of the commenters were already connecting me to your lack of scoring."

He guffawed. "You're the reason I *did* score last night. Hell, I've been wondering all day about asking you to kiss me again, just to see if it works more magic."

"You have?" She cocked her head, making her ponytail sway. He resisted the temptation to tug it.

"I need to keep scoring, Katie. I've heard of stranger pregame routines."

"Hmm. I have an idea." Her gaze darted sideways, to where her brother was still talking to the color commentator. The crowd around Connor had grown. And the captain's intense study of Liam and Kate persisted. If the guy was aiming *not* to draw attention to them, he was failing hard. Unless…

"Do you think your brother's talking about us?"

"To the media? He wouldn't. Ever."

"Right." Liam groaned. "The minute he gets me alone, he's going to be up my ass about this. Only you saying you'd be here after practice gave me a reprieve this morning."

Kate glanced at her brother. "He's not that bad. But…things with Vincent were messy. His default setting is still set to 'protect.'"

"Yeah, I picked up on that."

One of the journalists started striding toward them.

Liam grabbed Kate's elbow and turned her, making sure both their backs were toward the reporter. He bent his head to Kate's ear and guided her toward the double doors that led out to the concession area. It wasn't empty, but it was at least free of reporters.

"So, what's your idea?" he asked.

She shook out her hands a few times. A nervous tic, or a calming strategy? "We can't control what people say about us, but we can control what we show them."

"What's there to show?"

"Nothing much…yet," she said, pushing the swinging door open a second before he did the same to its mate.

He scanned the common area. No one sat on any of the benches, and a metal guard was still pulled down, blocking off the concession counter. To the right of that, Estelle was chatting with a younger man who was fixing rental helmets in the equipment locker.

Safe enough. "Seems like a loaded *yet*."

She blinked at him, luminous eyes casting a warm glow over him. He wanted to bask in that glow for a long, long time. It made him forget his problems, his—

Responsibilities. He groaned and checked the digital clock on the wall. "Natalie's going to be waiting."

"Right, right, right. I'll be quick. We need to get our story straight before you talk to her, Liam."

"Five minutes. I'll put off showering until after."

"Mmm, sweaty glove smell," she teased, then cocked her head. "Honestly, it's not that bad. You… I mean, I… Er…"

She waved off whatever she was going to say.

"You're into hockey equipment stank?"

"I'm used to it. And you…you really don't—"

She was turning bright red.

Time to give her a break.

"What's your idea? Tell the truth?"

"No. Embellish it." She turned toward him, placing her hands on his chest. Her gaze dipped. "Amplify."

He still wasn't sure what she was selling, but with the searing look she was giving him under her lashes…he'd buy whatever it was.

He tipped up her chin. "Amplify *this*?"

"I don't see a way out otherwise. No choice makes us look like saints. But if we stretch the truth and let people think we're serious about each other, if we make it look romantic, it lets us control how it plays out."

"Wait, what? We aren't *anything* about each other." Except that delicious kiss. And his inability to stop staring at her.

"I know we aren't. That's why I said *embellish.* If the world, including the team, thinks we're serious about each other, you won't look off base for fooling around with the coach's daughter. Everyone will believe it's the real thing. We can prove I'm not affecting your play. Important if, correct me if I'm wrong, you're in the market for a new contract. And a lucrative one."

He nodded sharply.

"So I could help you, *and*, I can use the added press to draw attention to my academy. My summer enrolment will rise, and I'll be able to secure my ice space for the fall." Her smile tilted. "And if you really think there's something to your new superstition… We can keep doing that."

"Kissing, you mean?" he said.

"Yep." She cupped his jaw and stroked a circle on his cheek with her thumb. Heat flared. Goddamn.

"You're right. It's not a hardship," he croaked.

"It's a…situationship."

"Which means…"

"Dates. Hanging out. Some well-placed affection in public. From now to the end of the season. With you moving on, it's a natural exit strategy. But it'll be long enough for me to know I've met my school's financial targets. Does that work for you?

It wouldn't be getting in the way of any actual relationship plans of yours?"

"Don't have any of those. Hockey takes up enough of my time."

"Gotcha. Hockey, and for now…me."

"You." Jamming a glove under his opposite arm, he took it off and traced the backs of his fingers along the side of her neck. "How far are we talking here? Are we going to elope the next time we play Vegas?"

She swatted him. "Stop it. No. You're done playing Vegas this year, and we don't need to drag it on past the end of the season."

No, they wouldn't be able to. He'd be looking to move on the minute the Daggers' season ended. That date wasn't predictable, though. They could be done in two weeks, or it could go until mid-June.

"What if we make the playoffs?" God, he hated *if.* The uncertainty, and the knowledge he was part of the reason they weren't guaranteed a spot yet, kept him up at night.

Kate got an earnest look on her face. "I'm good with being a playoff 'girlfriend' if you're good with having one." She sobered. "Just know I won't have time to deal with dry cleaner runs and keeping your fridge stocked and the like."

Dry cleaning and groceries? He lifted a brow. "Wait, we aren't planning on living together, are we?"

"Of course not, but…" She waved a hand. "Never mind."

"I wouldn't treat a girlfriend like a hired errand service, Katie. I have one of those." Curiosity burned. What had her marriage been like? "One glitch I see—there have to be people in your life who won't believe we've been together before today."

She nodded. "Sophie, my sister-in-law, for sure. But she won't say a word. I promise."

"What about Maude? And Connor?" His captain's clear guard dog routine around his sister left Liam's gut in a knot. "Plus your dad."

Air hissed between her teeth. "I don't want to lie. But... I don't want others to have to cover for us, either. And with Maude, it's too complicated for a ten-year-old to understand. What about being vague on details? Saying that we were hiding it?"

Doubt crawled up his throat. "Will that work on your brother? I literally asked him and Lars for your phone number last night. Which I never did get. Nor did we seem too familiar with each other when we were chatting with Connor outside the security entrance."

"It's believable we'd be hiding it from him and my dad, especially. Let's stick to the truth as much as possible." Her guileless, optimistic expression was at absolute odds with the fallacy she was creating. He couldn't help but smile in return. "The fewer details about how we 'got together' the better. And if there is something we have to fabricate, we text it to each other right away so that we can keep our stories straight."

"'Fabricate' sounds so much more creative than 'lying.'" He chuckled.

"We'll be honest about what's happening in the moment," she said.

"Other than how serious we are about each other."

She nodded. "Couples are allowed to have private truths."

"Caldwell." His coach's voice boomed from the doorway behind them. "You're late."

If Kate was bothered by her dad's irritation, she didn't show it, peering around Liam with a grin. "Hey, Dad. Sorry. It's my fault Liam's late. We were ironing something out."

Coach Sullivan crossed his meaty arms over his chest. "Katherine, I don't know what the hell has gotten into you, but between yesterday and today, I'm getting concerned—"

"Nothing to worry about. Promise." She bracketed both Liam's biceps with a firm grip and rose on her toes, brushing her lips over his cheek. "Sorry to make you late, babe."

"Do you think you should come to the meeting with Natalie?" he asked. "She's your friend, and—"

"I'm not a Daggers employee. I'm sure you've got this. Call me later."

She backed up, still smiling sweetly at her father.

Call me later. Liam jolted to attention. "Wait. Katie. Give me your phone for a second."

She looked at him, dark eyebrows high, but handed over the device.

"I want to text myself that picture," he said.

And in doing so, make sure he had her number, and vice versa. After sending himself the screenshot of the two of them kissing, he added himself as a contact and handed it back, winking at her as she noticed the nickname he used.

She squeaked.

Damn, she was adorable.

"*Caldwell,*" Coach repeated. "*Move.*"

"Yes, sir." He was tempted to wink again, to earn another Kate-squeak. "I'm all yours tonight, love. Promise."

"What did you call her?"

Liam didn't need to turn around to see his coach's expression. He could feel the man's lava-hot censure burning into the back of his jersey.

Kate blinked, clearly frozen.

He turned and plastered on a smile as he walked past her father, thumping the other man's shoulder twice. "Sorry, Natalie's waiting for me."

"You're all hers?" Sullivan thundered. *"Love?"*

"No need for endearments, Coach!" Liam called over his shoulder as he passed through the doors to the ice.

He was going to pay for that one. But it was safer than trying to lie to his coach and floundering. He and Kate still had a whole lot to hash out.

Chapter Six

KISS ME, KATE?
Liam Caldwell spotted kissing Kate Sullivan. Has the coach's daughter reentered the romance arena?
Picture below the cut.
Denver Daggers Blogger Babes, March 31

<3 <3 <3
@DaggerDamsel

Nice boys don't kiss like that
@RomComMom

We can say goodbye to Caldwell cuz no way is Sullivan keeping him around now
@frank1974

@frank1974 maybe this time Sullivan will ditch his daughter instead of screwing over the team
@DenverHockeyTillWeDie

Kate waited until the doors swung shut behind Liam before bestowing an innocent look on her dad. She had no clue what she wanted to say yet. Her hammering heart sounded like the discordant bedlam of lining her students up on the blue line and letting them take slap shots into the end zone for fun.

But if she didn't say something, the red creeping above the collar of her dad's royal-blue warm-up jacket was going to end in an explosion.

"Need a hug, Dad? One of the good, twenty-second ones that close a stress cycle?"

He rubbed his temples. "Katherine…"

"It works. Science," she said.

"How long has this been going on?"

"Science? Well, forever, if you think about it, though from the Western perspective, the Catholic Church was a heck of an obstacle in the Middle Ages, but—"

"Kate."

Her throat tightened. She could do this without lying. She could. She and Liam had a plan. It would work.

"It's been going on long enough to know I'm serious about being with him." No lie there.

Her dad groaned.

"It's not against any rules," she said. "I'm not a member of the Daggers organization."

"I have half a mind to put you on the payroll so that I can stop you from making another damn mistake."

She lifted her chin. "I thought we agreed we wouldn't dwell on my divorce anymore."

"And I thought you'd sworn off professional hockey players."

"You're a hockey player. You raised two NHL players, and one who got close." Her younger brother, Jake, played in Switzerland. "Almost all the men in my life who I love strap on skates for a living."

He gave her a you-know-full-well-it's-not-the-same look. "You told me you don't want to deal with the uncertainty of being married to the game. Not again."

The truth choked her. "Liam and I aren't talking marriage yet, Dad."

He lifted his hands, palms forward. "I'm just saying. You know that the NHL comes first."

"I know that as much as *anyone* in our family."

"So why are you putting yourself through this again?"

Oh, if he only knew.

"Because I enjoy being around him, Dad."

Another easy truth. In the short amount of time they'd spent together, he'd made her smile and laugh. Last night, he'd even listened when she'd talked about Toby.

Her dad pointed a thick finger at her. "That's not enough, and you know it. Seriously consider what you're doing here. Before it gets out."

She pressed her lips together. "It's already out."

"You're almost thirty. I'm not going to insert myself into your business. You won't hear another word from me, unless it becomes a problem in my dressing room. But Christ, Katherine, be careful."

The shake of his head was a hundred percent disappointment. Waving a dismissive hand, he stalked away.

She rubbed at the sting in the center of her chest. Was it weird to wish he *would* get involved in her life more often?

For once, it's better he stays distant.

Easier to pull the wool over his eyes.

Heading for the door, she tried to focus on the current benefits of him being hands off instead of on the closeness she wished she had with him.

"Kate! Hold up." The perpetually beleaguered president of the Hollow Valley Minor Hockey Association barreled over, a clipboard in one hand and an oversize equipment bag in the other. Her steel-gray pixie cut was somewhat askew, as if she'd been chasing after her twin grandsons. "We need to talk about next weekend's fundraiser."

Kate nodded and let Marja guide her over to one of the empty benches. They spent a half hour hashing out details for the joint fundraiser, a ticketed skate with some of the Daggers and fun fair activities in the parking lot of the arena. Half the proceeds were going to the league and half to Kate's school.

"Is your boyfriend going to join us for the skate?" Marja asked, almost giggling while tidying the stack of papers they'd waded through. "He isn't on the list."

"Mmm." Kate didn't want to sign Liam up without knowing

his schedule, but it would look odd if he wasn't there. "He said something about a prior commitment, but I'll check."

"He is gorgeous," Marja gushed. "You sure catch the pretty ones."

Kate cringed.

"Oh, sorry. I never like to bring up Vince. I just figured with you seeing someone new..."

"Absolutely. It's fine," Kate said. Time to start milking this thing with Liam for all it was worth. Use public opinion to her benefit for once. "Liam *is* gorgeous. And he's the biggest sweetheart."

A few minutes later, she managed to pry herself away from Marja. She hurried out the door and headed for the path back to her dad's neighborhood.

She unlocked her phone and pulled up the most recent text screen.

LOVE OF MY LIFE.

That was the nickname he gave himself in her contacts?

She didn't want to know what nickname he'd given her in his contacts.

Shaking her head, she replied. Cute, Liam. Cute.

Love of My Life: Getting into character. When's my first curtain call?

She couldn't blame him for the silly analogy. It did feel like performing on a stage. Or at least it would, once they got serious about pretending to be serious.

Kate: That comes after a performance. You mean first act.

Love of My Life: Are you a thespian, Katie?

Kate: Afraid not. But my mom loved the theatre. More than she loved hockey, so she used to take me to musicals whenever she could. It was our thing. As much as my dad worshiped my mom, he hated going to anything that wasn't competitive. And they never expected my brothers to go. She was...old fashioned.

She wasn't sure why she'd given him so much detail. Sorry, more than you were looking for.

Love of My Life: No, I like learning about you. Part of the gig.

Kate: Shouldn't you be in the meeting?

Love of My Life: Natalie just finished reading me the riot act.

Kate: Ah, she gave you a warning about besmirching the Daggers' good name?

Love of My Life: No, about not breaking your heart.

Kate couldn't help but smile. Nat's a loyal one.

Love of My Life: And a die-hard romantic, apparently. She's lamenting that we have no good ship name options.

She stifled a laugh. She didn't like Katam? Callivan? Litherine?

Love of My Life: That last one sounds like someone with a lisp is talking about mouthwash.

She snorted, and scrolled through the emoji menu.

A wall of bark flashed in her vision. She stopped short, inches away from the tree trunk marking a fork in the trail. Yikes. Walking and texting with a cute boy was more of a hazard than she'd thought.

Yeah, Liam Caldwell is a hazard, all right.

One she could manage, though.

Taking the path to the left, she sent him a laughing emoji, and then, You're right, Litherine won't work. We'll have to workshop it.

Love of My Life: See, another theatre term. Are you sure there isn't poor quality video of a preteen Kate acting as Juliet somewhere?

Kate: Preteen me lived at the rink. For my brothers' practices and games as much as mine, at least until Toby and Connor were old enough to drive themselves.

Love of My Life: The scheduling must have been wild. Even with just me, it was a strain on my dad. With my mom overseas for long stretches of time, the taxi service fell to him.

Kate: At that age, I would have envied being an only child. Not that having more time to drive me to practice would have convinced my mom that hockey was anything but a hobby for me.

The second she pressed Send, regret flooded her stomach. For one, even joking about having wanted to be an only child felt awful, knowing she would do pretty much anything to have Toby be alive. Nor did complaining about her mom sit right, given she wasn't here to explain her perspective. Rehash, more accurately. Kate had heard it all, from her mom *and* dad.

You're too small to make it in a men's league.

You'll get an academic college scholarship. You don't need an athletic one like Jake will.

I can't be in three places at once. Connor's elite camp comes first.

None of these things were untrue.

But she couldn't help wondering where she would have ended up if she hadn't been in the Sullivan boys' shadows. The IIHF World Championship games? The Olympic Games?

She shook her head. No point focusing on anything except

what she could do now: remove barriers for Maude and other girls to excel.

A new text notification popped up.

Love of My Life: Damn, Katie. That's a rough attitude to have to fight against. You must have put up a good one, though. I saw your jersey on the wall at Sullivan's.

She grimaced. It's there because Sophie insisted on hanging it.

Love of My Life: It's there because you're a superstar in your own right. And not because you happen to share a name with a certain Saturday Night Live character.

Love of My Life: Unless sticking your fingers in your armpits and sniffing them is your thing, of course.

She laughed and stopped walking, right before she got to the metal gate at the end of the path. With the arrival of spring, both sides of the trail were lined with bright green growth. Soaking in the vibrancy, and the scent of new leaves was one of her favorite ways to de-stress.

Most days, it worked. Not so much on the days she spilled about her past to Liam Caldwell, apparently.

She sent him a tongue-sticking-out emoji, and then typed, Here I am, telling you all my childhood secrets.

Love of My Life: Tell you what. On our first date, I'll spill one of mine.

The pressure in her chest lifted by a few pounds. Good trade. When will that be?

Love of My Life: What time does your hockey practice end tomorrow morning?

She narrowed her eyes at the screen. He knew what she did on Tuesday mornings? Had she mentioned it?

Back when she'd started coaching Maude's teams, Vincent had never bothered to remember her coaching schedules, claiming they always changed. She'd gotten used to tiptoeing out of the bedroom in the morning and showering and getting ready for the day in their second bathroom. Then she'd come home to a husband who hadn't been sure if she'd been at the rink or out getting an early start on errands.

Liam asking about it now triggered something she didn't like to face.

She kept her reply simple. How do you know I'm coaching tomorrow?

Love of My Life: Natalie

She sent him a facepalm emoji.

Love of My Life: I managed to hedge my way out of sounding like a completely inattentive boyfriend. And then she said something about me at least remembering *that* you coach, let alone knowing when. And then she wouldn't elaborate, so I left it be. What's the deal?

Her pulse thunked.

Kate: You're going to need to give up at least five of your own embarrassing truths before I explain that one.

Love of My Life: Noted. I'll keep track. So what time?

Kate: 7:30.

Love of My Life: K. See you then.

She couldn't lie to herself. She was looking forward to seeing Liam. The sooner, the better.

Chapter Seven

NEW MAN, SAME FIGHT FOR KATE SULLIVAN?
Coach Sullivan spotted arguing with pair after Monday's practice.
Denver Daggers Bloggerista Babes, April 1

On Tuesday morning, Liam arrived at the Hollow Valley sports complex early to cajole Kate and put in a bit of work.

He had a girlfriend to impress.

Or a woman he needed to appear to be trying to impress, anyway. He wasn't sure if he'd be able to do anything about the text she'd sent him an hour ago—heads up, haven't had the chance to talk to Connor yet because he was out on a date last night—but he did have a plan. Back in November, he'd recognized Estelle Zvarych as the beating heart of Hollow Valley's sports complex within ten minutes of walking into the facility. He also knew she had a soft spot for Daggers players, and he wasn't too proud to lean on her favoritism to gain some help.

Parents and skaters stood on and around thc built-in benches in the waiting area between the rinks. Leg warmers, helmets, hockey gloves and equipment bags were strewn along the floor and wooden seats. Looked like the figure skating club occupied one of the public ice sheets and minor hockey the other. A typical morning of being sports parents, going off all the lace tying and coffee in to-go cups and socializing. His dad had been one of those parents during Liam's minor hockey career, shooting the breeze all over small-town Saskatchewan, essentially a single parent during Liam's mom's deployments.

Liam pulled his baseball cap a fraction lower over his eyes but shucked the hood of his plain gray sweatshirt and shifted his duffel bag on his shoulder. There was a difference between hiding in plain sight and sticking out because a disguise was too complicated. And as much as he was here to be seen with Kate, his plans for the morning would be easier if he could prepare for them uninterrupted.

He skirted the crowd, keeping his gaze low, only tossing out a smile when Rika Tiimonen's wife, Anneli, lifted a hand from where she was wrangling one of her sons out of his chest protector.

His target, the concession, was still closed.

Estelle was behind the equipment rental counter. *Excellent.* Time to turn on the charm. He hated to think of it as a weapon. More a tool. One to wield with care and respect.

He leaned an elbow on the counter and slapped on a tilted grin. "Estelle, mauve is your color."

She dropped an armful of helmets into a rolling bin and scurried over.

"Flattery will get you everywhere, Liam Caldwell."

"I know. But I'm also serious about the mauve."

She patted the bright beanie covering her shoulder-length silver hair. "My granddaughter knitted it for me." Her eyes narrowed. "In fact, she's close to your age. Have you met her?"

He put a hand to his chest. "I have, and she's a gem. But sadly—well, not so sadly for me, in fact—I am a taken man."

She brightened. "I heard that rumor. From my granddaughter, in fact."

And she'd still hinted at setting him up with Natalie? He raised an eyebrow.

"Had to test you," she explained. "See how serious you are about our Mary Kate."

"Making me run a gauntlet, and it's barely 7:00 a.m."

"Worth trying."

"I can tell you this much—I'm still trying to impress Kate. And I have a favor to ask of you."

"You need an accomplice." Her gaze sparkled. A woman who liked a good gambit, Estelle. He'd remember that.

"Yup. An accomplice with the keys to the concession, who's willing to warm up the hot chocolate machine and teakettle early and to let me in there so that I can make a team's worth of hot chocolates and one chai with soy milk. If you have it."

"I do. I bring it in special for Kate." She cocked her head. "You're going to make them, dear? I could ask one of my employees to do it."

"And lose my chance for a romantic gesture? No, ma'am." Or, at least, it would look like a romantic gesture from the outside. Only Kate would know it was for show. "Also, you're looking at Desolation Cove's fastest hot-drink slinger. Had to pay for elite registration fees somehow, and the only place hiring was the diner on the water."

After his mom had come home wounded from her last tour of duty, money had been tight. They'd moved to British Columbia—to the small, coastal town where his dad inherited his childhood home—trying to stretch his dad's salary as a high school teacher and his mom's disability pension as far as they could. Keeping Liam in hockey equipment and extra skills camps had been a major sacrifice, one he never wanted to forget. A big advantage to his higher-value, shorter-term contracts was setting his parents up with financial security and medical support, both for now and into the future. He might not stay with any one team for very long, but at least his bank account was in order. And he'd make sure it would remain that way, so long as he could swing another lucrative signing after July 1.

Estelle blinked in surprise. "Liam Caldwell, pouring coffee for a bunch of small-town locals? What do you know. I bet you working at that café increased their sales."

"Now who's the flatterer?"

"When it's deserved. Follow me, dear. It's a one-button machine. Easy peasy. Nothing that'll require your advanced training."

She winked at him and then came out from behind the

rental desk to lead him through the back door of the concession. Right before the door swung shut behind them, heavy footsteps clomped in the hall.

"Hey! Weller!"

He groaned under his breath and held the door open for his captain, who was dressed in a hoodie and sweats similar to Liam's. Goddamn Connor and his early rising. He had an hours-long routine before morning practice and was always the first player at the arena.

"What the hell are you doing here already? And in the concession?" Connor demanded.

"Let me get set up so that I'm not wasting Estelle's time. Then I'll explain."

His captain seemed mildly mollified, so Liam put his bag down and focused on Estelle's instructions for making the hot chocolate and Kate's chai.

"I'll come back after practice to pay for it all," he offered. "That way you don't have to open the till early."

"Let me see Kate's face when you show up with a tray of drinks, and I'll let you have them for free."

"I couldn't let you do that, Estelle, but if you want to see Katie's reaction, I'll be taking those drinks over at the end of her practice."

She sighed. "*Katie.* What a sweetheart, you are."

His ears warmed. "Pretty common variation on her name."

"But not one anyone else uses."

He half expected her to pinch his cheek.

She smiled and left, insisting he holler if he ran into any trouble.

After she was out the door, Liam busied himself setting up cups on a tray and ignoring his captain. With Kate not having had the chance to talk to her brother yet, pulling the wool over Connor's eyes was falling on Liam's shoulders. He held in a shudder.

"*Katie*?" Connor echoed. "What in the actual hell is that about?"

"Common for people to use nicknames in general, but especially when they're dating," Liam said mildly, putting the first cup under the spout and pressing the button. The machine hissed and hot liquid streamed out.

The sound resembled Connor's annoyance.

"Yeah, *dating.* That's the part that isn't making a lick of sense. I've never seen you together, other than earlier yesterday. And last night, you asked me for her number."

"We hadn't decided to tell people yet," he said.

Huh, Kate was right. Being vague did mean saying something technically true but alluding to something that wasn't.

"You pretended you hadn't met? And you know each other… well?" Connor's disbelief was loud enough the kids probably heard him through the windows separating the lobby area and the rink.

Liam switched cups, then filled the new one. "Jesus, if you want to broadcast it to the whole arena, you could have Estelle get you the mic for the PA."

"Brave words from someone hooking up with my sister."

"It's not like that." Liam grabbed one of the cups too hard and sloshed searing liquid onto the back of his hand. "Ow! Damn it."

Connor crossed his arms. "What's it like, then? Are you into her?"

"Thanks for the concern, Sully." He wrung his hand rapidly, swearing at the sting.

"A little pain from a burn will be the least of your hurts if you're messing around with my sister for laughs."

"As if I would date your sister if I didn't have genuine feelings for her. I do not have a death wish."

Another half-truth—he and Kate might not be in love or anything, but the attraction sparking between them and the protectiveness rising the longer he argued with Connor was damn genuine.

He stared at the cups he'd filled so far. Hopefully, a treat for her team would make those warm glints in her eyes surface. And the sweet pink in her cheeks.

A butterfly—*one,* not a flock or anything—fluttered in his stomach. Okay, maybe the romantic gesture wasn't *entirely* for show.

His captain grunted, jaw set. "Whatever it is you two are doing, do not screw it up."

"Christ, man, I'm planning on the opposite."

Ugh, would this machine not work faster? If he had to face the third degree for the time it took to make another eleven cups of hot chocolate, he'd be bound to say the wrong thing and make Connor more suspicious.

"Last night was a hell of a soft launch, then," Connor said.

"Yeah. I did not expect Kate to kiss me at that exact moment," he admitted.

"Probably easier not to have to hide."

"You could say that."

Connor exhaled, the sigh of a man who thought he'd been deeply inconvenienced. He made a give-it-to-me motion with a hand. "Here. I'll fill the cocoa. You go deal with whatever fancy crap you're making for Kate."

Less than fifteen minutes later, Liam was making his way into the public part of the arena, drinks on a tray, his duffel over his shoulder and his captain in tow.

"You have a rapt audience," Connor remarked in a low voice, tipping his chin toward Estelle, who was making her way through the stands with a broom and stick-handled dustpan.

No doubt hoping for a show.

Liam made his way along the front row of seats and called out "everyone okay with the kids having a little treat?" to the parents and trusted adults in the stands.

The reactions ranged from surprised yeses to the odd thumbs-up. A few mouths twitched into smiles.

"I hope you have a Sharpie in your pocket," Connor said. "I watch Maude play all the time, so I'm old news, but you won't be."

"No, I didn't think to bring one."

"What are you, a rookie?" Mouth fighting disdain, Connor fished one out of the pocket of his sweats and handed it over, then made his way to a group of moms in the stands.

He'd never really processed how his captain was a father figure, but if Kate had stepped up with Maude when Toby died, Connor probably had, too. Today, though, Liam wasn't sure if his captain was there to watch his niece or if he was sticking around in hopes Liam would make a fool out of himself.

Too bad for Connor, Liam's plan couldn't fail. Kids never said no to hot chocolate after practice, and he sensed Kate was way too much of a softie not to be touched.

Free from his glowering shadow, and with the necessary permission from the adults in the vicinity, Liam made his way around one of the ends and along the stretch of boards to where the players would get off the ice.

Kate was standing at center ice, with a net bag filled with soccer balls. The team formed a wide circle around her, shifting on their skates in anticipation. None of them held sticks, and all were grinning like Muppets. Liam sat in a folding chair behind a stanchion, not wanting to interrupt the magic.

"Ready?" Kate called. "Remember, you're getting timed as a team. Get the balls in the nets faster than last practice, and you get to vote on what fun activity we do for our away tournament."

Nineteen heads nodded.

Kate emptied the bag on the ice, blew her whistle and started kicking balls to all four corners of the rink as her players darted after them.

Liam chuckled at the mayhem. They were hooting and hollering, encouraging each other. A few fell, of course. The point of the drill, aside from teamwork and fun, was probably to improve their footwork, and some of them were still getting there. Maude caught his eye from the corner. Having watched her the other day, he knew she was skilled enough to round up all the balls and score herself, but instead, she was collecting the balls from the boards and passing them to her teammates.

A leader, as well as talented. No wonder Kate was so invested in giving her niece the opportunities she needed to succeed. Might be related to Kate's text from yesterday, too, about her mom seeing hockey as a hobby, not a career. Curiosity still simmered in his chest, but he'd wanted to have the conversation in person, not over text.

With one ball to go, Maude finally kicked her own in.

Kate blew the whistle. "Two minutes, seventeen seconds! You shaved twenty-one seconds off your time!"

She gave them a muted round of applause with her gloved hands.

They swarmed her at center ice, whooping and cheering.

"Katie, send them my way when you're done with them," he called, standing and sliding out from his hiding place. "I have a little something to help celebrate their victory."

Kate's gaze landed on him. Her jaw dropped.

He held the tray high enough for her to see.

A corner of her mouth rose and her eyes lit, and *yes*, there it was—pink in her cheeks.

His own little victory.

A second butterfly flew in to join the first, the rioting in his stomach closer to the reaction he'd expect from scoring the goal he was desperate for, not from bringing a smile to his fake girlfriend's face.

"Oh, man, Liam Caldwell?" one kid exclaimed.

Maude waved, and Liam grinned back.

A couple of minutes later, practice ended. To say he got

mobbed was an understatement. He distributed hot chocolate to some intense grabby hands, and then got busy signing sticks and cups with the Sharpie Connor had lent him.

After a few minutes, Kate took control back. "Kiddos! School bell's in forty-five. Get your patooties in gear. And say thank you to Caldwell. Both for the drinks and for getting you out of cleanup."

He winced an apology.

She shrugged.

Maude nudged him on her way past. "Nice goal on Sunday. You even showed up Uncle Connor."

Oh, Connor would love that.

"There's no one-upping each other when we're on the same team, Sullivan. I wouldn't have scored without your uncle's pass."

"I guess." Her dark eyes danced. "You gonna do it again in your next game?"

"That's the goal," he said, faking a cymbal riff and making a *ba-dum-tssss.*

Maude laughed and made her way to the dressing room.

Kate shook her head. "Hell of a dad pun, Caldwell. And guess who's on cleanup after that show."

"Even with me making you a milk-foam leaf?" He handed her the tea he'd balanced on the lip of the boards.

She took the lid off to inspect his latte art. "Wow. You know what you're doing."

"My barista skills were *kryptonite* to the girls at my high school."

"Yeah, I'm sure your face had nothing to do with it," she muttered, taking a sip and then sighing happily.

He leaned forward, elbows on the boards, serving her with a smirk. "What's wrong with my face, superstar?"

"Nothing, and you know it."

Christ, she was cute. He was about to lean even closer and

give her a kiss on the cheek, but out of the corner of his eye he caught Connor and the rest of the parents filing around the walkway past the end zone toward the kids' locker room. His captain didn't literally point at his eyes and then at Liam to signal "I'm watching you," but it was close.

He straightened and sent Connor a sarcastic salute.

Kate choked out a laugh. "I'm so sorry you had to deal with him before I could."

"I handled it," he said. "He thinks we've been together for an undefined amount of time, and that we were hiding it on purpose. Until last night, when you got all cheeky."

She cocked an eyebrow.

He held up both hands in defense. "I am not complaining, Kate. Let's be real about that."

Her lips pressed in a brief, thin line. "You got your skates in that bag?"

"A spare pair. Figured I might need them," he said.

"You sure do." She was oddly stiff, her gaze flicking between Liam and the straggling parents.

He stepped closer and caught her under the chin with a finger. "Hey, Katie. Relax."

Fear flashed honey gold under her dark lashes.

"Have a little fun with me," he whispered. "Cleanup gives us an excuse to play. I was getting jealous of your team being so silly on the ice. You're multitalented, getting them to have a good time without them realizing the point was to improve their footwork."

Her throat bobbed with a swallow. "Th-thanks for seeing that."

"Yeah. Of course." He caught a strand of hair off her cheek and brushed it away. "I also see that you're nervous. So you let me know what's next."

He'd wanted to get another kiss before his game tomorrow,

but he wasn't going to do anything she wasn't ready for, not with that streak of terror he'd glimpsed.

"It's the unknown, you know?"

"Well, let's make it more known. Take control."

She shivered, and he stroked his hands down the soft fleece sleeves of her jacket.

"Control. Right," she said.

He lived for it. This was just one more element to master.

After getting his skates on, he joined her on the ice. She bossed him around, directing him to clear away the nets and then the soccer balls. With every order, her shoulders settled more, until the only thing left on the ice was green and purple marker left over from the bingo-dabber routes she'd scribbled in each end.

"Estelle will clear the marks when she runs the Zamboni over the ice," Kate explained. Her gaze dipped down his body.

Wait, was she checking out his sweatpants? Or, more precisely, what was under them?

Another flick of her gaze.

Ha, she *was*.

He lifted his brows.

Blushing, she grabbed his hands and skated backward toward the far end of the rink.

"I know, I know—unreasonably hot for an equipment boy," he teased.

"And a model of humility."

Spinning her around, he tugged her back against his front, grabbed his phone and took a selfie of the two of them while she was still wearing her flustered smile.

"A little morning socials activity to fan the flames?" he asked, holding up the shot. In it, she was looking at the camera. He was looking at her.

"Post it," she whispered.

He uploaded it to the stories on one of his socials apps and then pulled her back with him for a short video of them skating in reverse, which he shared on one of the apps that got more video traffic.

"No caption?" she asked.

"Better to be mysterious," he said. He pivoted around her, crouching into an exaggerated defensive position. "Get past me, superstar."

Annoyance flared on her face. "You don't have a stick. Or a helmet."

"So don't knock me over."

She faked him out twice, but he spun her around and drove her gently into the corner. With her back pressed against the boards, and no pads on either of them, feeling every curvy inch of her against him was way too easy.

"Ha," she murmured. "I beat you to the boards. I'm the champion."

No, I am.

Holding her to the cold puck board and plexiglass was a hundred percent a win.

"Next time we get together, we need to spend some time getting to know each other." he suggested.

She nodded. "After your morning skate tomorrow? I'll have an hour before my shift at the bar."

"How late are you working? I was going to ask if you wanted to come to the game."

Her cheeks lost their rosy glow. "Until eight. And it's been a while since I watched a game at the Dagger Den. It'll be expected, though. It's tight to switch tomorrow's shift, but I could try."

A hitch in her tone warned him to tread carefully. "Don't worry about tomorrow, Kate. Maybe you can catch the one next Thursday. So, you work day shifts, too?"

"Once or twice a week."

"See, this is what I need to know. Time for a crash course in Kate, and vice versa."

"Okay." She bit her lip, her lashes downcast.

The closeness was too tempting. He leaned in, a silent invitation.

Her hand stopped him. "Not…not yet. It might have helped you score the other day, but we were in the tunnel at the Dagger Den, right before a game. This won't check any of your superstitious boxes."

He straightened. "All good. Of course. But once you give the go-ahead, I'm going to kiss you in other places than at the Denver arena, Katie. And for other reasons than luck. Part of appearing to be your boyfriend."

"I know." She palmed his cheek and peeked around him. "But I think this has been enough of a show for today. I should clear out. My 'boyfriend' brought me tea, after all. And it's getting cold sitting on the bench."

Lips quirking, she scooted out of his arms and skated away.

He snapped another shot, catching her ponytail in flight as she picked up speed.

Chasing Kate Sullivan could keep a guy occupied for a lifetime. Good thing she didn't want that from him. *Lifetime* wasn't in Liam's repertoire.

Chapter Eight

The next morning, Liam stood in front of his locker after the team's game day skate, staring at the dozen or so pictures some cheeky asshole had plastered on the wall behind the hooks where he hung his clothes. Each shot was identical, a color copy of Kate and him kissing in the tunnel.

Oskar Larsen, one of Liam's locker neighbors, stood next to him, head cocked at the impromptu collage. "Someone was busy."

"Who, Kate and me or whichever of our teammates decided they're now an *artiste*?"

"All of the above, I guess," Lars said before stripping out of his plain blue jersey and shoulder pads.

Across the room, Jonesy and Jay Johnson were leaning against their lockers, killing themselves laughing. Brian Boyle sat next to them, glaring.

"Does loyalty mean nothing anymore?" The defenseman threw his towel in a laundry bin. "She was Vince's *wife.*"

"I don't have to be loyal to a prick like Vince, Boyle," Johnson said calmly. "He was in the wrong, not Kate. She deserves to be happy. And so does Weller."

Boyle spat out a curse and stomped off.

Yeesh. That dude was never going to be Liam's biggest fan.

Liam slotted his gloves onto their drying posts and ran a hand through his hair, examining the collection of pictures. What would a guy in a relationship do in this situation? Ignore Boyle's tantrum, for starters.

"Nice, gentlemen," he said with a lazy salute at Jonesy and Johnson. "Saved me the trouble of bringing a picture of her from home. Now that she decided we should go public and all."

"Did she ever!" Johnson called over, cupping his mouth with

his brown-skinned hands and letting out a whoop. "In all seriousness, though, Kate is a gem. You're a lucky bastard."

"You know it." Liam cracked a grin.

Unlike the Dagger Den in Denver, where both the main dressing room and the dry locker where they kept their clean clothes to change into were devoid of personal belongings, the Hollow Valley practice rink allowed for individual touches.

With careful fingers, Liam peeled off the white hockey tape the jokesters had used to stick the paper to the wall. He took the picture in the best condition and centered it at the back of his locker, squarely in view. The rest, he kept in a neat stack. The prank was funny enough to share with her, once he was showered and dressed and ready for their rapid-fire "learn as much as we can about each other in an hour" date.

Lars, who was now down to his shorts, athletic shirt and shower shoes, nodded at Liam's cleanup efforts. "Best to be proud, dating a person like Kate."

"I sure am."

The Norwegian sobered. "In case any of the lies made their way to Carolina, anything Vincent said about Kate and me was precisely that: Lies. Hurtful ones. Messed up a friendship I valued."

"I believe you, man. Not that I put much stock in locker room gossip, especially when it involves wives and partners."

He'd paid so little attention, in fact, that he didn't know what the hell Lars was referring to. Whatever it was, though, his teammate's sincerity was obvious. He'd have to get Kate to fill him in.

Lars nodded. A hint of relief crossed his face as he made his way to the showers.

Liam finished taking off his gear, showering and dressing, and then made his way to the arena lobby, the stack of pictures safely in his hand.

There must have been a lull in the lessons and public skating schedule, because the lobby was empty but for a few adult skaters tying on skates and one beautiful woman lingering by a glass trophy cabinet, hands jammed in the pockets of her navy, zip-up hoodie. She wore her glasses. Maybe she only wore contacts when she skated? He'd have to ask. As he approached, her smile tilted, a hint of nerves.

"Hey, love," he said. They were in public, so he was going to do it up good. Even though there wasn't much chance the small number of people in the vicinity were paying attention.

She blinked. Her cheeks flushed.

He approached until he was close enough to greet her properly, then pressed his lips to her forehead.

"Liam…"

Leaning in close to her ear, he murmured, "Keep saying my name like that, and I'll be even more impatient to give you a real kiss."

She inhaled sharply, the sweetest little sound he'd heard all day.

Threading his fingers through hers, he guided her toward the doors. "Let's get outside. I learn better in fresh air."

She nodded, peering at the papers in his other hand. "What are those?"

"Present from Jonesy." He held up the stack so she could see it better.

She snorted. Also an adorable noise. God, she was full of them.

"I'd take his efforts as a compliment," she said.

"Yeah, probably." He stopped by the garbage and recycling cans right by the front door. "Want one before I toss the rest?"

"Uh, sure."

He let go of her hand and folded one of the ones he'd managed not to rip when peeling it off his locker. He handed it to her and dropped the remainder in the bin.

She unfolded it for a second, shook her head with a fond look on her face and tucked it into her hoodie pocket.

Before she could put her hands in her pockets, too, he tugged her left back into his grasp and squeezed. "Time to teach me the basics, Coach Kate. Rapid-fire. A shoot-out."

"Let's walk down the path to my house and back. Uh, my dad's house, I mean. I live in his pool house. Definitely something you'd know."

He nodded and followed her lead toward an asphalt trail through a forested area hugging the south and west walls of the arena. With the sun out, he didn't need to zip his jacket. And even with the scent of fresh-cut grass in the air, he still caught a trace of vanilla-citrus.

"Is that your shampoo? Whatever smells like a Creamsicle?"

She blinked. "Uh, yeah."

He nodded. "I use some fancy crap from the salon around the corner from my condo, where I get my hair cut. Couldn't tell you what it smells like, exactly. It's supposed to help with thinning. Not that I've started to, yet, but a guy starts to worry, once he turns thirty. My mom's dad was bald as a cue ball, so I might be screwed."

She stopped walking. "Bend down."

"Huh?" But he followed her lead, pausing next to a thick-trunked evergreen and ducking his head for her.

She leaned in, sniffing. "Juniper. And mint of some kind?" She scooted closer and inhaled again.

"You like it?" he asked, his voice raspier than a few seconds ago. Sue him, but having her this close made him want to get even closer.

"Yeah." That breathy tone again.

He barely held in a groan. Straightening, he gave her a mischievous smile. "See, learning all the important stuff already."

"Right." She started walking again, faster this time. The trees thinned out, leaving space for houses to peek through on either side. "Uh, my favorite color is blue."

"I don't have one," he said. Though it might soon become

deep honey-amber, if he wasn't careful. "We're going about this wrong, though. No one's going to quiz us on our favorites. Personality stuff, though—if we don't know that, it'll look weird. And habits."

"Like?"

"Side of the bed."

"Left," she said.

"Middle," he said. "Cuddling?"

"Yet to be determined," she said. "Back to side of the bed—I won't put up with a bed hog, Caldwell."

"And we're not going to be testing it out, so it's moot, Sullivan."

"Of course," she said quickly.

Too quickly.

"Wait, did you think we *would* be?"

"No! I was just… It's more information for you. I would not put up with a bed hog. Neutral data for your files."

"All right then. Uh, are you a chaos goblin, or a silly goose?"

The look she dealt him could have dried up a bin of sweaty equipment.

"I'm serious," he insisted. "Key personality trait."

She shook her head, but her mouth screwed up in thought.

"Silly goose," she finally said with a definitive nod.

"Final answer?"

"Yes. I'm not really chaotic. Or impulsive."

He guffawed. "You kissed me on a whim, in *public*. Chaos behavior to a T."

"I did it for *your* sake!"

Lifting her hand to his lips, he kissed the soft spot between her thumb and finger. "If you're taking anything from my point as a complaint, you're reading me wrong."

A long breath shuddered between her lips. Her hand tensed in his. "I am so not good at this."

"You feel good to me. *Seem* good."

She didn't call him out on his quick correction, but the small lift of the corner of her mouth hinted at satisfaction.

"I have another question. Not sure you'll be willing to answer," he said cautiously.

She worried her lip. "What question?"

"What rumor did your ex spread about you and Lars, Katie?"

Her jaw hardened. "What lie, you mean."

He nodded.

She sighed and pulled her hand away, then crossed her arms over the bottom of her ribs.

His phone buzzed in his pocket. The trail was quiet enough he could hear the hum. He ignored it and waited for her to say something.

The cell stopped for a few seconds, then started vibrating again.

"You should answer that," she said quietly.

He checked it and made an apologetic face at Kate. "It's my mom."

"Take it. Of course. Living away from your parents can't be easy."

He answered. "Hey, Mom."

"Li, honey. Glad I caught you. Do you have a moment to talk?"

"Sure." Kate didn't seem to mind, and there was a bench ten feet away where they could pause. He strode over to it and sat. "Everything okay?"

"Enh," his mom said. "I've had better days. But I can't expect them all to be pain-free. Also, we need to talk about your dad."

The strain in her voice choked him up. Her willingness to admit it, too. She always put on a brave face for him, even when he asked her not to.

Kate sat next to him on the bench and took out her own phone. It looked like she was checking her email.

"Can I do anything?" he asked his mom. Goddamn it, he

was limited in how he could help. He'd bought their house, had it renovated and paid for any ongoing care not covered by their pensions. The extreme solution—him quitting hockey and moving home to be an extra set of hands—would put them all in a terrible financial place. Not to mention giving up the game he loved and shitting on all the sacrifices his parents made to get him here.

"Yes—you can play your best tonight. Score another goal. Maybe get another kiss before your game?" she teased. "How many daughters does your coach have, anyway?"

"Only the one," Liam said, matching her joking tone. "But even if he had more, it wouldn't matter. I'm keeping the one I have."

"You are, are you?" Deadly serious.

He glanced at Kate, who had stilled at his side and was studying him with wide eyes. Could she hear his mom's side of the conversation? He winked at her. "Yeah, I kinda like her."

Kate drew in a quick breath.

His mom chuckled. "I see. It's like that. I knew when you eventually fell, you'd fall hard."

"We're taking it one day at a time," he said lightly, his gaze still on Kate. "My contract is at the forefront of my thoughts, and it's all but guaranteed I'll have to sign elsewhere because of the salary cap. But it's looking like more of a possibility we'll make the playoffs. I feel good about this team."

Kate gave him a thumbs-up.

"We'll be watching tonight," his mom said. "Unless your dad takes a turn this afternoon. He's been..."

He waited for her to finish. What cognitive decline was the most recent? Had he lost interest in history documentaries, or was it getting harder for him to bathe himself? Liam didn't know what was worse—being there every day to witness his dad disappear or going longer stretches and then being walloped by the drastic changes the few times a year he made it home.

Home.

It would never be the same, not without his dad.

Clearly, his mom wasn't going to finish what she'd been about to say, so he asked, "Yeah, what about Dad do we need to discuss?"

"He wants to talk to you," she said.

Hope lightened his chest. "Great. It's been a few calls since we've been able to have a proper conversation."

Too often these days, his dad was somewhere other than the present.

"Ah, Liam… Like I said, it's not a good day."

He didn't bother fighting to keep the corners of his mouth up. His mom couldn't see his face, anyway. "I'll meet him where he is."

"Somewhere in the early aughts, is my guess. Let me pass him the phone."

Kate's hand caressed his shoulder. Sliding her hand to the middle of his back, she rubbed a slow circle.

The small touch eased some of the tension building in his gut. He leaned into her touch.

"Liam! Kiddo."

Oof. Was he going to have to pretend he was in elementary school? High school made it a little easier. Regardless, it was brutal. He sucked in a breath. "Hey, Dad."

"Wow, son. I swear, you go away for a weekend and you sound like you're a full-on adult. How's your tournament going? Sorry I had to miss this one. So much marking to do before report cards are due."

"Uh, yeah," he said, tone gentle. His eyes shuttered closed and he grimaced. "Hockey's good. I scored a goal in our last game. Have you been gardening yet? The, uh, bulbs are starting to push up here."

The question, and his dad's lengthy response about their plans for the garden, gave him a few minutes' reprieve. So long as he alternated between empathetic humming and surprised, 'oh, really?' noises, yard work was a safe topic. From time to time, his mom made noise about assisted living, but Liam would be happy to hire all the nurses in the world if it meant his parents could stay in the space they loved.

With Kate's hand still splayed between his shoulder blades, he slumped further on the bench.

"How many games do you have left to play, Liam?" his dad said, switching away from the health of the rhododendrons.

"Uh, three?" he guessed, aiming for something reasonable.

"You're finding time to study, right? That math test on Monday won't care how many goals you scored. Even though we love to hear that you're winning."

His throat tightened. "Yeah, I studied for hours. Mr. Brar's been helping me all week."

"Math is important. Your hockey performance is all applied math."

Liam dragged a hand down his face. "For sure."

"And your essay on *The Chrysalids*."

Ah. Solidly in grade ten. He racked his brain, his chest aching. "That's due Wednesday. I'm on top of it. I promise."

Goddamn it, how did his mom do this every day? Screw his earlier doubt. Having to dance around dementia all the time was miles worse than seeing it from afar. Christ. Guilt nagged him for being far away, but also for the part of him he'd buried deep. He was a shitty son for being even remotely thankful he didn't have to witness every moment of his dad's decline.

They went in circles for a few more minutes about some long-forgotten thesis statement tying the themes of persecution in the novel to the historic context Wyndham had drawn from.

He shot Kate another apologetic look. He was eating into the scant hour he'd get with Kate today, but his dad needed him, too.

Sorry, he mouthed.

Her gaze was nothing but empathetic. She scooted closer, sliding her arm farther around him, a full half-hug.

The second his dad switched back to Liam's math test, he couldn't take it anymore. "Hey, Dad? I have another question for Mom. Can you pass the phone back to her?"

"You can't avoid your schoolwork, Liam—"

"I'm not. I promise. I'll study extra hard this week." He scrubbed his free hand down his face and tried to keep the ugly mix of frustration and sorrow and hopelessness from bleeding into his tone. "I love you. I'll see you soon."

With a grumble, his dad said goodbye.

"Liam." His mom wasn't doing much better at keeping her anguish out of her voice, either. "Thanks, honey. It sucks, I know."

"I haven't caught a lucid moment with him in a while," he said quietly.

"There aren't that many of them." She cleared her throat. "We need to increase his care, Li. It's time for round-the-clock nursing."

"I'll arrange that with the service, Mom." He could at least take that off her plate.

"But Liam—"

"I can do it before my nap this afternoon. I'm off to Calgary tomorrow."

"I'm not sure it's best for us to stay in the house anymore," she blurted.

"Let's not make decisions now, yeah? If you have a nurse with him all the time, it'll be better."

She was kind enough not to point out it would never be better.

"I love you, honey."

"Love you, too, Mom."

After a goodbye, he put his phone down on the seat next to him. The device felt like it weighed twenty pounds and his arm was tired. Hell, his *soul* was tired.

"I'm sorry," he said to Kate, staring at the trees on the other side of the path and trying to get back to level. “That took way longer than I expected. I guess you’ll have to show me where you live another day.”

“Those conversations must be exhausting.” The gentle observation felt like as much of a hug as her arm, still secure around his shoulders.

He nodded and sucked in a breath through his nose. “There’s no point in trying to correct him. He gets agitated when I do.”

“Is he remembering real homework assignments, or is he making them up?”

“Oh, they’re very real. He probably won’t be able to recall my children’s names if I finally get around to having them, but he could tell you every project I ever did in social studies class. Comes with having been a humanities teacher, I guess. Sometimes, his nurse will print out essays off the internet for him to ‘grade.’ They swear he calms down when he has a stack of marking on his desk. Or when he’s watching old recordings he took of me playing. Mom puts them on for him. Sometimes he knows they’re from fifteen years ago. Sometimes he doesn’t.”

She hissed out a sympathetic sound. “We have boxes of tapes and DVDs from when my brothers and I played, too. More of them than of me—my dad wasn’t as worried about me learning from my mistakes. But still, lots of memory lane.” She paused. “Sorry. Didn’t mean to shift the focus onto me.”

“It is one hundred percent fine.” He loved any excuse not to focus on his grief. “My mom would sympathize with how much you struggled with having to prove yourself in a male-dominated environment. She had to fight against gender expectations all the time in the military. And on the stretches she was at home, she got side-eye from the other soldiers’ wives for saddling my dad with being the primary parent when she was deployed. They could never understand how she could handle being away from me. But serving was important to her. Until someone who’d strapped an IED to a donkey took the decision out of her hands.”

"Oh, my God, that's… *Whoa*. It's not the same, Liam. I was only fighting to play a game and to be seen as my brothers' equal."

"It's not the struggle Olympics, Kate. You're allowed to acknowledge it was hard for you, even if others had it worse. Not feeling like you were as important as your brothers is a massive load for a kid to carry."

She nodded, glancing at him under her lashes. "Want to talk about your dad more?"

"Not much to say. Dementia is an asshole. And it's progressed faster than we expected."

"I'd say *sorry*, but it never does much, does it?"

He shook his head. "And it's not only my dad. My mom's injuries limit her physically. Her pain fluctuates, and the chronic nature—it wears on her. Recovery was tough. And she worries that the strain it put on my dad contributed to the speed of his decline."

She winced. "Carrying an unknown like that would be heavy."

"It's probably unfounded, but either way, she's hurting; he requires a lot of care; and even if I played in Vancouver, I couldn't help them much more than I can from here. It's still a four-hour journey up the Coast, unless I charter a float plane. Which I do whenever I have an away game there."

"I didn't know that," she said.

He shrugged. "We haven't played Vancouver in a while. Anyway. My salary gives me the ability to hire them in-home nursing care and to make changes to their house whenever they need something more accessible."

He needed to fix it and butted up against the truth too often: it wasn't fixable.

"I can't imagine how tough that feels," Kate said quietly.

"I bet you already know. You must have run into moments where you wanted to support Sophie in her grief after Toby, but all you could do was hold her, because there wasn't a solution other than going through it. We both know what hopelessness feels like." He dug his hands into his hair. "I shouldn't complain. I'm lucky enough to be able to provide them some measure of comfort."

"You can complain to me, Liam. Anytime."

"Careful. I might take you up on that," he said.

He hadn't unloaded on anyone except the team therapist in a long time. Something about Kate holding him made him feel like he might be able to face the phone call with the private nursing service more easily than usual.

"I need to get ready for work." She glanced down at his casual sneakers. "Race you back to the arena?"

"I might even let you win."

Chapter Nine

TWO-GAME GOAL STREAK FOR CALDWELL
Here's hoping he makes it three in a row by focusing more on opponent's game tape than on videos of Kate Sullivan.
Denver Star, April 3

The hum of the plane engines normally lulled Liam into a nap during late-afternoon flights. Not today. The highs and lows of yesterday—his walk with Kate, his talk with his parents and the ensuing call to increase his dad's nursing care—had wiped him out. And after winning last night's game, and scoring again, he'd woken up this morning feeling wrung out. He'd crashed in a chair at the private gate while the team waited to board their flight. Now he felt like he'd chugged a liter of energy drink.

He made his way back to his seat after visiting the john, his limbs still restless. The aisle was wide enough for them to stretch and do some dynamic exercises midflight, and he dodged Connor, who was working on his hip flexors, earning a stern look.

When Liam had left for the bathroom, he'd been sitting in the window seat. Lars had been in the aisle. But when he got back to his row, Lars had switched seats.

"Problem, man?" Liam asked.

"You have the bladder of a toddler," his teammate groused, firmly turning the page of his novel and then loosening his tie. He was one of the few players who didn't change into sweats and a T-shirt the moment they hit altitude. Club policy stated they had to wear professional duds to and from games and on travel days, but they relaxed the policy once the airplane door closed. Today, Liam had a hoodie and shorts on, plus a pair of flip-flops, but the casual outfit wasn't doing anything to help him relax.

"I'm restless," he admitted.

A head poked over the row in front of them, face pale and freckled.

Jonesy. "Figured you'd be exhausted, not keyed up."

"Eavesdropping is rude." Lars's gaze stayed glued to his book.

"Piss off, Lars. Aren't you curious about what new guy here is up to with Kate the Great?"

"Nope."

Liam narrowed his eyes. Was the nickname fond or sarcastic?

"I haven't heard anyone call her that before," he said mildly. Remarkable, really, how every little interaction was an opportunity to layer in a convincing nugget of truth.

"She's earning it, isn't she? You sacked out in the airport terminal like you hadn't slept in a week. Bet she kept you up last night."

Liam scowled. "How about shutting the hell up? Would you harass someone about their wife that way?"

Jonesy pretended to think. "Probably."

"Have some respect," Lars snapped.

"Hang on, though, is Kate wife material?" Jonesy prodded.

She would be, if I ever planned to marry. Liam's face grew hot.

"Yes, she is," Lars said, saving Liam the trouble of answering.

"A whole week away," Jonesy said with a whistle. "You going to survive that long without a good ol' bedroom rodeo?"

Liam swept a middle finger around, circling Jonesy's aggravating face for a few seconds. "I don't know, will *you*?"

"That's the thing—I won't have to. Calgary has been so good to me in the past. And Edmonton."

"And let me guess—Montreal, too."

"You know it." Jonesy snapped his fingers. "You *would* know it. I bet you got so much Canadian tail when you were in Winnipeg."

"Adam," Lars growled, "if you don't shut the hell up, I'm going to tell HR to sign you up for another round of consent culture training. Now turn around. I'm almost at the end of a chapter."

Jonesy mimicked jacking someone off in Lars's direction but sulkily turned around and slid into his seat.

Liam let out a breath and settled back against the headrest.

"Been a while since you've been ragged about a partner?" Lars asked quietly.

"Never have been," he admitted. "I've moved around too much to try on a committed relationship."

Lars whistled. "And now you're running class five rapids."

They would be *if* their feelings were involved.

He pulled out his phone and swiped to the text thread with the contact he'd labeled *Superstar.*

I might owe you an apology, he typed.

It didn't take her more than a few seconds to reply. Oh?

Liam: Had some time to kill when I got to the airport, so I sacked out in one of the chairs.

Superstar: And my dad got after you for spending time with me instead of having a nap at home?

He wasn't sure if that would be worse.

Liam: No. Everyone's giving me a hard time about a certain pretty brunette keeping me up all night.

Kate replied with a blushing emoji, and then, At least they bought it?

He grinned at his phone. Fair point. The more convincing they could be, the more serious they would come across, and with it, his chance to prove he wasn't fooling around. And now I'm glad I avoided your dad.

Superstar: He promised he'd stay out of our relationship. The only hard time he'll give you is for your on-ice performance.

Liam: I'll keep my head down. And I'll call you when we get to Calgary.

Superstar: Don't mess up your routine on my account.

He snorted. She was blowing all his usual practices to hell. He couldn't help typing, Kissing my girl is my routine.

Superstar: Girl? <gag>

He chuckled. Noted. To be negotiated: terms of endearment.

Superstar: Amongst other things

Liam: You have my attention

Superstar: Degenerate

Liam: If you want me to be.

The reply probably crossed the line, given how well they *didn't* know each other, but he couldn't resist.

Superstar: Proving my point

"You're grinning too loudly," Lars muttered. "It's more annoying than Jonesy's yapping."

"Love you, too, Lars!" Jonesy called from the row ahead.

"Kate's funny," he said to his seatmate.

He wasn't going to lie—he was flirting on purpose. If they were going to be convincing in this farce, they'd need to be comfortable with each other. The more she got used to him flirting in private, the more she'd be able to handle it in public, where people would expect it.

That, and they had to make up for their lost getting-to-know-you time. And there was still an hour until they landed in Calgary. He had nothing better to do than twenty questions.

Liam: Given you're a superstar, what was your university major?

Superstar: Wouldn't you like to know.

Now he was curious. Might not be hard to find out. She was enough of a public figure herself, with playing college hockey and being a Sullivan. And no doubt her divorce had earned some press, and not in Kate's favor. She'd hinted at it, but he already knew the power balance rarely shifted toward women when the media covered conflicts between professional athletes and their intimate partners. A dynamic he'd need to be mindful of with their own gambit.

He flipped to a browser and searched for her name. Easy results. She had a Wikipedia article and everything.

The first chunk was about her grandfather, dad, uncles, brothers… Seemed unfair, how much of the focus was on the male members of Kate's family instead of on her own success. The cost of being a woman in a hockey dynasty? He read on. Grew up wherever her dad's career had taken them. Played for more than one high school team, went to university in Minnesota, and took—

Ha.

He flipped over to his text app and typed,

Hang on. Kinesiology? For a hockey player? Cliché, Katie. CLICHÉ.

He kept reading, then stalled at the subheading about her personal life. Longer than his own. Ouch. He wasn't going to take Wikipedia's word for it, though. Flipping back to the page of search results, he scrolled down. It only took three entries to start hitting on headlines about her divorce.

The protein shake the flight attendant had brought him curdled in his stomach.

Kate was taking a while to reply, which gave him the chance to read through almost a dozen old articles. The Sullivans had no-commented their way through the split, but Vince had fed into rumors by implying Kate hadn't been a supportive partner. And—wait—the rumors about her and Lars were about *cheating*? And from her husband's mouth? *What kind of fool was Vince, anyway?*

"The asshole kind of fool," Lars said in a low voice. "Or the hurt kind, who moved through life thinking he should be the perpetual center of attention. But mostly the first."

"Huh?" Liam blinked at Lars.

"You were asking about Kate's ex-husband, right?"

"I wasn't asking about anything. Or I didn't mean to."

"Thinking out loud," Lars mused. "Embarrassing."

"I'm lucky I'm not sitting next to Sully. Or Coach."

"Because they'd be pissed you were invading her privacy? Or because they'd wonder why the hell you don't ask her instead of creeping on her online?"

He reached up to twist the air vent open. *Definitely* getting hot in here. "We've been focused on other things more than talking?"

"Classy, Weller."

He stifled a groan. He meant to keep it light, but his words sounded crass when he played them back in his head. Not the "serious boyfriend" impression he wanted to give.

"She and I were good friends, before all that." Lars flicked his fingers in the direction of Liam's phone. His face wasn't his usual mystery-blank. More wistful.

Liam felt for the guy. "Damn. I can see why this got in the way."

Lars nodded but didn't reply.

Searching for her history had hammered home for Liam how

careful they needed to be. If coverage went sideways, she'd face more backlash than he would. And the last thing he wanted to do was hurt Kate Sullivan.

Kate was sitting in a circle of book clubbers at Page + Bean for their monthly get-together, half paying attention and half addressing the onslaught of texts from Liam. The smell of books and coffee took her back to college, cramming in the library between practice and classes. Unlike Vince, she'd never seen her degree as a backup option. The better she understood human motion, the better she'd be as a coach and teacher. And unlike so many programs, she could focus her training on helping girls excel and feel like limits didn't exist. But until she'd moved from Denver to Hollow Valley last year and started to explore building an academy, her ideas had remained theoretical.

Now she was using what she knew to create change, which was a bigger thrill than anything she'd done in her life, even winning the Women's Frozen Four in college.

"If we're going to read another romance next month, let's make sure it has dragons or magic again. Monsters, even," Sophie said from her spot at Kate's side.

"Sounds like Kate wants to give hockey romance another try."

The circle cackled at Natalie's jibe.

"I get enough of hockey players at home," Anneli Tiimonen lamented. She was a new addition to Hollow Valley and the book club. Her husband had signed with the Daggers over the summer, a few months before Liam's trade.

The woman had three sons, a daughter, a husband in the NHL… A family dynamic Kate knew intimately. "Your house is probably a lot like mine was growing up. I was always chasing the boys, desperate to fit in."

Anneli's light blue gaze was sharp, analytical. "I feel like that sometimes, and I'm their mom. Driving them all over town for hockey and skating lessons. At least the boys can play at the rink here most of the time."

"Does your daughter play, too?" Kate asked.

"She wanted to but didn't have a good time last year. Disappointing, given she's only ten. But she was on a team that included the coach's twin boys, along with a group of their friends. They decided they didn't want to play with a girl who was still learning. Barely passed to her, iced her out whenever they could. Rika and I both talked to the coach, and to the league, but he wouldn't do anything about the team culture. She quit."

"Would she like to give my spring league team a try? 10U, a mix of girls and boys, and I have lots of beginners." Kate motioned across the circle at her friend, Pavneet. "Pav's daughter hadn't even put on a pair of skates before last summer, and now she's scoring goals. Or if your daughter isn't ready to be on a team yet, she could test out one of my classes."

"Don't you only teach power skating? She's not ready for that, yet."

"I have space in my beginner-level skills classes this summer. Two will be girls-only. Plus a 3-on-3 camp. I hired teachers from a women's college team in Denver."

Anneli pursed her lips, clearly contemplating the option.

"Take a look at our website," Sophie suggested. "And my daughter's on Kate's 3-on-3 team, too. She loves it."

"Isn't Rika skating at the fundraiser on Saturday?" Natalie added. "Kate's giving mini skills lessons. Your daughter could come see what it's all about."

Anneli nodded.

Kate's phone lit up again.

She bit her lip and glanced at the screen.

Sophie's dubious expression landed on her.

Natalie, on the other hand, seemed titillated. She elbowed Kate. "Your boyfriend is bored on his flight."

"Put your phone away," Sophie said grumpily.

"I can't. My book's on my library app."

Plus, as much as she knew she should focus on her friends, the back and forth with Liam wasn't only helping the academy. It was…fun.

Love of My Life: I'm sorry

Wait, why?

Her gaze flicked up the text thread. He'd last mentioned her college degree. If he'd kept googling her, who knows what he'd found.

She groaned.

Kate: I should have mentioned not to look me up online.

Liam: I probably needed to know. Being your boyfriend and all. But…damn. I should have waited for you to tell me. I suck at twenty questions.

She felt a little lightheaded.

Natalie's dog nudged her hand with his nose. Natalie had POTS and experienced dizziness and heart palpitations. One of the tasks Scone was trained for was to sense Natalie's heart rate. Maybe he was picking up on Kate's too, or maybe she smelled stressed to his sensitive nose. He didn't have his vest on, so he wasn't working during book club, but he was never truly "off."

"Thanks, buddy." She scratched the soft fur between his ears.

"You okay?" Natalie asked.

"Yeah. Well, no. I'm tired of carrying my divorce around like a kettlebell."

"So put it down."

It was a good point. And it wasn't like she hadn't done a little poking around about Liam, too.

Even so, her thumbs were twitchy as she rapped out the text.

It's okay. Saves me from having to talk about it.

Love of My Life: You got thrown under the bus badly. Are you sure you want to be a headline again?

Kate: Bit late to back out now. And my school is worth it.

“So,” Sophie said loudly, breaking into Kate’s thoughts. “Predictions for the third book? Is Callie going to stay with Edric after he transformed into a fae?”

“Oh, she can’t turn her back on him,” Natalie said. “They’re fated mates.”

Sophie stared at Kate. “But Callie swore off fae after the Great Betrayal.”

“Would you two stop?” Kate hissed. She woke up her phone screen to look for the place in the book where it foreshadowed Callie had suspected Edric was going to transform. Before she could find the quote, another text popped up.

Love of My Life: Need me to throw down with Vince the next time we play Tampa?

She rolled her eyes. Since when do you fight?

He’d had all of four penalty minutes since the start of the season.

Love of My Life: Since my girl’s honor was impugned.

Kate: Again with the ‘girl’ crap

“Well, I think second chances are deserved,” Natalie’s nan announced. “Even if it’s the first time at a second chance.”

Kate arched a brow at Estelle.

“What?” The older woman smirked. “We’re all invested in your—er—Callie’s well-being, Kate. You should know that by now.”

“Good grief,” she said. “I didn’t think me dating Liam would be national news.”

A lie. She'd counted on it.

Sophie choked on her coffee. "And yet, you literally *made* the news."

"I heard Maude was playing matchmaker," Natalie said.

Scone huffed and put his head in Natalie's lap.

"You get me, don't you, buddy," Kate whispered to the canine.

She stroked one of his silky, floppy ears and glanced at her phone again.

Love of My Life: The offer stands

NO. Best behavior, please. She couldn't press Send fast enough. Thankfully, Tampa wasn't on the Daggers' schedule for the rest of the regular season. She did not want Liam to even talk to Vince, let alone get in a scrap. *Not* the kind of attention they wanted.

Love of My Life: My Katie, the pacifist

Natalie peeked over. "Hang on. *Love of My Life?* And *My Katie*? Oh, my heart…" She put a hand to her chest.

The half of the room in the loop concerning Natalie's POTS looked at her with concern.

"Not *literally*. Geez. But you have to admit—Liam's sweet."

Kate bit her lip and covered her heating cheeks. She couldn't deny Natalie's claim. Not one bit.

Chapter Ten

CALDWELL LIGHTS UP WINNIPEG WITH A TWO-GOAL NIGHT
Will the Denver dressing room remain free of the drama from last season?
Denver Star, April 9

The sun was shining when the wheels of the plane touched down in Colorado. Liam was antsy. He'd earned a glare from across the aisle every five minutes of the flight home. Apparently, Tal Sullivan did not appreciate Liam's restlessness.

More likely, the reason for it.

"Would you settle the hell down? I assume you're excited to see my daughter, but could you at least pretend to be calm?"

He blinked at the older man. "Doesn't Kate deserve someone who's excited to see her?"

Coach grunted.

"I'm going to go see her before I head to my place." He had no actual plans to meet up with Kate. But if he was going to convince Daggers management he was reliable—in hopes it would trickle down to other coaches and managers who may one day offer him a more lucrative contract—Tal Sullivan was the person to start with.

"It's a longer drive to Hollow Valley than to downtown," Coach grumbled.

"Kate is worth a thirty-minute detour."

"Yes. But..." The admission was testy. "Jesus. I said I was going to stay out of this."

"I get it. You want the best for your daughter." He grinned. "Good thing that's me."

Not for long term, but for now, he and Kate could save both of their reputations by appearing to be serious.

"Being away for a week has felt like a month," he continued.

He was asking for it. No doubt, he'd be put through heinous drills next practice. He was being honest, though. He'd been eager to get back to Colorado since the second they'd been wheels-up on their way to Calgary. The texts he'd shared with Kate all week had buoyed him through three tough games. Seeing her face would be even better.

He pulled out his cell and shot her a quick message. I'm going to call you. Play along.

She answered on the second ring.

"Hey, beautiful. We just landed."

"Welcome home." Her voice was quiet, but warm.

"Thanks. Where are you? I'm going to come find you."

"I'm at the Page + Bean," she said. "Are you really coming here? Don't you want to go home and unpack?"

"Seeing you is way more fun than unpacking."

"You're pretending, aren't you?" She whispered the question.

"I'm sitting across from your dad. He says hi."

"Ah, gotcha."

"What do you say about tonight, Katie?" He let his mouth curve into a knowing smile. "Your place, or mine?"

"Oh, my God," she said in the same low tone. "You're incorrigible."

"You mean *infatuated*."

The noise from the taxiing plane drowned out any sounds from Tal Sullivan, but by the look of his tense jaw, he was doing a number on his molars.

Coach plucked the phone out of Liam's hand. "Katherine, honey? Could you decide what bed you're planning to sleep in when I'm *not* sitting three feet from your boyfriend?"

Liam couldn't hear her response, but it dragged on long enough, and Coach Sullivan had a hell of a wince on his face. She must have been tearing him a new one.

"Mother of—sorry. I know. Grown-ass woman. Yes. *Sorry.*

Yeah, dinner on Friday. I'll grill burgers." Coach handed the phone over and stared straight ahead. "She says her place."

Kate was laughing when Liam put the device to his ear.

"If your plan was to irritate my dad, you succeeded."

"I prefer to think he's grimacing with love," Liam said.

"When will I actually see you next?"

"Soon," he said.

"Text me when you get home and we can figure it out," she said.

"You bet, beautiful."

They hung up. But a thought persisted.

You live in your dad's backyard. If he thinks I'm staying over, won't he notice if I don't?

He pressed Send.

She didn't reply.

Twenty minutes later, he was retrieving his suitcase from the charter terminal when a deep voice barked his name.

He turned to face Coach, who stood next to Connor. Both men looked grumpy. Had he overdone the infatuated act on the plane?

"You got your car here, Caldwell?" Sullivan asked.

Liam nodded.

"Good. My car service messed up the schedule and Conn and I are out a ride. Do you have room for us?"

Liam swallowed. "Uh, yeah."

"Terrific." Coach strode toward the doors, suitcase in tow.

"Great," Liam said under his breath.

Connor slapped him on the shoulder. "You get to see my sister *and* get in my dad's good graces."

"Bonus," he said dryly, following his coach out the door and pointing the men toward his BMW parked nearby in one of the valet pickup spots. "And here I thought scoring twice on the road trip would be enough to keep him happy."

The two games where Kate had sent him a picture of herself with her lips pursed. He chose to believe it wasn't a coincidence.

For the first half of the drive, small talk about hockey kept them occupied. Talking shit about their opponents the past three games, mainly.

Then his Bluetooth chimed, and he pressed the button for the system to play the text by habit.

"*Text from Superstar: I'm sure we could figure out a way for you to stay over, if we needed to,*" came the feminine, British-accented voice Liam had set for his auto-reads. It didn't sound a thing like Kate. Somehow, the accent made the statement sound more suspicious.

The car went silent.

His stomach sank.

Both Sullivans were staring at him.

"What the hell does that mean?" Coach snapped.

"It means I'm picky about mattresses and hate Kate's," he said, scrambling for the best answer possible.

"Princess," Connor said with a snort.

"That's me." He'd agree to any insult to keep Connor's attention off the truth.

"How the hell have you stayed in my pool house without me knowing?" Tal bit out. "Actually, don't answer. I don't want to know."

Pretending indifference, Liam shrugged, pressed the reply button and started dictating. "Hey, beautiful. I'm in the car with your dad and Connor. And maybe the solution is I buy you a new mattress. Since I'm the fussy one."

Connor swore in complaint from the backseat.

Coach Sullivan sighed and dragged a hand down his face.

Irritation burned the back of Liam's neck. He gripped the steering wheel with both hands. "You know, I'd have thought the fact Kate's been married and divorced would have demonstrated she's an adult who participates in consensual relationships."

"It's not her, asshole, it's you. We all know you're planning to move on at the end of the season," Connor bit out.

His breath caught. "I—"

"Do not respond, Liam," Tal said, his voice suddenly even. "Not without your agent present and the management team and an official contract extension offer from the Daggers. Who knows where your head will be at in a month. Hell, we're getting close to a playoff spot."

The tension in Liam's throat eased. "Thanks, Coach."

A few seconds later, another alert chimed.

Oh, hell no.

And again.

"Play it, Weller," Tal demanded.

"It might be private."

"It's my daughter. And she knows we're here. She wouldn't say anything inappropriate."

Liam sighed and pressed Play.

"Text from Superstar: Hi, Dad. Hi, Conn-sternation. Be nice to Liam. Meet me at the bookstore, babe. Love you all!"

"She *loves* you?" Coach Sullivan asked in disbelief.

Liam lifted a shoulder and channeled the overconfident smooth talker people expected him to be. "I am lovable."

"Am I going to need to invite you over for dinner Friday night, too, to get the chance to see my daughter?"

"Uh, I wasn't planning to join her Friday," Liam said carefully.

"You don't want to take me up on my hospitality?"

"Might look like favoritism," Liam said.

His coach's mouth flattened. "I think that ship has sailed."

Far too many minutes later, he peeled away from Connor's house, having first deposited Tal in his driveway, and headed for the bookstore.

He came to the small town all the time for practice, of course, but always went straight to the arena. Many of his teammates chose to live in the sleepy bedroom community, especially the ones with kids. He did not.

He didn't need to live amongst constant reminders of the love and good times of being part of a close-knit group of people. Those reminders couldn't conquer reality: it was too easy for life to snatch away the people who mattered and the sense of home they created.

He slowed his car to the posted twenty miles per hour. Key word, *slow*. For ten blocks, give or take, structures stretched down either side of Hollow Valley Avenue, mostly two-story storefronts with an old-timey, mining town feel. He parked where Kate had suggested and made his way back down the block on foot. Page + Bean was on one of the corners.

He could smell a gossip haven from a mile away.

He pushed open the old-fashioned, single-pane glass door. The entrance was set on an angle to the corner of the street, with the coffee shop inside to the right and the bookstore branching off to the left. Half of the two- and four-person tables were filled. Acoustic guitar twanged on the speakers. The bookstore side, however, appeared to be empty but for the familiar, take-Liam-out-at-the-knees woman standing behind the counter.

He couldn't remember her mentioning working here, but with Kate, who knew? She seemed to be part of the glue holding Hollow Valley together.

She didn't look up. Her gaze was glued to a thick, hardcover book on the counter in front of her, open to about the halfway point.

He approached and was about to say her name to get her attention, when she gasped. Squealed. Full-on bounced on her toes. Her jaw dropped and her hands covered the lower half of her face.

"Shut the front door," she mumbled between her fingers.

"I didn't leave it open," he teased, leaning an elbow on the counter.

She startled, her hands falling from her mouth to her chest.

"Caught you at a good part?" God, she was adorable with her breath coming quick and her eyes wide behind those cute blue glasses.

Bookish Kate was a recipe to decimate his sanity. More so than Hockey Coach Kate? Probably not. Claiming a favorite version would be impossible, but this one was damn irresistible in a bulky, pale yellow cardigan over a thin white T-shirt. The built-in shelf behind her, filled with face-out covers on stands, provided an Insta-perfect backdrop, had he been taking a picture.

The mental capture would have to be enough.

"I didn't know you had a third job," he said, leaning closer.

"I don't. My friend runs this half of the shop, and she needed to pop home quickly. I offered to watch the counter. I like to read here on my days off, but usually at one of the coffee shop tables."

He glanced down at her book and indicated it with his chin. "What was the big plot twist?"

Her cheeks flushed. "Just fan service."

"Oh, yeah?"

"The enemy fae prince called the wool-spinner's daughter his—" She cleared her throat. "It doesn't matter. You don't care."

"Try me."

"You read fantasy romance?"

"No, but I want to know about this big prince reveal. I'm intrigued."

"I don't know what it means, yet. He told her their souls are tied… The book came out today, so it's my first read-through." She tipped the hardcover up to flash the title at him.

"Looks like the Daggers' logo, if you shrouded it in smoke and mist."

"I guess," she said. Her forehead knitted and her gaze traveled along the length of him. A glint of appreciation lit her eyes. Maybe Kate liked the sweater over a dress-shirt look. He'd have to try it with the sleeves rolled up one day. Test out the forearms-are-irresistible theory.

"It's nice artwork," he said.

"Liam, I'm so sorry I dragged you here," she blurted. "I wasn't sure how you'd feel about actually having plans with me, but I rolled the dice, given you had a captive audience."

"It's really okay. Makes sense I'd want to see my girlfriend after a week away."

And something about spending an evening with Kate appealed a hundred times more than going to his condo alone.

"You didn't want to go home first?"

He shrugged. "No point in driving into the city and back."

She pressed her lips together in a wince. "I should have figured out a way to check, first."

He took her hand. "It's fine. And hell, if the woman I'm infatuated with is working the counter, even temporarily, I should buy something."

One brown eyebrow rose.

"What?" A defensive edge lined the word, one he hadn't meant to wield. He relaxed his tone. "I read. Mostly by listening to audiobooks on the team plane these days, but still, it counts. My parents and I have been reading and listening to the same books concurrently since way back when my mom was deployed. It was a way for us to escape the realities of deployment together. We kept up the practice after Mom's accident because, to be honest, there was just as much of a need for escape as she healed as there'd been with her across the world." He pressed his lips together. "My dad can't always participate now. Less and less recently. But Mom and I still try."

Her gaze softened. "I love that tradition. But you don't have to buy something today."

He put a hand to his chest in mock offense. "I'll seem like a better boyfriend if I do. Trickle-down reputation effect. What do you recommend?"

Please say you.

She pointed over her shoulder at a small sign proclaiming "Reader of the month: Coach Kate." Two other signs advertised selections from what he assumed were Page + Bean employees. One was mostly political themes, both nonfiction and fiction. The second circled around cookbooks and stuff to do with knitting. Kate's, however, were all imagination-and-people-focused—fantasy, romance, children's lit, athletes' memoirs. She was a dreamer. Something tugged in his chest.

He shook off the feeling and pointed at the same silver-and-metallic-blue cover as the one she was reading. "You're already recommending that one, and you haven't even finished?"

"Oh, I knew I'd love it before I flipped to page one. I'm a hardcore Windweavers fan."

He motioned to it with hand-it-over fingers. "Sold."

She eyed him, those magnetic honey pools fixed to him like she was expecting him to shape-shift into a villainous fae prince himself, but didn't question the request. She plucked one from the stack of the shelf and slid it toward him. "It's book three. You should go back to the beginning. The first two are behind you."

Artfully arranged stacks of red-and-gold and bronze-and-green books filled a table at the end of a shelf. He'd missed the display when he arrived—gave himself a pass, because why would he care about an array of books when he had the chance to watch Kate react to a plot twist?

He snagged one of each color and made a stack on top of the one on the counter. "There."

He'd probably end up buying them on audio instead, but it never hurt to have paper copies.

She rang through his purchase.

"I guess I shouldn't come behind the counter," he said.

Her gaze was suspicious. "Why?"

He leaned in close. "Because those people over there are watching us. So maybe we should give them a show."

Chapter Eleven

Kate nearly dropped Liam's books.

Why, though? She'd *asked him* for this. She shouldn't be surprised by his suggestion of a public display of affection.

And yet, her stomach jittered like a kids' tap-dancing class.

"Katie…"

The nickname was spoken in such a low register, it approached subsonic.

Oh, no. None of that nonsense, vulnerable and awkward.

"Want a bag for these?" she asked. "There's a twenty-five-cent surcharge."

His mouth tilted. "Uh, yeah, sure, but—"

She named his total, keyed it into the machine and held out the terminal for him to tap.

He fumbled in the pocket of his dress pants and pulled out his wallet. His hands were clumsy as he extracted his credit card.

Is he—

"We don't have to perform for the masses," she assured him. "Not if you're nervous."

His gaze fixed on her, solemn and earnest. "I'm not nervous. But there is a lot on the line."

"Ah, there it is," she said. "This is about hockey."

Not me. Ouch.

"Everything's about hockey," he said. "My contract, your school… Isn't that why you suggested this gambit?"

His mouth quirked further.

She felt that twinge all the way through to her marrow.

Those lips. Devastating. Even the hint of his wintergreen gum drifting across the counter made her a little melty. She couldn't lie to herself—she'd enjoyed every millisecond of their first kiss. He'd tasted like the thrill of the chase, of stolen moments, of more.

Liam Caldwell was the primary ingredient in the recipe for bad decisions.

She nodded. "Yes. The gambit."

He reached across the high counter and stroked the back of a finger down her cheek. "I didn't say thanks for those pictures you texted me before my games. The two times you did, I scored."

"Because of your killer wrist shot, not me," she whispered. Her skin was on fire. She tilted her head toward his palm.

He cradled her jaw. "Nah. It was luck."

A hint of good luck from Bad Luck Kate. The universe sure had a sense of humor.

So laugh along with it. Enjoy a no-strings moment with this beautiful, beautiful man.

She took a paper bag from under the counter and slid his books and receipt into it. He held out a hand.

Instead of passing it over, she scooted out from behind the counter and closed the distance between them.

"Welcome home, Liam," she murmured.

With him in shoes, not skates, she didn't need to rise so high on her toes to meet his lips. Her hand met the warm wool of his sweater, not an embroidered crest over a chest protector. And without his gloves on, nothing got between his fingers and her skin as he cupped her face, the rough heels of his palms on her cheeks, his fingertips teasing through her hair.

He devoured her. Like he was relishing every spark kindling between them.

Her knees wobbled, and she had to grip his waist to stay steady. The bag of books thunked against his thigh. He dropped a hand from her face to her lower back and pressed her closer.

Skillful, careful lips took her apart. Her senses sharpened wholly on him, like standing in a spotlight of Liam Caldwell.

A noise erupted behind her. Applause?

She jolted, pulling her lips away enough to focus on her surroundings.

Not applause. Giggles.

Liam rested his forehead against hers for a second. A breath shuddered from his lungs, and he stroked his thumb along her lower lip, his gaze flicking to something over her left shoulder.

"Not the audience we anticipated," he murmured.

She glanced back. Two black-haired heads peeked around the middle-grade and YA bookshelf. One belonging to her errant niece. The second, to her errant niece's bestie and teammate, Shayla.

More giggles, and the girls ducked back.

Kate peered around Liam, spotting Shayla's mom standing at the counter to order something from the café. She shot Pavneet a sheepish smile. Pav lifted a hand, her mouth perking up in amusement.

"I mean, at least they refrained from 'Coach and Liam sitting in a tree.'" Liam ran a hand through his hair. He retreated enough to put a foot of space between them. The instinct to follow, to lean in and kiss him more, simmered in her veins.

They couldn't take it further here.

But somehow, it felt unfinished.

And if she went and found a dictionary from Page + Bean's reference section, the entry for *nonsensical* would begin with *Kate Sullivan: forever attracted to inadvisable men.*

Inadvisable hockey players, to be specific.

She swallowed and looked up at Liam's crushingly handsome face. Kissing him wasn't the problem. Loving him would be the death knell to her intelligence.

Which I will not *do.*

Another giggle came, and the girls peeked around the shelf behind Liam.

"The Page + Bean isn't for hide-and-seek, Maudie," Kate chided gently.

"But it's for kissing?"

Liam choked on a laugh.

Kate gave her niece a stern look. "It's certainly not against any rules. For *adults.*"

The pair was full of laughs as they bopped their way through the café to a beckoning Pavneet.

Liam took the bag of books from Kate.

"My friend should be back any minute to retake the helm of her literary ship. Head home. You don't need to do something with me tonight."

"Tell me." He tucked a piece of hair behind her ear. "How likely is it your dad wouldn't notice if I split early?"

"Next to zero," she said. "Part and parcel of living in his backyard."

"Mmm, thought so," he said.

"I could always tell him we went back to *your* apartment," she said.

He shook his head. "Too many ways to get caught in a lie. You're stuck with me tonight, Katie. At least until after dinner."

What a shame.

Thankfully, she managed to keep the sarcastic quip inside, saving herself from inflating his ego.

"I walked here," she said. "Once I'm free to leave, can you give me a ride home?"

"Of course." With a wink, he strolled over to a café table, sat and pulled out the first of the three books he'd just purchased. She could barely keep her eyes off the shifting, interested expression lighting his green eyes as he got absorbed in the pages.

Fifteen minutes later, her friend had returned and relieved her. She almost felt guilty tearing Liam away from the story.

"Already on chapter three. Impressive," she said.

"I doubt you'll be surprised to hear it's engrossing." He offered her his hand and opened the front door of Page + Bean for her with the other.

Kate slid her fingers into Liam's and tugged him out onto the verandah and then the sidewalk.

"I parked over here," he said, motioning to a peridot green BMW sedan.

Sleek. Sexy. Fast. But not a smack-you-in-the-face-with-my-seven-figure-salary statement.

"And here I would have pegged you for a Ferrari or a Lambo."

A brow arched. They stopped on the sidewalk in front of the hood. "A BMW coupe isn't enough of a sports car for you?"

"It's electric," she said, recognizing the special license plate.

"Isn't that a good thing?"

"Yeah, of course. But I wasn't expecting…practical."

He hissed out a breath. "I'm not going to spend hundreds of thousands of dollars on a car, Kate. Who knows what my dad's nursing care will cost a year or two or five from now?"

Yet another reminder there was more to him than she'd given him credit for.

Her face burned. "I implied you're irresponsible or at best frivolous, and you're not. I'm sorry."

"I appreciate the apology. And all this proves is you don't know me well enough." He coaxed her a little closer, then lifted her knuckles to his lips. "Do you enjoy driving?"

"Yeah, why?"

"I feel like she needs to prove herself to you. Want to take a turn behind the wheel?"

"Seriously?"

"I share my toys, Katie."

Why did her mouth go dry?

She gulped. "Uh, sure. Sounds like fun. And while you're playing passenger princess, you can tell me the thing people get wrong about you the most."

"Only one?"

"It's like, a three-minute drive. *If* I go under the speed limit."

Snorting, he went over to the passenger side and unlocked the door. "Hop in. It's keyless, and the fob's in my pocket." A wistful softness crossed his face. "I almost miss being in high school and being able to toss someone a handful of keys. That metal *clink* was so satisfying."

Nodding, she opened the driver's door and got behind the wheel.

"God, I'm getting old," he complained, sliding into the passenger seat.

She rolled her eyes. "At thirty-one? Oh, yeah. *Ancient*."

Though some guys washed out of the league in their mid-twenties, or didn't make it far into their thirties.

"The clock moves too fast sometimes," he said, sliding his seat back to the furthest position. Seated, his dress pants clung to his thighs. Her pulse sped up and she pressed her lips together. God bless hockey players and their quads and glutes.

She forced herself to hunt down the location of all the important buttons and indicators rather than staring at his too-hot body. "You've built your career on speed."

"It's worked for me up until recently," he murmured. "Got me a professional contract and keeps me moving."

Six professional contracts. He seemed to stake his value as a player on being the temporary fix. And she couldn't blame him for seeking stability for his family, even if it came at the expense of his own.

Came at the expense of an actual relationship with him, too. Kate was *not* going to fall for another man who refused to plant roots—but neither of them were in this to fall in love.

Kate followed his instructions for adjusting the seat and mirrors.

"All right," she admitted, soaking in the rich scent of leather, the smooth feel of it under her fingers. "This is pretty sports-car-ish."

He smirked. "Just because she doesn't roar doesn't mean she isn't sexy."

She dished him some quick side-eye, guided the car out of the parking spot and headed in the direction of her dad's house.

"Didn't realize until I dropped Connor off that he lives a half a block from you and your Dad. Quite the little Sullivan compound you have going on," he said.

"Especially when you add in Sophie and Maude. They're across the street from Conn."

He nodded. "Did you and Vince live nearby?"

"No." Her yearning to move to Hollow Valley had been one of the many disagreements between them. "We had a place in Denver. Sold it after our split."

"You didn't roll your half into a place of your own?"

Regret rolled low in her belly. She shook her head.

"What happened, superstar?" he said.

"Pretty simple. I would have felt sick taking money from him. I figured I could support myself. And I can. I know having more of a nest egg would make starting the school easier, but coming from him, it would feel tainted. I haven't taken financial help from anyone in the family, let alone my ex. I don't want a hint of his toxicity mixed up in my dream, especially given the efforts I'm making to get *away* from the double standards girls and women face in hockey."

She drummed her fingers on the steering wheel. "But enough about me. Weren't you going to enlighten me on the things people get wrong about *you*?"

"I think you're going to need to tell me what it is people assume, and then I'll refute it."

"Or confirm it."

"Or that," he allowed.

Her throat tightened. "On second thought, I don't like this. It feels as if I'm being set up to say something mean."

"Then stick to the little stuff, Kate."

"No, I want to know how *you* feel misunderstood. None of this 'guess a thing about me' BS."

"Ah." He pointed at the elementary school. "Did you go to school there?"

"No. My dad's from here, but he was playing in St. Louis and Toronto when I was school age. After Toby died, I traveled back and forth between Calgary and here, helping Sophie and Maude as much as I could. Didn't move to Colorado full-time until about three years ago." She cleared her throat. "Nice evasion, by the way."

"Yeah. Uh…" He examined his thumbnail, picking at the edge. "What people get wrong…"

"You don't have to divulge," she said, turning down a residential side street in the direction of home. Driving his car was fun, but this conversation was awkward.

"No, it's fine. It's a hard question, when you think about it."

"Yeah, it is." And probably too deep for a manufactured relationship.

She turned the last corner onto her dad's street.

A thought popped into her head, and her heart thrummed. "I thought of one—with how often you've moved between teams, it seems you *like* being temporary."

He glanced out his window as if the willows lining the half block to her dad's house were the most interesting trees he'd ever seen.

"Liam?"

"Yeah." He cleared his throat and connected with her gaze. "Moving around makes things easier."

His tone was convincing. His eyes? Not so much.

If she'd thought he looked full of longing when talking about being a teenager, it had nothing on the brief but intense flicker she'd just glimpsed.

"Easier how?" she pressed, pulling into the empty driveway. "It can't be easy to be so far from home, and never to be anywhere long enough to create one."

"Like I said, Katie, it's easier." Emphasizing the "er," he looked away, somewhere between the main house and the path cutting into the landscaping to the left. Follow it, and they'd get to her pool house door.

She'd exposed a layer of Liam Caldwell, one it would be safer not to study.

"Still want to come in?" she asked.

"Of course." His grin was brilliant. How the hell did he flip the switch so quickly? "Mind if I bring my suitcase inside. If I'm going to be hanging around for a few hours, I'd rather be comfortable."

"Please. As much as I like the sweater you have on," she said, returning the wink he'd given her at the bookstore. If they were going to survive the evening, they had to get back to a lighter mood.

They both got out of the car, and he retrieved a large, wheeled case.

He looked a bit sheepish. "It was a week-long trip," he explained. "I don't always pack so much."

"I am not like my brother and his carry-on only ways," she said. "When I travel, I account for every possibility."

She led the way down the path and through a locked gate. They passed her dad's greenhouse, and Liam stared at it with curiosity.

"Does my dad not wax rhapsodic about his zucchini at the end of team meetings?"

Liam halted, his face a silent "what are you talking about?"

"He gardens," she explained. "The whole yard during the summer. His greenhouse and Dutch lights during the winter. You haven't seen the real Tal Sullivan until you've seen him babying a bed of pansies."

Mouth open, Liam examined the yard with a new intensity.

Before they could start moving again, the door to the greenhouse opened. Her father emerged. He glared at Liam's suitcase. "Moving in, Caldwell?"

Chapter Twelve

Kate was having none of her dad's grumpy, overprotective routine today. It was her business alone if Liam stayed over, for however long. "When it comes to me having houseguests, Dad, you're no different from any other landlord."

Her dad crossed his arms over one of the flannel shirts he wore when he did yard work. "Sue me for being curious, Katherine."

"Sorry," she said. "But every time you doubt Liam, you doubt me. And I promise, all is well, okay? Liam isn't Vince."

"I know, otherwise I wouldn't have advocated to have the team trade for him," Tal said. He regarded Liam, face more neutral than during his first greeting. "My daughter is precious to me, you hear? *Precious.*"

"Heard, Coach," Liam said quickly. "And if you ever want to trade tips on cold climate vegetables, my parents know enough to fill a book as thick as the ones Kate reads."

Tal looked intrigued.

"Have a good night, Dad," she said, tugging her "boyfriend" along by the hand.

"Gotta say," Liam whispered, "when I thought we'd be needing to win people over, I was expecting more of a challenge from the general public than from the men you're related to."

"Ugh, I'm sorry."

"I'm not, Katie." He lifted their hands and kissed the back of hers for the second time since they left the coffee shop. The first time, she'd wondered if it was for appearances. Now she was thinking Liam Caldwell was simply affectionate. The sweet gesture sent tingles up her arm.

"Well, you're here now, and you've more than survived the gauntlet. You can relax for the rest of the night."

"I plan to."

She made sure he did.

By seven o'clock, they'd eaten a stir-fry she cooked up and were two episodes into the first season of *The White Lotus*, which he'd never seen and she never passed up the opportunity to rewatch.

He sprawled diagonally across her extra-large, teal chaise in the great room of the pool house, wearing a T-shirt and sweats. One of his arms was slung behind his head. His sleeve had shifted almost to his shoulder, exposing his entire biceps and triceps.

Snaps to the training staff—the man was fit.

And extra snaps to his tattoo artist—his ink sleeves swirled and slashed from his shoulders to his wrists. She'd never gotten a close-up view of the intricate artwork before, and *wow*. The minute he'd shucked his dress shirt and she'd glimpsed the bold mix of color and black, she'd been dying to study the details close-up.

Idle fingers stroked the velvet upholstery by his hip.

His tactile nature made her wonder about better places for those fingers to stroke.

"It feels like this chaise has a story," he said.

"Everything has a story."

"Yeah, but something about bright velvet clashing with a whole bunch of navy blue and rattan makes me think this piece wasn't your dad's choice."

She sighed. "I bought it after my divorce. Sold the black leather monstrosities Vince had insisted on buying and used the cash to get the chaise. The rest of the furniture was here when I moved in, but I brought that with me."

"Mmm, a spite couch. Excellent." Humor danced across the angles of his face. "You know what the best thing is to do on a spite couch, Katie?"

She swallowed. The possibilities seemed endless, and exceptionally unwise.

"I can see you getting specific in that mind of yours."

"Well, you were suggesting…"

He held his hands up in mock surrender. "You are putting words in my mouth."

"Fine, what's the best thing to do on a spite couch, Liam?"

"Whatever the hell you want," he said. "Best way to get revenge is to live every moment exactly how you want to live."

"I'm not out for revenge," she said quietly. "I'm still hurt by what he did, but the more I focus on retaliation, even something petty, it gives the past power over my present. But you are right about living how I want to live. He and I weren't happy. I was so unhappy without a long-term home and being unable to build my academy. I could only make so much of a difference with volunteer coaching or working for other skating schools. And none of that worked into what he wanted for his life." She blew out a long breath. "I wish we'd figured that out before he got traded here. His animosity with my dad spread through the locker room faster than the stink of sweaty socks on game day."

"Let's make sure we don't cause that kind of drama, then. And, because we know this will end when I leave Denver when my contract expires, no one will get hurt." He patted the seat next to him. "Come join me."

Her ass was already smarting from the rattan love seat's firm cushion. She'd always viewed her stay at her dad's as temporary and hadn't bothered to redecorate. The chaise would be twice as comfy, but having a sore butt was safer than being near those arms.

She shook her head at his invitation.

"Katie." His voice was criminally low. How was it possible to feel like he was growling her name along the skin of her neck when six feet separated them? "Isn't it easier to get comfortable with each other when we're alone?"

Easier. *Ha.*

"C'mere," he urged.

"But no one's going to know what we do here."

"And thank God they won't, because I need some privacy."

Her heart softened.

"Sit with me. Not because it's an act. Because it feels good to be physically close to another human. And if we're stuck together for a couple of months, potentially until July—Lord Stanley's ghost willing—then we might as well enjoy it."

Fine. *Fine.*

She scooted from her spot and removed a throw pillow to make space next to him. With him stretched out on an angle, she couldn't do the same without draping her legs over his, so she curled up with her knees bent instead.

"See?" His arm slid lower, looping around the middle of her back. His muscles tightened, drawing her against his side. "No big deal."

"Sure," she whispered.

Ugh, why did she feel so vulnerable? Neither of them was going to catch feelings, if they chose not to. And like he'd said, they knew their end game, and it wasn't *being* each other's end game.

"So, uh, how come you're as stiff as a board, then?"

"Because I'm too nervous to enjoy this, Liam!"

His fingers tensed around her upper arm. Not a threat but matching the surprise on his face.

"Can I ask why?"

She soaked in the wary tilt to his mouth. His perfect lips, parted enough for her to trace her tongue there if she kissed him. The jaw that could double as a diamond cutter, and the lock of hair falling across his forehead, softening what could seem like a hard stare.

There were a thousand parts to him she wanted to explore. But she didn't know if she'd be able to stop, were she to start.

"I need safe boundaries."

"Safe from what?" His expression was guarded. "From me?"

"From getting attached to you."

He paused, his mouth stretching in uncertainty. "Enjoyment doesn't mean getting attached."

"You can't be sure."

His thumb traveled a gentle path down her biceps. "I know I'm not going to ask it of you."

"Good." She nearly choked on the word.

"Katie." A bare amount of pressure urged her closer. "Are you not sure if you can trust me, or your own feelings?"

She didn't know.

Didn't want to answer, either.

She'd already kissed this man twice. And he was right—it wouldn't do for her to get all squirrelly when he put his arm around her in public.

She was already only inches away from him. A slight lean, and her lips were pressing against his. The lemon sparkling water she'd served him lingered on his mouth, teasing her tongue.

He smiled against her mouth. "See? Audience or not, it's the same. Just me."

"It is the same." She slid a hand between his pecs. "Mainly because I don't want to stop."

A rumble of agreement vibrated under her palm. "So don't."

"We shouldn't get too carried away," she said.

"Says who? Do you ever do what *you* want, Katie?"

When he put it that way…

Tangling her fingers in his hair, she guided his mouth back to hers.

So much of him was hard. Not his lips, though. Soft and pillowy, first slack, then taut and searching. With a firm hand behind her head, he dominated the kiss.

She kissed him back, savoring every ounce of bliss from his mouth.

His hands skimmed her hips. She braced to end up on her back with six feet of hot hockey player between her thighs, but instead, he lifted her into his lap, settling her over his hard quads. Her knees slid to either side.

The movement broke their kiss. With the fraction of distance, she caught his gaze. An unspoken question of *Is this okay*? marked the curious set of his reddened lips.

She answered by planting her hands on his chest, leaning in and stealing another taste of him. The angle brought her forward.

Oh. *Oh.* His quads weren't the only hard thing. Pressed right against more than his fair share of thickness, heat pooled in her core. She rocked forward.

The pressure… *Mmm.* Sparks shot through her limbs.

His fingers were ten tight points, thumbs right below her hip bones and the rest along the curve of her ass. Holding her in place. Support, yes, but also keeping her from moving, and oh, God, she wanted to move.

The feeling of him, right where it counted, was too good. Her core muscles tightened, protesting the emptiness, wanting more.

He stilled his lips and skimmed his mouth across her cheek, featherlight and teasing, then gave the barest hint of a swirl around the shell of her ear. "Is this what you want, Katie?"

Her breath caught. "Kissing you? Yeah."

"No, do you want me to make you come?" Grip steady, he lifted his hips enough to drag the fabric of her leggings and underwear along sensitive flesh.

"Yes. I mean…" her cheeks burned "…not sex. Just… *Argh.* I want…"

A corner of his smile lifted, and he rocked her in a slow, teasing slide.

The sound that escaped her was almost a moan.

A flutter in her chest flirted with embarrassment, but his satisfied grin replaced it with something closer to pride. To be able to put that look on Liam Caldwell's face… A woman could get used to such power.

He rewarded her by guiding her hips forward and back, forward and back. Pleasure built, hot and consuming.

"Liam…" she said, almost slurring.

"Take what you need," he murmured.

"I was only going to kiss you."

"But this is what you really want."

He was right, damn him.

This tiny moment for herself, to chase everything he could give her… Maybe it was selfish. A little careless.

Too fast.

But irresistible. She normally wasn't this sensitive, but the angle was just right. *He* was just right. With every hitch, she edged closer to release.

"Are…are *you* okay?" she asked.

"More than. I love seeing you like this, Kate." His eyes were the darkest green, like diving into a lake at twilight. "On the edge."

She bit her lip and squeezed her eyes shut. Her existence distilled down to the warm scent of masculine deodorant on cotton, the tease of his chuckle, the lingering lemon from his mouth. His hands were only on her hips, but she felt the glide of his arousal against her sex across every inch of her skin.

"Can you come apart for me?" he said, voice low. "Like this? Or do you want me to…"

"I feel like I'm taking advantage," she moaned, cracking an eye open.

His heat-fraught gaze flared. "Use me. *Please.* I love it."

He reached for the waistband of her leggings.

She braced her hands on his shoulders. "No, like this."

The angle, the friction, the impulsive urge to fall into something she'd thought out of reach.

She rode his thighs, chasing her release. His expression, heated, fascinated, burned through her last threads of resistance.

She shattered, tumbling into a world of white light and endlessness.

He swore, his arms holding her together, her body threatening to drift away. "Holy God, Katie. You're so damn beautiful. Thank you for…oh man. *Christ.*"

"Uh-huh." Her mouth couldn't form whole words right now.

If coming in Liam's lap had been good, using his chest as a pillow while soused on postorgasm euphoria was like floating down a river in the high heat of summer. Skin sun-kissed, thoughts drifting lazily, the faint scent of the forest on his T-shirt.

"You good?" he whispered against her ear. Long fingers stroked her back.

Good? Try rearranged like a mosaic. Seemed safer to be light about it, though. "Five stars. Would come here again."

He chuckled.

"Are *you* good?" she slurred. "Want me to—"

"Nah." He kissed the top of her head. "This was for you and you alone."

She shot him a surprised look. "You sure?"

"One hundred percent." He shifted, tucking her into his side. "Get comfy. Let's watch another episode."

Her blood had been rendered to molasses. Hell, all of her melted against him.

Over the course of the hour, his breathing slowed and his body relaxed. His arm got heavier on her back. Had he fallen asleep? She had to assume but didn't want to wake him by moving to peek.

But when the episode ended, she was yawning, too.

She craned her neck. Oh, my goodness. Sound asleep, he was the most adorable. Thick lashes resting on his cheeks, plush mouth parted, jaw a little softer, but still so damn sharp.

Her heart skipped. She should leave him to sleep. Even more, she should wake him and see if he wanted to head home.

His arms, though. Even in sleep, they anchored her. A welcome harbor.

Five more minutes. The equivalent of a snooze button.

Then she'd summon the will to detach herself from the comfort, the satisfaction, of snuggling against a slumbering Liam Caldwell.

Chapter Thirteen

REVEALED: LIAM CALDWELL'S SECRET ROMANTASY ADDICTION
We stan a hot man reading. Picture below the cut.
Denver Daggers Bloggerista Babes, April 10

A trilling noise filtered into Liam's head. Waking up was like coming out of a fog. Where was he? The weight against his side… Katie. Holy crap, she smelled like heaven in the morning.

They were still on her big-ass, long couch. He had to give the piece of furniture credit—it had been decently comfortable, considering they'd been passed out on it since ten o'clock last night. Sure, his shoulder ached from having slept in a strange position, but he couldn't remember the last time he'd crashed so hard, especially with a pillow that wasn't his.

The woman in his arms wasn't his, either.

But she didn't seem to mind pretending to be.

And last night… Unexpected. A damn joy, bringing her pleasure. A bigger sense of satisfaction than breaking his no-scoring streak.

The look on her face had been worthy of a painting in a museum.

Earning those responses could creep toward addiction level, if he wasn't careful. The moment she'd come, he'd wanted to make her do it again.

Maybe her orgasm explained why she was still out like a light, even though the high-pitched trill persisted in her bedroom. A good toe curler could knock Liam out any day.

He hadn't needed his own last night—didn't want her to get him off because of obligation—but maybe they'd get there.

He rotated his wrist fast enough to get his watch to light up. Five thirty. Ouch. Had she meant to have her alarm set?

"Katie?" He tightened his arms around her. "Your alarm's going off. Do you have practice or something?"

She roused, rising on one elbow and rubbing her eyes with a fist. "Liam?"

He smiled softly. "Hopefully not a bad surprise."

"No, but—I didn't mean to fall asleep. Is that—holy crap, we slept through the whole night?"

"Hate to break it to you, but it's *still* night. It's bringing back memories of driving to the rink with my dad in the pitch black of a Saskatchewan winter."

Her small smile was fond, as if remembering her own car trips at the ass-crack of dawn. "You don't have to get up. Do you want to stay for a couple more hours? You're welcome to my bed."

He'd rather be there with her in it.

He shook his head and slid a hand behind her back as she sat up. After having had her against him for hours, losing close contact left a hole in his chest. *Christ.* "I'll head back to my place. I need to get organized after being away for a week. I'll skip the optional game-day skate, I think. Catch an extra hour's nap."

She winced. "You're sure? I'm so sorry I've thrown off your routine."

"Katie. I chose to be here. I loved last night. Promise."

"Okay. Can I at least make you coffee?"

"Yeah." He kissed her forehead right before she slipped away. She was soft, still rumpled. The perfect wake-up treat. "Sure. I'll clean up a bit and be on my way."

By the time he emerged from the bathroom with brushed teeth and wearing a clean T-shirt from his suitcase, she had a to-go mug filled and waiting on the counter.

"I'll get the mug back to you later." He paused. "Did you, uh, manage to align your work schedule to come to my game tonight?"

She bit her lip. "I did…"

Oof. Her obvious hesitance chafed, even though he knew that was unfair.

"Still nervous about going to the rink?" he said.

"Yeah. I built it up in my head. Beyond rationality." Clutching the edge of the counter, she blew out a long breath. "Cutting it down to size is difficult."

"It's a big arena," he said. "You could always stay up in the fan areas. Not come down to see me, if you want to avoid any of my teammates who stayed close to Vince."

Her chin lifted. "I'm not hiding. He doesn't live here anymore. My family are Daggers. My friends are. It's my home, not his. And I'm going to be there. To be seen, and to give you a goddamn kiss before you play."

Well, damn. A determined Kate Sullivan was a turn-on and a half. He circled the kitchen island and lowered his mouth to hers, tasting her until he earned a moan.

Her hand clutched his T-shirt. "You're going to make me late for practice."

He stepped back a bit. "Can't have that."

She made the face of a person who wished they could be in two places at once.

Her hand was still on his chest, and her fingers tapped a gentle rhythm. "Maybe if I'm in the crowd, I'll be able to avoid making small talk about my fricking ex-husband."

He smiled. Even better. His designated seats were close enough to the ice for him to see her, a few rows behind the bench. "My tickets will be waiting for you."

"Two?"

"Sure, bring whoever you want."

"Okay. But I have a trade for you."

He lifted a brow.

"There's a fundraiser at the arena on Saturday. Would you come skate with the kids for a few hours on the weekend?"

"Uh, sure." The tit-for-tat of it left his stomach uneasy. "It doesn't require a trade. I want to help your school."

"Thanks. I'll let Natalie know to add you to the list. A few of the other guys are attending, too."

"Sounds like fun."

She looped her arms around his neck. "If you sneak out now, you'll escape before my quasi-roommate sees."

He cringed. He hadn't even considered Coach Sullivan this morning. "Probably best."

One more kiss.

He doubted it would hold him over.

"Tell you what," he said. "Why don't you spend your day making a list of reasons why it isn't smart to let me make you come again, and later, I'll tear down every one of your arguments. Right before hearing you moan my name"

Committing her dazed expression to memory, he grabbed his coffee and suitcase and wound his way out past the pool and the extensive garden. He was putting his stuff in his trunk when the front door to the house opened and an ornery scowl greeted him.

"Morning, Coach!" he said, throwing in some extra oomph to sell the story of a carefree lover.

"It's going to be like this, is it?" his coach said, crossing his arms over his zipped-up running jacket.

"Seems so," Liam said, closing his trunk and making his way to the driver's side. "See you at the rink this afternoon."

"Not coming to the skate?"

"No, I have some things I need to do at home," he said.

Coach scowled. "Good. One less reminder you spent the night in my pool house."

Liam shook his head. "Destined to be a thorn in your side, I guess."

Maybe the fundraiser would help.

Hmm. "Hey, Coach? Are you going to be at Kate's fundraiser this weekend?

Tal frowned. "She hasn't asked me to be."

"Ah. Well, I bet she'd love it if you were there."

Coach jerked out a nod. "Thanks, Weller."

Genuine gratitude, for once.

If he'd thought being serious about her would win points with Tal Sullivan, in hopes of a trickle-down effect through the league, he'd been dead wrong. Hopefully the rest of the world would be more on board with the romance than Kate's grouchy father.

Kate's team's practice ended on time for the kids to get to school. Spring league wasn't as intense as winter hockey season—only two practices a week—and the space in her schedule was a breath of fresh air. Still, she went hard on her team during drills and scrimmages. By the end of the hour, she had a gaggle of sweaty kids, some out of energy, some raring for more ice time. Shayla had managed to stay on her feet for the entirety of the soccer-ball dash, which was huge progress. Maude, with her natural talent, wasn't the only one who mattered. Kids like Shayla, who were all enthusiasm and willing to work hard to make incremental progress, were just as much of a reminder of why Kate put in the work.

"Five more minutes, Aunt Kate?" Maude pleaded, skulking by the gate.

"Ma'am. You're about to get run over by a Zamboni," Kate said, jerking her thumb behind her. "To the changeroom with you."

Maude made an exaggerated sulk face, but followed instructions.

Sophie was lurking in the stands. She stood and climbed over benches to make her way down to Kate. "Feel like picking up a shift tonight?"

"I..." Her cheeks burned, and not from the exertion of keeping up with her tiny skaters. "I'm going to the Daggers' game."

Sophie did a double take. "Ready to face the fire?"

"It's not a big deal," she said.

Last night had been the big deal. But she wasn't ready to give her friend the details yet. It felt private. For her, but also for Liam.

"Forgive me if I disagree." Sophie wiggled a finger in Kate's direction. "Ten days ago, you didn't even want to go to the arena."

"I know. But it's important to Liam."

"And all of a sudden he's important to you? I thought you were only making it *look* like you're serious about each other."

"We are… And… *Argh*." Her brain was still scrambled. "And that is exactly why I need to be at the game tonight. Want to come with me?"

"Can't. If you can't bartend, then I'll have to."

Kate faked a pout. "Can I take Maude, then?"

"Using a ten-year-old as a shield?"

Guilt rose. "I could go alone."

"I didn't say that. Maude will love to go," Sophie said. "Just… make sure she doesn't get caught in the spotlight."

"Of course not." After the attention from Toby's death—well-meaning, but still difficult to take—the family kept Maude shielded from public view whenever they could. "Hot dogs, popcorn and aunt-niece time, coming up."

"But no soda on a school night."

"When do I ever give her soda on a school night?"

Sophie's eyebrow cocked.

"Spoiling her is my job," Kate said. "But I hear you. Sleep comes first."

"Especially since the game will wind her up," Sophie said. "You'll have a hyper ten-year-old on your hands without sugar to help."

By the time Kate and her niece got out of the car at the Dagger Den that evening, Maude, true to her mother's prediction, was a ball of blue-clothed energy, bouncing on the toes of her striped Chucks. In honor of her uncle Connor, she'd pulled a pair of pizza-printed socks up to her knees, over the tights she had on under her blue skirt. A Daggers jersey with "Sullivan" and Maude's own number sixteen completed the ensemble.

She'd been dismayed to see Kate was only wearing a Daggers athletic jacket and jeans, but even when Kate had been married to an NHL player, she hadn't been much for dressing up for games. She owned one of Connor's jerseys, but she didn't want to give her brother the satisfaction of her wearing his sweater instead of Liam's.

"We're going in through the staff entrance?" Maude asked as they approached the gate in question. "I thought we were sitting in the club seats."

"We're going to go see your grandpa first."

"And Liam Caldwell." Maude's eyes twinkled.

"Yes, and Liam Caldwell."

"You said you weren't going to kiss him, but I saw you did." Maude's glee was undeniably victorious. "It was on TikTok."

"*You* aren't on TikTok."

"No, but Tyla in my class has a phone, and she showed me."

Ugh. If it was up to Kate, kids would have to wait for phones until high school.

"You are growing up too fast. *Too fast,*" she said, keeping her tone light.

"Mom said he's your boyfriend."

"Mmm." *Thanks, Soph.*

"He wasn't your boyfriend the day he practiced shooting with me."

"Mmm."

"You always make that sound when you're avoiding a topic."

"*Or*, you're not even eleven and so aren't privy to everything going on in the lives of your trusted adults."

Maude sighed but then switched to chattering about Tyla-in-her-class, who, in addition to having a phone, also had a boyfriend, and Kate was struck by the fear of Maude showing romantic interest in one of her classmates before she even made it to sixth grade. Spilling the elementary school tea made for plenty of preteen drama as they made their way through to the restricted-access area where they had to flash their passes to get in. She'd take Maude's drama over her own any day.

Ten or so players were standing in a circle in the basement concourse, all in technical shirts and shorts or warm-up pants, passing a soccer ball between them. Liam had his back to her, his riot of waves sticking out the back of his royal blue cap. Connor was across the circle facing them. When he noticed Kate and Maude approaching and beckoned to them, Liam turned their way.

Jonesy gave him a teasing nudge. Liam returned it with an exasperated headshake.

He walked over to them. His gaze was fixed on Kate's, dancing with surprise and satisfaction. "I thought you were steering clear of our lair tonight."

Kate's pulse jumped. "Like I said, it's *my* home."

Maude's gaze was darting between Kate and the approaching player like Christmas had come early.

"Miss Maude!" Lars called from his place next to Connor. "Come take Weller's spot."

Her niece rushed forward to join the circle. She immediately launched a hell of a header across to her uncle.

Liam wasn't paying any attention to his teammates. He stopped right in front of Kate and kissed her forehead.

She could get used to that.

"Hey," he greeted, scanning the area behind her. His eyes lit on something over her right shoulder. "C'mere."

He slipped his hand into hers.

Shivers danced on her skin.

My God, why? It was hand-holding. Had it really been so long that something so innocent excited her? Good grief.

She let him guide her around the curve of the concourse, far enough to still be in the employees-only area, but out of sight of the warm-up circle.

"You came early," he commented.

"Maude would revolt if we didn't get food first. This gives us time to come say hi and load up on chicken fingers and nacho fries."

"Time for snacks, and this." A mischievous eyebrow rose as he tugged her into an alcove. He leaned back against a maintenance door and guided her in between his feet. Slouching, he was closer to her height. Gripping both her hands, he stroked playful circles along her skin with his thumbs.

"And here I thought the point was to be *seen* being romantic."

"I think the mystery is more convincing."

"Ah, *pretending* to make out in the machine room, then?"

"I wanted to give you privacy, not pretend."

Ugh, his voice was so sexy-low.

His eyebrow quirked. He caught her hip and pulled her closer, catching one of the sides of the open collar of her jacket between a thumb and forefinger.

"Didn't want to wear my jersey, superstar?"

"You didn't give me one to wear," she said.

"Next time," he said.

"Again with the 'next time.'"

"There's another next time I'm wondering about. Where's your list?"

"I don't have one yet," she admitted.

"Better yet, don't make one." He cupped her face, and it was like he was holding her up with his fingertips alone. She was wax between his fingers, melting under the heat of his gaze.

His lips were cool, though, a tiny shock. In a flash they heated. Their tongues tangled. A little suck of her lower lip. Her breath hitched and she rocked onto her heels, breaking the kiss. He followed as she pulled away.

"Not sure what it is about this," he murmured against the

sensitive skin by her ear, "but I can't even think about hockey right now."

"Not sure that's a good thing."

"Oh, this is a very good thing."

He mouthed her earlobe and along her neck, sending a shiver through her whole body.

"Liam…"

"Don't worry. I'll be able to focus just fine when I get on the ice."

Must be nice.

She was in the clouds after that kiss.

Still was hours later, as the second period was coming to a close. The tie game was keeping everyone on the edge of their seats. The Daggers had killed off a slashing penalty on Brian Boyle and were now energized and on the attack.

Maude was still bouncing in hers. "They'll score on the next shift, Aunt Kate. I can feel it."

A canine nose appeared in the aisle on the other side of two seats that had sat empty the whole game. Scone sported one of the specialty vests Natalie had made for him—half alerting people to his service dog status, half cementing himself as an Insta fashion plate. Natalie held his leash. A woman around her and Kate's age followed in Natalie's wake.

They took the two empty aisle seats next to Kate and Maude. Nat sat in the aisle seat to create a little extra space for Scone, who squatted between Nat's knees like a Great Dane in a clown car.

This put the new woman next to Kate. She looked a bit familiar somehow. Her eyes, maybe? Deep brown, framed by luminous brown skin and midnight lashes thicker than even Liam's. Her super thin box braids, black shot through with blue highlights, were gathered in a thick knot at her crown.

She offered Kate a hand. "Florence Johnson. I'm shadowing Natalie today."

Kate accepted the gesture and introduced herself and Maude.

"And here I thought Maude would be flagging by now," Natalie commented.

"Psssht." Kate waved a hand. "The kid is fueled by hockey."

"Like aunt, like niece."

"She'll go further than I did," Kate said.

"If she chooses to," Natalie said carefully.

"Of course." Kate's cheeks burned.

"I'm going to the Olympics, Auntie Natalie," Maude said mildly, her gaze tracking the puck.

"Not the Professional Women's Hockey League?" Florence asked.

"Oh, that, too." Maude could not have been more matter of fact.

Natalie chuckled.

"Are you in PR?" Kate asked the newcomer.

She shook her head. "I'm almost done with my journalism degree at CU Boulder. I'm writing a feature on the women of the Daggers organization. I love seeing women working in hockey. And it helped to have a small in." Florence motioned to the ice.

"Helped you're a brilliant writer," Natalie said.

"Naturally." Florence smiled.

Kate's brain caught up, snagging on Jay Johnson's number 54. "You're Jay's sister." She winced. "Sorry. It's the worst when the first thing out of anyone's mouth is something to do with my dad or brothers."

"Hard to avoid their shadow. Not that Jay's is as large as the one cast by the Sullivan name."

Kate nodded.

"You have your own shadow," Florence continued. "Your college stats were fire."

Kate blinked. "You know my college stats?"

Florence looked taken aback. "I've been obsessed with women's hockey since I was about your niece's age." She pointed at Maude, whose attention was on the play, entirely ignoring the adults' conversation. "Always wanted to keep up with my brother, but skates and my feet are mortal enemies. So I learned to narrate. I'm going to do play-by-play instead, hopefully for an outlet covering the PWHL." Her striking face screwed up in thought. "If the league had existed when you finished college, you'd be playing for them, I bet."

"Couple years too late," Kate said. "But I'll admit, when I was younger, it killed me to know I wouldn't play professionally."

Especially since her parents had brushed off that inequality.

"Must've hurt," Florence said.

"I made my peace with it," Kate assured her. "I've found a way to make hockey my profession. Like you, I just had to be flexible with my vision. Even with growing up in the family I did, finding opportunities in girls' hockey was tough. And I can't improve the system everywhere, but I can at least make sure it's easier for girls to play in my community. Hollow Valley took my family in our lowest moments after Toby died, and I want to be part of the town's fabric."

"You mean that," Florence said.

Kate nodded. "I'm halfway to my goal to secure my ice time for the fall semester, and the fundraiser we're holding this weekend will get us even closer."

She gave Florence a rundown of her school's goals.

"Your school sounds like a venture worthy of some journalistic magic," Florence said.

"Sports section, or a business magazine?" Natalie mused.

Florence snapped her fingers in agreement. "Let me make some calls. I'd love my name on that byline. And I love the direction you're taking."

Kate rubbed the back of her neck. She didn't want to count her chickens, but this seemed like a hell of an opportunity to get attention for her school without having to try to beat the media at their own game.

A whistle sounded, stopping the play, which had been back and forth with nothing to show for either team. The light came on for a TV commercial break.

Maude peered around Kate to grin at Florence. "Which PWHL team do you like more, the New York Sirens, or the Boston Fleet?"

"Minnesota Frost," the journalist answered.

Maude nodded seriously. "Good penalty kill."

Florence's gaze twinkled. "And my girlfriend is their goalie."

The game resumed, and Liam took the ice with Lars and Connor. Florence's brother, Jay, was out, too, on defense.

"*This* time they're going to score," Maude said.

"You said that last time, and it didn't come true," Kate reminded her.

"I can feel it."

The energy of the crowd seemed to spur on the play. Blades slashed and blocky numbers sped by, the puck a blur.

"Can you do commentary?" Maude asked Florence.

The journalist smiled and leaned forward. "Sure. Well... Oskar Larsen carrying the puck over the blue line, passing to the cause of my childhood angst, over to Sullivan, to Lars, back to my brother and his smelly feet—" Maude laughed "—chipped to Caldwell in front of the net. He takes it around, to Sullivan, to JJ, to—score! Wow, what a wrist shot."

Maude whooped, clapping and hollering along with the roaring crowd. "It was Liam!"

Kate jumped to her feet and cheered, trying to drown out her niece. He'd *buried* the shot. "That's right, Caldwell!"

He was skating back to the bench and pointed toward the stands. To her.

Kate's cheeks seared. She pressed her cool palms to her overheated skin.

"Not subtle, is he?" Natalie teased.

"Aunt Kate's in love," Maude joined in.

"Neither of you have any chill," Kate complained.

"Why should we? Love's meant to be celebrated," Natalie said. "As fleeting as it can be sometimes."

Fleeting. Or utterly fake.

Chapter Fourteen

KATE SULLIVAN SPOTTED AT DAGGERS' GAME
Fans hoping for a Kiss-Cam worthy moment left disappointed.
Denver Daggers Bloggerista Babes, April 11

Bright and early Saturday morning, Liam trailed Connor through the public entrance of Hollow Valley's arena complex.

Connor eyed Liam with suspicion. "They're *kids*. Why are you turning green around the gills?"

"Half the town is here, from what Kate said. And fans from the surrounding area."

"Which is good for minor hockey in Hollow Valley. And for Kate."

Hence the green.

He wanted to make this happen for her, beyond their agreement. He genuinely desired her success. Kids would benefit from her leadership and mentorship for years. People like Kate were what hockey needed—generous, genuine difference-makers, stripping out the lingering toxicity from generations past, making space for kids struggling to stay in the game. How many times had he overheard his parents crunching numbers and debating how to pay for rep hockey fees or new equipment? He couldn't fully know the frustrations Kate had faced as a young girl trying to be taken seriously, but he did understand the uncertainty of wondering if his current season would be his last. Having to give up hockey—and the time and bond it had given him with his dad, too—would have destroyed him. If her school kept even a handful of girls from having to experience those feelings, she'd be making a world of difference.

And with his own need to be a literal team player, visible to the Daggers brass—and hopefully to other interested teams in the league—it seemed a lot was on the line.

Connor couldn't know most of that, though, so Liam stuck to "It's a big day for your sister. I'm nervous for her."

Natalie bustled over, her Great Dane a hulking shadow at her side, replete with his assistance-dog vest. This one was royal blue, decorated with Scone's name and badges with the Daggers' logo. "There you are. My final two."

"We're early," Liam defended.

"Borisov, Rik, and Lars were earlier."

"Brownnosers," Connor griped.

"You're just annoyed you aren't the earliest for once," she said to Connor. "Take your skates and go join the others in the arena."

"Not me?" Liam asked.

"Nope," Natalie said. "We have enough skaters."

He followed her, Connor's footsteps fading behind them.

"It's not a dunk tank, is it?" Liam asked.

Natalie gave him a scolding look. "It's barely April. We're not in the business of giving hockey players hypothermia."

"No different from ice bath therapy. And it would be a moneymaker."

"So are the rest of these events. We considered having you sling hot beverages at the concession—my grandmother can't shut up about how efficiently you make cocoa. But Kate mentioned reading is a passion of yours. So, for kids who are less into street hockey or the skate, we assigned you somewhere special."

She led him to a classroom-sized multipurpose space lined with mats, including squishy crash pads, and beanbag chairs as well as folding chairs. All seats and mats were filled with the six-and-under set, plus parents.

"What, uh, am I doing here?" he asked Natalie. "A puppet show or something?"

Her eyes lit. "Do you want to?"

"No," he hissed. "Jes—jeez, no."

"How about reading aloud?"

"If that's what you need me to do."

He should have guessed he'd be reading from the get-go. A comfortable-looking armchair stood at the center of the semicircle of adults and kids. The velvet almost matched Kate's chaise.

He narrowed his eyes at it. "That looks familiar."

"It's mine." A happy realization dawned on Natalie's face. "You've been to Kate's place."

"Of course, I have," he said, pretending like it would have been weird otherwise.

"Oh, yes, of course. *Of course*," she said.

He half expected her to wiggle her eyebrows. Did she know the truth?

She shuffled him toward the chair, where he eased onto the cushion.

She clapped to get the crowd's attention. Scone sat patiently at her side. "Do I have a treat for you today, kids. How many of you like stories about hockey?"

A forest of hands shot up.

"What about one read to you *by* a hockey player?"

More waving.

He picked the one off the top. "*Z is for Zamboni*," he read, scanning his rapt audience and holding up the book with the cover facing them. "Let's guess what the letters might be before we turn the page. What's a hockey word starting with *A*?"

Nervous faces looked back at him.

"How about…the building we're in is called an…"

"Arena!" a kid of around six called from the back.

"Good prediction. Let's see if you're right."

He started to turn pages, reading through the first part of the alphabet. Every time he turned a page, one of the girls in the front row, around two, with the reddest hair he'd ever seen, scooted closer to his feet.

He got as far as *K* when she stood and put a hand on his knee. "Up?"

"Uh…"

"Up!"

The girl's dad rushed forward from the side. "Sorry, I—"

"I'm okay with it if you are," Liam said. As soon as he got a nod from the father, he bent toward the girl. "Want to help me turn the pages?"

"Turn!" the girl echoed.

The dad looked a little embarrassed but shrugged. "Sure. Her name's Georgia."

"Come on up, Georgia," Liam said, lifting her into his lap. She barely weighed a thing and was clearly used to being read to because she reached for the page. His heart panged. Being an only child, and lacking in the close-friend department, he rarely got the chance to be around kids outside of the occasional children's hospital charity visit. And damn, there was something pure and perfect about reading a picture book with a tiny human using his bent elbow as a backrest.

"Do you think *L* will be for Liam?" he asked the audience.

"Lightning!" one of the kids suggested, leading off a torrent.

"Left wing!"

"Lunch!"

The neighboring boy jabbed what looked like his twin brother in the side. "That's not a hockey term, stupid."

"Hang on, now," Liam said gently. "Lunch is a big part of a hockey player's day. Can't skate fast with no gas in the tank."

"You drink *gas*?" the lunch kid said in disbelief.

"No," Liam said, suppressing a chuckle. "But food is to our bodies like gas is to some cars and trucks."

Georgia, done waiting, lurched for the next page. Liam had to curl his arm around her to keep her from ejecting onto the floor.

She skipped a few pages, showing off *Slash* and *Trip* for *S* and *T*.

"Aw, and here I was hoping for *Sullivan*," came a voice from just left of Liam's peripheral vision.

He tilted a smile toward his new arrival. "I happen to love *S* for *Sullivan*."

A few titters escaped the parents in the crowd.

Kate's cheeks turned a distinct pink.

And with her reaction, any lingering nerves dissipated. Even if no one from the Daggers' front office, save Natalie, noticed he was here, it didn't matter. By the number of people packed into the various parts of the arena, the day was going to be a fundraising success.

Plus, he'd made Kate blush.

Somehow, that mattered more than any of it.

An hour after Kate finished running her ten-minute long, complimentary private skating lessons and with all the other activities wrapped up, she waved goodbye to her dad, who'd showed up to help with the concession.

"Thanks, Dad!" she called, smiling at him as he headed out the front door of the arena.

"Proud of you, Katherine," he called back. His expression was stern as always, but he sounded like he meant it.

His praise was the cherry on top of the successful day. Warmed by his words, she headed to the multipurpose area to clean up.

She halted in the middle of Liam's story time circle. Earlier, she'd loaded the folding chairs onto a wheeled storage cart and now had the two, thick, rectangular mats to contend with.

A throat cleared behind her, and she whirled to face the low, masculine sound.

"Casing out the joint for a nap?" Liam asked, coming around the table. He slid in right behind her and pulled her back to his front. He buried his nose next to her ponytail.

"Oh, my God," she protested, snuggling into his chest. "I had my helmet on not long ago. I cannot smell good."

He took a long, exaggerated whiff. "You smell like the ice. And a vanilla-orange milkshake. I love your shampoo. Perfection."

"As if." She couldn't manage more than a half-hearted rebuttal. His compliments were too specific to be total lies.

"You did good today. Every kid in the place had a huge smile on their face."

She sighed. "I hope we raised enough."

"You did. Guaranteed. The place was packed." He kissed behind her ear.

A squeak escaped her before she could muffle her reaction. God, the shivers from this man's lips. They danced down her skin.

"No one is watching," she said.

"Nope. This is for you and me alone," he said. "So long as you like it."

"I do."

"Good. You feel just right, like this." He tightened his embrace. "Need help putting these mats away?"

"You'll have to let go."

"Not for long." The promise in his voice was intoxicating.

They started with the flatter ones, stacking them in a nearby storage room full of equipment for the small, attached gymnasium. A few minutes later, they slid the two crash mats side by side.

She was about to walk away when he caught her by the hips and pulled her backward. They landed on the cushy surface, his laugh echoing in the cement-walled room.

His *laugh.*

It leveled her. The world came to a screeching halt when Liam was holding her in his arms with a wide smile on his face.

"What are you doing?" she said. Instead of trying to get up, she rested her head on his shoulder and tucked right in against his side.

"I watched the kids bounce on these mats for over an hour. Looked like fun," he said.

"Oh, so we're taking a bounce break?"

He smirked at her. "If you want to."

Heat simmered in her belly. "What kind of bouncing are you talking about?"

"The good kind."

"That's subjective." Give her five minutes, though, and she could provide him with an itemized list of the "good kinds."

"Whatever kind you're up for?" He sounded so hopeful.

She shot him an apologetic smile. "None, right now. We have cleanup to do."

"Such a shame. Ever since you used my lap to have the prettiest orgasm I've ever seen, I haven't been able to think about anything else."

"Liam. Not here."

"So, later?"

"We'll see."

He cupped her cheek and leaned in. "No bouncing then. A quick break. Five minutes. They can do without you for five minutes."

"Liam," she warned again.

"Please?"

She was close enough so she could see the myriad shades of green in his irises. "Argh, why can't I resist you when you say *please*?"

"I'll remember that."

An admission she'd probably regret.

Or will greatly enjoy.

"Fine. A *quick* break," she said, caving.

He dropped a light kiss on her mouth. His lips were soft and carried a hint of salt. Butter, maybe.

"Were you sneaking popcorn from the snack table?" she accused.

"I paid for it," he said, amusement clear.

"You worked up an appetite reading, I'm sure." She walked her fingers up his chest.

"Exhausting work. Nearly broke a sweat during the argument about lunch. Thought those brothers were going to start throwing elbows."

He was minimizing his efforts. But she'd watched him for more of his story time than she should have, given how many tasks she'd had to accomplish herself.

"I think any adult in the room who is into guys fell a little in love with you as soon as you started doing the voices," she said.

"Including you?" he asked mischievously.

Ack, no. "You know what I meant."

"Mmm, yes, I'm irresistible."

"Good thing you're moving on come summertime," she teased. "Otherwise, I'd have to face my utter inability to resist good-looking hockey players."

"Is that *so*, Katie?"

She'd been joking, but in reality, it wasn't a joke at all.

He seemed to clue in to her discomfort, as his expression turned teasing. "No wonder you agreed to fool around while we play up our narrative. You like a jock."

"On the outside," she grumbled. *And* on the inside, when they were sweet with kids and devoted to their team and—gah. He was *not* permanent.

"Speaking of fooling around," he said, "when can I see you next? Tonight?"

"I'm working. Tomorrow, too."

He looked legitimately disappointed. "And here I was going to invite you into the city. Spoil you after the success of today."

She grimaced. "No rest for the wicked. I'm sorry to miss tomorrow's game. Might be a big one."

With the two points from a victory, and if Utah lost their own game, the Daggers would creep into a playoff spot.

"With any luck. If we don't make the playoffs, this will be the first time I've missed the chance at the big prize. Every team I've ever been on has at least made it to the first round. So we're depending on that good luck kiss, Katie."

She lifted a skeptical eyebrow. "Don't you think we have it well covered by now?"

He shook his head. "Tomorrow's Sunday. Where are you going to be after my morning skate?"

"My 3-on-3 team has a game at eleven."

"Home, or away?"

"Home."

He grinned as if he'd won the lottery. "Am I going to be a distraction if I come by?"

"Without a doubt." She smiled, though. The kids had loved his last visit. "What, this isn't enough?"

She kissed him.

He deepened it, sliding his tongue along the seam of her lips.

She let herself enjoy it for ten seconds, twenty, thirty, before insisting, "You're going to get us in—"

The door flung open.

"Oh, good grief," came a dry voice.

"—trouble," Kate finished.

"You're needed, Katherine," Sophie said. Natalie stood at her side. So did Scone, dishing out his usual, healthy serving of disdain.

"You're not hiding my niece back there, are you?" Kate said weakly.

"Fortunately for your eardrums, no," Sophie said. "Her level of preteen embarrassed glee would be supersonic."

Looking entirely unapologetic, Liam sat up and offered Kate a hand.

As much as she wanted to, she couldn't very well disappear into the crash mat.

Why was this a big deal? She wanted to be seen with him.

But kissing him just now had only been about her and him. Not the rest of the world.

"You didn't feel your phone buzz?" Sophie said.

"Must have missed it." She got up and brushed herself off. Her limbs were jelly. Damn, she'd rather have the time to sink into that feeling.

She'd get a better opportunity if she took Liam up on his offer of a night in Denver, whatever his definition of spoiling her entailed. Something delicious, no doubt. Maybe soon. Though if all went to plan, the Daggers would make the playoffs, and in a couple of weeks, the quest for the Stanley Cup would consume his free time.

"Forgot we were planning to count the money?" Natalie asked gently. "It's your big moment."

She gave her friends a sheepish look.

"I mean, I get it, Kate. I do." Natalie winked at Liam, who chuckled.

Liam squeezed Kate's hand. "Sorry to distract you, superstar. I'll take off. Call me as soon as the count is done to crow about your success."

It was the kind of thing a boyfriend would say.

And too much of her wished he meant it.

Chapter Fifteen

Kate's team's 3-on-3 game was wrapping up, and she couldn't help but feel excited about their tournament the following weekend. They weren't winning this morning, but at 3-2, it was close. No matter the result, they were looking sharp on the ice. Maude's mid-shift communication had been dynamite. So much progress, especially from the kids who were also enrolled in her skating class.

"Nice pass, Shayla!" A familiar voice rang out from the door to the common area.

Liam approached the bench. He must have walked all the way over from the other ice sheet right after his morning skate, because he still wore his full practice gear, minus his helmet. He'd tousled his hair after taking it off, but it was still a sweaty mess.

He came to stand at her side. "Hey, Coach Superstar."

"Weller." She crossed her arms over her chest and ignored the flare in her chest urging her to scramble up his frame until her legs were around his bulky hockey pants.

"Put me on, Coach."

"I'm sure the kids would love a new line mate, but there's only a minute left in the game." Her niece fumbled with the puck, then scurried to keep it from one of her Eagle opponents. "Head up, Maudie!"

Maude scrambled to follow the instructions, stole the puck off the kid who'd taken it from her, then passed it to Rika Tiimonen's daughter, who took a shot. The goalie saved it, but barely. It was Kesia's first game—Anneli had signed her up to join during the fundraiser yesterday—but the girl had natural talent. Kate was thrilled to have her as a River Otter.

Soon after Kesia missed, the horn sounded, ending the game. A few of Kate's kids groaned.

"Want to give them some encouragement?" she asked Liam. "Both teams?"

"Yeah, sure."

"Gerry, you okay with Liam joining them on the ice for a few minutes?" she called to the other coach.

He was a bro-looking dad in his late thirties who she ran into more often than she'd like. He usually carried a near-visible chip on his shoulder. Tended toward the hard-line angle of coaching, which made Kate want to take him by the shoulders and shake some sense into him. Anytime she saw it, she was taken back to the times she'd been chewed out by one of her high school coaches.

Gerry shrugged. "I'm sure they'd love it."

Liam nodded and skated out onto the ice. Wide eyes greeted him. Sticks dangled from loose arms, matching their dropped jaws.

"Eagles," he said. "Solid win. Apex predators. Earning your name."

The Eagles players shared another round of fist bumps.

"But we learn as much from losing as from winning, right? River Otters, remember, you are a keystone species! The ecosystem is shaped to your existence. Make it impossible for the other team to ignore you," he instructed, then started to glide backward. "So, Eagles, let's give your opponents a cheer, too, yeah? They gave you some fierce competition."

The encouragement paid off, and the Eagles players gave a whoop and some applause and back pats to the River Otters who were close enough.

"Follow me in a skating drill!" Liam called. "I want to see your best *head and shoulders, knees and toes*."

"Is this guy serious?" Gerry muttered. "They're too old for nursery rhyme crap."

"Balance. Muscle building," Kate said. "It's not all about arm day, Gerry. It's about functional movement. And being kids. Letting them be silly and joyful. Even when they're ten or eleven. *Especially* when they're ten and eleven."

"You're too soft on them, Kate. It's why they don't win for you."

"They win. Not every game, but they do. And this year, I have a number of beginners. Not every kid has the advantage of learning to skate and joining a team when they're five. Especially the girls. If they finish the season and still love showing up and getting a sweat on, I've done my job."

Gerry scoffed. His gaze was fixed on Liam, who still glided backward and was smoothly transitioning from touching his shoulders down to his knees and toes. He was *effortless* on the ice.

His skill...but also his ease with the young players and his commitment to sharing his love of the game with them. He was easy to admire. She pulled out her phone and sneaked a clip of him, then texted it to Sophie with Can you use this?

The gaggle of kids reached the end of the ice, slipping and sliding and looking far less coordinated than Liam. Some had smiles on their faces. Others grimaced in determination. From her team, Shayla looked frustrated—she'd take her aside later to remind her to be patient when trying an old skill in a new way. Maude wasn't smiling, but wasn't frowning, either.

Liam clapped his gloved hands and motioned for the kids' attention. "How about... Freeze tag?" He pointed at a few skaters at random, two Otters and an Eagle. "You three are it. Annnnnnd...go!"

He took off, speeding at first and then slowing to let the smallest of the three tag him. He froze, limbs and face splayed in a comedic "oh no." How the hell was he going to hold that pose for any length of time? His abs would be screaming.

Or, given how fit he was, he might not even feel it. His six-pack was probably something to behold.

You could find out.

Yes, yes, she could.

Maybe soon. Hopefully before his next road trip.

Liam goofed around with the kids a bit more, freezing twice for comic relief. He spent a minute with Shayla at his side, giving the girl gentle pointers on her stride as they chased Maude around the rink. By the time he shooed them all off the ice to their dressing rooms, Shayla had a smile on her face again, and all of the kids were laughing. He signed a few autographs for Eagles players—including Gerry, who was almost bashful when he asked for one—and then came to stand in front of Kate.

"Hey, there, lucky charm."

"We're still sticking to that?"

"We sure are."

He kissed her. Then went for a second. Then a third.

Not even intense. Public appropriate.

And yet, she was a breathless puddle in a tracksuit.

"For tonight, and then loading up for the road trip," he claimed.

"Plus an extra?"

"Whatever it takes."

"Thank you for taking the time to play with the kids. Especially helping Shayla. They were all so happy."

"Hey, leading ten minutes of fun? *I'm* the one who got the best deal. Loosened me up, too. If I get stressed out during the game tonight, I'll remember to do a mental *head and shoulders, knees and toes.*"

She looped her arms around his shoulders. "I'm sorry I can't be in the stands."

"It's okay. Your work matters, Kate. What you do with the kids, *and* what you do for Sophie."

A message she hadn't gotten from Vince and still didn't always get from her dad. It filled her well.

"I'll be watching," she promised. "Every TV in the bar will be on the Daggers' broadcast."

"No pressure," he said with a wink she didn't quite believe.

* * *

Hours later, the televisions at Sullivan's were, as promised, tuned in to show the Daggers giving the Edmonton team a damn clinic on offensive zone coverage. Despite that, Borisov hadn't had the best night, and the score was tied at three. Kate and Sophie were both on tenterhooks watching.

Kate kept getting distracted in the middle of making drinks. By the Daggers' collective skills, of course, not the occasional between-play glimpses of Liam's face.

"Maude could not stop talking about Liam coming by your game this morning," Sophie commented, in the middle of the third period.

Kate lined up three glasses on the bar. She was known around town for her Blue Dagger, a cocktail she managed to make the right shade without it being sickly sweet. She crafted more than her fair share of them on game nights. "Oh, yeah, Liam put on a show, alright."

Sophie stilled. "What does that mean?"

Oh, dang. She forced a laugh. "He likes making the kids happy. It was only a few silly skills activities."

"Like he was there for the kids. The two of you can't keep your mouths off each other, or so arena lore tells me."

"*Lore.* I hardly think this has gone down in the annals of history yet. It's not foundational."

"Hot goss, then," Sophie joked.

Kate rolled her eyes and measured indigo-tinted gin into the shaker with a jigger and followed it with grapefruit liqueur, dry vermouth and butterfly pea tea.

"We should be thrilled," she said. "A few of the parents posted videos of the freeze tag match to their socials, and two of them tagged the school."

"We don't want people thinking he's offering regular clinics to our students," Sophie said, biting her lip as she entered something in the point-of-sale.

"I agree, and nothing we're putting out would suggest he is. But if Liam's name catches someone's attention and gets parents looking at us, and then they like what we *do* offer, well, my ruse has come to fruition."

"So evil genius of you." Sophie sobered, her hand falling away from the screen. "Are you sure you're not into him, Kate?"

Kate sighed. "Falling for him would be asking for heartbreak."

"Which doesn't answer my question."

"Using this media attention to benefit the school was my idea. And I wouldn't have done it if I didn't feel some sort of pull toward him and at least find him fun to be around. But I won't let my feelings get involved." She jammed a pint glass onto the cocktail shaker and agitated it over her shoulder.

If she shook hard enough, she might be able to forget how much they'd gone beyond "fun." He was too easy to confide in. And she loved being a safe place for him to share his frustrations and grief, too. But she'd do that for any of her friends. Just because she'd been open about some of her past, it didn't mean she was head over heels.

"I just don't want him to hurt you like Vince did."

Kate put the overshaken cocktail down and frowned. "You think I'm going to put myself in that position again?"

Sophie glanced at one of the TVs positioned in the corner closest to them. "Well, whatever you're doing, Liam is sure on fire tonight."

"Still hasn't scored," Kate said.

"Pssh. With two assists, I don't know he'll care."

"He cares."

Sophie studied her. "And *you* care. Stop pretending you don't."

Her hands shook a little as she measured the drink into the glasses. "Yes, I do. He's one of the best. I want to see him succeed."

"And he's going to take his hotshot reputation and ride it all the way to a new contract. Somewhere *else*."

"He sure will," she said, managing to keep her tone more stable than her hands. "I'm not lying to myself, Soph. He won't be able to pull the rug out from under me like Vince did."

On the screen, his jersey number caught her eye, heading for the net.

She froze, then reached out to grip Sophie's forearm.

"Come on, come on," her friend muttered.

He missed the shot. The crowd in the bar groaned. Kate deflated. "No, no, no, this can't go to overtime—"

Connor got hammered in the corner and ended up on the ice.

Both she and Sophie gasped.

A flurry of bodies followed, scrapping for the puck. Connor got up and hooked the puck out and across to a waiting defenseman.

Damn. The speed of hockey never failed to mesmerize. Watching it was only second to playing, and Connor, Lars and Liam were at their best tonight, cycling the puck. The Edmonton players looked tired, trapped in their zone. Their superstar was injured, a boon for any opponent.

Kate clenched Sophie's arm harder.

"Oh, my God, this could be their whole season," Sophie said. "You should be watching in person."

Connor passed to Liam, who sent it back to Connor—

"I wasn't going to let you down—*yes!*"

Holy hell, her brother could score a beautiful goal.

Connor raised an arm and accepted his teammates' congratulations.

Kate jumped, nearly knocking Sophie over in the process.

Sophie was grinning, laughing. "Easy, killer."

"They're going to the playoffs!"

"I know, I know." She smirked. "You sure weren't this excited last year."

"Yeah, but…"

Sophie rang the bell hanging in front of the mirror, specifically installed for this purpose. "A round on number ninety-six!"

The bar patrons cheered.

Whenever Connor scored, he covered a round at Sullivan's.

The camera zoomed in on her brother, skating awkwardly for the bench, grimacing as he headed down the tunnel.

Sophie gasped. "He's hurt."

"Don't say that," Kate hissed.

"Why else would he head for the dressing room with a minute left in the game?"

"Equipment problems?"

"No, it was the check to the boards."

Sophie pulled out her phone and sent a text.

"Trying to reach him?" Kate asked. "You know he won't be on his phone anytime soon."

"He'll get it eventually."

Kate shot one off to her dad. He'd be the better bet.

And one for Liam, though it was only right to congratulate him, first.

Three assists? Epic. So happy for you. I hope my brother isn't banged up too badly. Let me know.

The waiting was awful, making the shift drag. Neither Connor nor their dad replied. About twenty minutes after the game ended, Liam sent a quick message:

Thanks, superstar. Big night. I'll catch you up in a bit.

She flashed the screen at Sophie, and they exchanged an uncomfortable look.

The number of patrons who asked for updates on Connor over the next hour exceeded the number of drinks they served.

Just before eleven, Sophie checked her watch. "I wonder if he's home yet. Weird we haven't heard anything."

"I know," Kate said. She'd gotten nothing but radio silence from Connor and her dad. And Liam's definition of "a bit" differed from hers by a good half hour.

A few minutes later, she emptied her gin bottle. She went back to the storeroom to replace it. When she returned to the bar, a familiar set of hulking shoulders occupied one of the empty seats by the beer taps. She glanced toward the Daggers usual table, but it was full of college students, still enjoying Connor's generosity. No other hockey players were in sight.

"You came alone?" she asked bluntly.

"Way to be welcoming, Katherine," Sophie said.

Liam laughed it off. "Most of the guys went to a place in RiNo." He cocked his head at Sophie's probing look. "Connor headed home. He's stiff, and his hip's probably barking at him something fierce, but nothing was torn or dislocated."

Both Kate and Sophie exhaled loudly.

"You didn't want to join the team festivities? Big deal, clinching a playoff spot," Sophie said.

"Sure, but Kate is *here*," Liam answered. Although he was replying to Sophie, his attention was on Kate the whole time. A heated stare, only for her.

What was she doing? She was supposed to be a supportive girlfriend. She needed to be all over him, not defensive and suspicious and trying to resist the pull drawing her to him by ensuring a bar's width of space separated them.

She darted through the gate and slid between him and the bar. The wood at her back, the warmth of him at her front… It was tempting and teasing and…secure?

"Hey," she whispered. "Sorry. I should have done this, first."

"*Should* is an ugly word, Kate."

She looped her arms around his neck. She lowered her voice.

"I didn't mean I felt obligated. Just that you deserve a big hello after your big game."

"Make it up to me by inviting me back to your place once your shift ends. I want to spend some time with you before I head out on the road tomorrow."

She caught herself right before she started chewing on her lower lip. Swallowing down the tightness in her throat and chest, she asked, "You sure you want to be up late?"

"I'm still humming from the game."

She expected him to kiss her. Instead, he angled forward, wrapped his arms around her and held on tight. He was almost shaking, as if emotion was coursing through him faster than he could process.

"Hey. You okay?"

"Yeah. I'm happy. And relieved. We have a chance."

He meant the Daggers. Surely.

Not *them*. Right?

Chapter Sixteen

"Tell me about your playoff routine," Kate said to Liam.

His head was too foggy to answer her properly. He was sprawled on her chaise, floating on the wave of the Daggers' massive win and in the sensory overload of holding Kate in his arms. Her light citrus-sweet scent wafting off her hair, her fingers tracing the logo on his T-shirt, her chest rising and falling against his. Christ, this was the best place to come down off his postgame high.

She'd brought him to her place after she finished work. They weren't bothering to pretend with the TV this time. She'd immediately cuddled into him. He wasn't sure where the night would take them. If it involved them being in her bed instead of on the chaise, he wouldn't complain. Especially if he got to slide her out of the oversize sweatshirt and fitted sweats she'd changed into when she got home.

Had she kept her underwear on?

Maybe not. *Hopefully* not.

Luck willing, he'd get the chance to find out.

But first, she seemed to want to hash out the real stuff. At least he got to enjoy the weight of her in his arms, her perfect ass nestled in his lap, while she grilled him.

"What makes you think I have a routine?" he teased.

"Everyone has a routine for the playoffs." She ran the pad of a thumb along his jawline. "Do you stop shaving?"

"Of course." He arched a brow. "Does a beard do it for you?"

Her scoff said "dream on." The way she licked her lips said "obviously."

He grinned.

"It was a serious question," she said. "You've been supporting me. I want to return the gesture, especially with the Daggers in the first round."

"And with the rumors about Toronto and Boston being interested in me. Super rumor-y of course—no one's breaking the rules and talking to my agent or anything. But you know how it is. News gets out."

"Two Original Six teams." The dimness in her eyes didn't match the encouragement in her voice. "Impressive."

"Yeah," he agreed quietly. "We'll see. But it's way too early to count even a chicken feather, let alone two whole birds."

She nodded. "We'll keep making you look devoted and hard-working. Which means, like I said, me being in on your routine."

"I try to keep things as normal as possible. I stick to the same diet I always eat. Follow my same superstitions. Work out like usual. Nap. Make sure to prioritize rest."

"You can't tell me everything will be the same. Vince always…"

His curiosity piqued. She so rarely mentioned her ex.

"Always…" he prodded.

"I don't want to bring him into this," she said.

"Okay, but if you ever want to, I'm here to listen."

She didn't say anything. Kissed his neck, though. Not passionate. A tiny, silent *thank-you.*

"You're right, though," he admitted. "The routine might be the same, but the feelings aren't. I probably get more intense."

She shot him a dry look.

"Sometimes I forget you've had a family member in the playoffs many times over."

"Since I was a kid. My dad made the playoffs the first time when I was five. Three times before I graduated. And then my brothers, and Dad as a coach… Honestly, I'd need a few minutes and a piece of paper to keep track of it all." She did a quick count on her fingers, passing a full ten twice. "More than twenty-one rounds. Plus my own. My college team made the Frozen Four once. Provided we're counting playoffs below the show."

"Of course we are." He chuckled. "What's it like to be hockey royalty?"

"I don't know, you tell me."

"Come now. A person needs to come from generations to count as part of a family dynasty. I'm only me."

Why did his throat get tight at those words?

"Maybe one day, you'll have a passel of kids who will follow in your skate strides. Maybe you're the beginning of a great string of Caldwells."

He choked on the image. Hard to create a family without being with someone long-term. And even if he toyed with the hypothetical—how the hell was he supposed to picture a passel of little Caldwells, knowing his dad would never really know them, would never be as proud of them as he had been of Liam?

A lump filled his throat, as round as one of the orange balls he and his dad used to shoot around in their backyard. All he managed to get out was a muted "Mmm."

"Oh, damn, I'm sorry." Red flagged her cheeks. "If you don't want… I mean, that could have been insensitive. Was it? I didn't—"

He cleared his throat and brushed a thumb across her lips. "Hey. No worries. You threw a *maybe* in there. And kids are something normal to talk about when you're dating someone."

"But…" Her hesitance hung in the air, a deflating helium balloon drifting halfway between the floor and the ceiling.

He cocked an eyebrow.

"We're not dating, Liam."

"You sure about that?"

"I mean, it's supposed to look like we are. But it's not for *us*, you know? It's saving face, or creating one, or whatever. But it's not about us *enjoying* it, right?"

He stroked a hand down her face, through her hair, loose now, still with a little kink from her ponytail. Soft between his fingers, sifting like strands of silk along his too-rough calluses. "I'm not going to tell you what you're supposed to feel, Kate, but I'm sure as hell enjoying this."

She tilted her face toward his palm and caught the inside of his wrist with her lips. Just a brush, but it seared.

"I like you." He pressed his mouth to her forehead. "I'd do many a thing to see you smile, Kate Sullivan."

"Yeah? Like what?" Her mouth sneaked up at the corner, a small, secret hint he hoped he was correctly decoding.

He shifted her onto her back, nestled into the collection of soft throw pillows. Kissing her neck, he started a slow descent. Her collarbone. The notch at her throat.

Sliding up her T-shirt and nipping at the soft perfection where her rib cage ended and her stomach began.

"Liam..." she said on a gentle laugh.

"See? You're already smiling."

"I guess you know what you're doing."

He chuckled, muffling the sound by pressing his lips to the slight curve of her belly. "Glad it looks like that from the outside."

Her hand caught his cheek, drawing his chin up until the golden brown seriousness of her eyes pulled him under her spell. "I don't have a clue, either."

"We can stumble through it together," he said. "No rules say we can't like what we're doing here, Kate."

He tugged at her waistband, exposing the top inch of hot pink, soft underwear.

"I like what *you're* doing," she said, breath hitching as he dragged her pants lower. Her hips rose off the couch.

He knelt at the foot of it, the exact right spot he'd need to drive her wild. Dragging a finger between her thighs, over the thin, damp fabric, he pressed a kiss to her mound. "Good. And you'll like this even more."

LIAM CALDWELL CELEBRATES WIN SOLO AT SULLIVAN'S BAR
Is team unity an issue going into the playoffs?
Denver Star, April 14

On Friday evening, right before Kate was supposed to usher her team from their hotel to their dinner reservation, a picture of Liam arrived on her phone, followed by a text: Next home game: you. me. nap. my bed.

Kate almost swallowed her tongue. Miles of his sharply contoured chest, bare, above the hint of a sheet. What was under it? Good lord. Liam's sheets probably had a stellar thread count, even on the road, as he was right now.

So was she, for that matter, in Colorado Springs for her team's tournament. Not the time for a debauched text thread with a flirty hockey player.

"Coach!" Pavneet called, jolting Kate back to where she needed to focus. "When is bowling?"

"Seven. Right after dinner," Kate said.

Her team and a handful of parent chaperones milled around her in the hotel lobby, getting organized for the short walk to Denny's.

Shayla raced over and threw her arms around Kate's waist. "Mom says I can have extra ice cream because I scored my first goal."

Kate hugged the girl back. "I think everyone gets two scoops after coming back from our first loss to earn a *W* in game two."

Shayla nodded and twirled away to join Maude.

After corralling the hyped-up team, Kate followed Pavneet out into the early evening sun.

She glanced back at her phone and typed a quick reply.

I'm up for suggestions. Off next Wednesday.

Love of My Life: Watching me play in game three next Wednesday, you mean.

Kate: Yes, I managed to switch my shift.

Love of My Life: You are a stellar girlfriend. Thank you.

Her cheeks heated. Ugh, what was it about praise from Liam? She shouldn't be reacting like this to something manufactured. No matter how much he'd talked about them enjoying themselves before nestling his face between her thighs and making every one of her functioning brain cells evaporate.

I'll pencil in naptime, she replied.

Love of My Life: Oh, no. Indelible ink only. I'm counting this as a promise.

She sighed. This didn't deserve a permanent pen. At least that was what she tried to convince herself.

Pavneet nudged her with an elbow. "Stressed about juggling coaching and your boyfriend's playoff season?"

She startled. "Oh! No, it should be okay. Not my first rodeo."

"Your first rodeo riding Liam," Pavneet whispered.

"Oh, my God, *Pav*."

The other woman smirked. "Seriously, though, I'm amazed you're still up for bowling, instead of holing up in a sports bar and cheering on your man. Or hopping on a plane to Minneapolis."

She sent her friend a chiding look. "I can't skip work and coaching to follow him around the country. Life goes on, even when the Stanley Cup is on the line. I can't shift my academy classes to accommodate the Daggers' schedule. Nor would I back out of a tournament our kids have been looking forward to. Traveling together builds camaraderie, because of the time they spend together *off* the ice. So I'm going to lead the way to bowling, and we'll have a great time."

"And if there aren't any TVs at the lanes with the game on, you'll be streaming it on your phone whenever you can sneak away."

"Maybe," Kate said, unable to hold in a smile.

"Liam's okay with you missing game one for some five-pin?"

"Yes," she said, an automatic answer. But as she sat with the answer through dinner and in the car on the way to bowling, she couldn't ignore the truth of it. He *was* okay with her prioritizing the River Otters' games over his own.

Hours later, she had a yawning Maude on her hands as she maneuvered her niece through the hotel hallway to their room. Sophie hadn't been able to take two weekends off from the pub in such short succession, so Maude was under Kate's watchful eye for this tournament. Sophie would catch the next one and was helping Kate organize it since the Hollow Valley hockey association was hosting.

"I don't want to go to bed," Maude complained, stifling another yawn. "I want to watch the third period."

"We'll put on our jammies and cheer on Uncle Connor."

"And Liam," Maude said impishly.

"Oh, yes. He owes me a goal."

"And maybe one for me, too." Maude rubbed her eyes and followed Kate into the room.

Once in pajamas, they perched on their beds and watched the Daggers defend their 2-1 lead. Kate's heart was in her throat every time Connor or Liam was on the ice.

Maude didn't look happy, though.

"What's on your mind, Maudie?"

"Uncle Connor can shoot harder than that."

Maude's ability to recognize puck speed at her age was impressive. Also, she was right. Connor hadn't looked the same on the ice since the hit he took last week. "I think he's a little sore, honey."

"You tell me not to play injured."

Bit different when millions of dollars are involved.

"Mom told him he was being irresponsible," Maude continued. Her eyes widened. "I wasn't eavesdropping on purpose. They were just talking really loud."

Kate let out a breath. Sophie had a hair trigger when it came to injury.

"You don't seem as worried as Mom does," Maude said.

"It's hard for your mom sometimes. She's learned to worry about safety."

Especially when it came to chronic injuries that may need surgery. Hard not to panic after Toby's shoulder surgery, which should have been routine.

Kate let Maude sit with her thoughts for a bit.

Reminders of Toby's death weren't as raw as they used to be, but the grief still hit her niece hard at times. She usually needed space to process.

On the screen, Liam missed a shot and Kate groaned.

"He should have had that one," she said. "And to think, Maude, a few days ago you were playing tag with—"

A small snore came from the neighboring bed.

Kate glanced over and chuckled. Her niece was curled on her side, sound asleep crossways.

She'd leave Maude until she'd settled into a deeper sleep before tucking her under the covers.

Shifting back against the pillows on her headboard, she watched the last ten minutes of the game, which ended 2-1. Not high scoring, but good enough for a win, and to go up 1-0 in the series.

She was desperate for Liam's take on it, but who knew when he would be free tonight? She sent him a text.

Kate: 1 down, 3 to go. You looked good out there

An hour later, she was in the middle of her millionth rewatch of *Notting Hill* on her laptop with her earbuds in, when her phone buzzed.

A call, not a text.

"Hi," she answered in a low voice. "There's the conquering hero."

He made a dismissive noise. "Game one. And it's not three to go, it's fifteen to make it *really* matter. Not worth celebrating, yet. *You*, on the other hand… How did the otterlets do?"

She giggled. Good grief. A little shift of focus and a cute animal reference, and she was melted butter. "I don't think that's a word."

"Off track, Kate."

"Right." She cleared her throat, trying to ignore how swoopy her belly got from him asking about her small tournament before recounting his own triumphant night. "Lost one, won one. Shayla scored. So did Maude."

"Excellent. Put her on?"

Something jolted in her chest. He cared enough to talk to her niece?

"Uh, sorry, she's currently passed out on top of the covers."

"Aw. A good day was had, then."

"Bowling was organized chaos. They were more competitive at the lanes than they'd been on the ice."

"You're good to plan those kinds of bonding experiences for them. I still remember how getting to go mini golfing or swimming in hotel pools with my friends made our weekend. With my dad, too." His voice cracked. "Not like now. When I talked to my mom yesterday, she said watching my games the past few weeks has been upsetting him. She didn't think she'd try to get him to join her tonight."

"Liam… Oh, no. How, uh, are you doing with that?"

"It is what it is, Kate. We knew he'd get here."

As *if* he wasn't bothered by it. His words sounded like he was running them over a grater. However, she wasn't going to force him to face his feelings. Especially not during the first round of the playoffs.

"I'm here if you ever want to talk about it," she said.

"Mmm. Speaking of dads, I didn't want yours to get the chance to tell you this before I could—my agent is expecting an official contract extension offer from the Daggers this week. But between you and me, I know it won't be good enough."

"You're still expecting to move on?"

"Yeah. I'm scoring consistently again, and the rumors out of Toronto and Boston aren't going away."

Something caught in her throat. Sharp enough to feel like disappointment, or the realization she'd been lied to.

But why? He'd never even hinted at planning to stay in Denver.

"Hey, I'm glad we're both getting what we wanted. My enrolment's continuing to climb, and you're on the cusp of getting a better offer than what you're expecting from the Daggers."

Saying it didn't make her *feel* better, though. Maybe after a good night's sleep, her emotions would get in line.

Chapter Seventeen

CALDWELL SAYS NO TO DAGGERS EXTENSION
After a bust of a mid-season with the Denver club, will the open market offer better?
Denver Star, April 23

Liam had just finished a workout in the Denver arena's gym when a familiar face entered—Paul Rebagliati, the Daggers' general manager.

Liam's pulse rose a few beats.

With the offer refusal still fresh, running into him felt a little awkward.

Liam toweled off his neck and said hello.

"Two games to one," Paul said. "Where we want to be. Though no one likes losing at home. We'll have them tomorrow, I think. And you looked good."

Liam nodded. The Daggers had won game two on the road but lost yesterday's game at home. Losing on a night Kate had taken off work to cheer him on felt like he'd let her down.

"We're playing well together," he told Paul. "Almost had them yesterday."

"I sure like seeing you light it up with Sullivan." The GM strolled over to one of the treadmills and started sanitizing the handles and screen. "Wish we could meet your price point for next year. You really think you can get better on the open market?"

After botching four months of your season.

Paul didn't say it, but Liam heard it in his tone.

His stomach twisted. "Yeah, I will. You know it, too."

"Sorry. That wasn't fair. I do know it. We brought you in to fill a scoring hole, knowing we couldn't afford to keep you. Someone will have a contract for you at what you're asking.

Probably for a longer stretch than what you usually get. But damn if I didn't wish we had less salary to contend with, to make room for you."

"My agent told me that."

"He knows his shit. But so do you. Listen to your instincts."

His instincts had always told him to aim for top dollar and keep moving.

"Sure hope he hasn't been talking to anyone," Paul continued as he started to walk briskly on the treadmill.

"Of course not. I'm looking for a contract, not a suspension due to tampering."

"We'll hate to lose you. If any of the other considerations we can play with catch your eye, know my door is always open."

Liam nodded but kept his expression firm. "I need to maximize this contract, Paul." At thirty-one, it might be the last time he signed for an increased sum. His last chance to set himself up for retirement, and to finance care for the rest of his dad's life.

"Common to think that way, until other things become a factor. Health. Family."

Health and family were the factors. But not in the way Paul was implying. He scoffed. "I'm a free agent in more ways than one."

Paul did a double take and nearly stumbled on the treadmill belt. "You are?"

Oh, shit. "Uh, not exactly what I meant."

"Yeah, what does Kate think about all this?"

"Kate and I understand each other's priorities. We support each other."

Paul nodded but didn't look convinced.

They said an awkward goodbye. Liam headed for the shower with Kate on his mind. With *family* on his mind.

In no world was she going to be his family.

He had to stay focused on his parents.

Once he was cleaned up and heading out of the building, he put his earbuds in for the walk to his condo and called them.

His mom answered. "Li. Hey." Her voice was strained.

"Pain high today, Mom?"

"So-so." A habit for them both, minimizing the realities they both knew existed—her disability and daily burdens alongside his father's wobbly reality.

He wouldn't ask if she could fly to Minnesota or Denver to watch a playoff game. Even if his dad could stay alone with nursing care, his mom's mobility and PTSD made the lights and noise and movement of flying too much for her.

"You looked good last night, Liam. You'll get them on the next one."

"Same thing I told my GM," he said. "Though you don't have to stay up to watch if you're tired."

"I've watched every minute of your games this season. We are so proud."

"Even the goalless ones from November to March?" That stretch of the year still stung.

"Especially those ones. You kept going."

One way to look at it. "Thanks for the optimism, Mom."

Her tone lightened. "So. Tell me about this woman who the TV flashed to when the cameras were filming players' families. Is she special?"

"She sure is."

He filled his mom in on the basics about Kate and how they were dating for a while but likely wouldn't last beyond the summer.

"Well, then. Will I get to meet her?"

"I don't see how," he said. "It won't last."

"So why are you with her?"

"Because she's amazing," he said honestly.

"So, don't write off the possibilities so soon."

"Mom. I'm not going to be able to stay in Colorado. I *just* talked to the GM a half hour ago. They can't give me what I want."

"Hmm."

"*That's* a loaded sound."

"Falling in love is a big thing."

"Mom," he warned.

"But you're not saying no."

"Even if I wanted to, I can't."

"*Can't* isn't *no.*"

It wasn't.

But Kate deserved the stability and connections and home she was so busy creating—nothing Liam could give her. How could he make a home with someone new when he was failing to hold the one he had together?

His mom sighed. "Your stubbornness aside, I'm glad you called. I was going to wait until after the playoffs to talk to you about your dad, but I think a delay could cause him more problems."

Concern crept up his neck. "What's going on? Is there an issue with the extra nursing care? We can hire more, or—"

"Shh, Li. Stop trying to guess."

He forced his breathing to regulate. "Sorry."

"Don't be. I love how much you care." She exhaled. "We had an incident earlier this week. His nurse was on her lunch break, and he and I were sitting in the living room. I… I'd been up a lot in the night, and I nodded off for ten minutes. And when I woke up, he was gone."

"Oh, damn—where did he go? Not toward the water?" The yard was fenced with a combination lock, but still.

"Down the road. Onto one of the trails. The neighbors helped, and we found him after about an hour. He was so confused."

Liam could hear the tears in her voice.

"Even with care, Liam, I don't know if this is the best place for him…"

"Mom. Hey. It's okay. These things happen, even at nursing homes." And his dad was too *young* to go to an extended care facility. "He asked me to keep him in the house, with the view and his garden and *you.* I want to honor my promise. We can get a second nurse, to cover breaks and things. You won't have to worry."

"Your promise to him isn't the only factor. The money—"

"Is *not* an issue. You'll have extra help by tomorrow. I will make it happen."

"No, I can talk to the temporary care people, while we wait for someone permanent. It's too much to put on you, sweetheart."

"It's not."

"Focus on hockey, Liam. And on this 'amazing' woman. I wish I *could* meet her."

Liam did, too.

He jammed that yearning into a locked compartment. Hockey, his home, his future—it all required keeping his emotions in tighter check.

DENVER DAGGERS DOMINATE GAME SEVEN
6-1 victory over an outgunned Minnesota squad promises a dramatic second round against a hungry Winnipeg team.
Denver Star, May 2

The plane back to Denver could not fly fast enough for Liam's liking. He'd be riding the high of the Daggers' game seven victory for days. He was damn near punch-drunk, though their 2:00 a.m. arrival time was partly to blame. They'd at least gain an hour with the time change flying west.

The texts he and Kate had sent a couple of hours ago, as he'd been getting on the plane in Minneapolis and she'd been finishing up at the bar, were imprinted on his mind.

Superstar: You did it. Let's paint the town red. Or Dagger blue.

Liam: I'll come find you tomorrow.

Superstar: No. Tonight. Come over.

He'd had to do a double take.

Liam: Is this what I think it is?

Superstar: If you're thinking it's an invitation, then yes.

A booty call, by definition, but whatever.

Liam: It'll be beyond late.

Superstar: I'll wake up for you.

Superstar: Unless you don't want to.

Liam: Oh, no. I want to.

He wanted to so much. He'd wanted to for weeks. Since day one. Making his hands—and his feelings—behave around Kate Sullivan was proving to be a far more challenging task than getting his scoring groove back. But his assurance to her about his playoff routine not being much different from his usual one hadn't been exactly accurate. His increased focus, plus a second out-of-town weekend tournament for the River Otters *and* her new class in the afternoon, had made seeing each other difficult.

For the rest of the flight, his ability to focus on a movie or a book, cards, even conversation with Lars vanished.

How could he devote a single brain cell to anything except Kate's promise to wake up for him?

And now it was three. Bedtime, by any definition of the word.

He was *headed* to a bed.

Just not his.

The drive to Hollow Valley was never-ending. Had she stayed awake, or would she be all warm and drowsy? Damn, would he have another awkward encounter with Coach Sullivan? Nah, the man wouldn't be out gardening at this time of night.

He parked in what was becoming his usual spot, next to a row of lilac bushes. All three garages were closed and only the porch light was on. Either Coach was already in bed, or he hadn't gotten home yet.

Liam grabbed his backpack and sneaked toward the gate. A hose was running somewhere, but it had to be a timed system. Solar lights illuminated the concrete, but not bright enough to light his face. If his coach saw him moving toward Kate's door and hadn't noticed his car in the driveway, he might think Liam was a burglar—or worse—and call the police.

Now *that* would be a headline.

"Make sure to get some sleep tonight, Caldwell."

Liam let out a yelp. Heart skipping triple time, he stumbled. His foot landed off the path, in some sort of plant.

"Graceful," Coach Sullivan said. "You owe me a creeping phlox."

He swore and righted himself. "Sorry, Coach. But, uh, what are you doing in your garden in the dark? At, uh…" he checked his watch "…three fifteen?"

"Watering my rhubarb. I promised Kate a crumble for Sunday dinner. And we won a hell of a game—a series. I'm still not tired."

Liam breathed to calm himself. "Yeah, me neither—"

"Jesus Christ, son. I do not want to hear it. Just try to get into Kate's place without killing any more of my flowers. And without falling in the pool." He paused. "Actually, go ahead and take a dive. I love a good laugh."

"Sure. Night, Coach."

"Night, Caldwell. Keep playing like you did this series, and we might make it to the third round."

After being very careful not to veer into the pool and make his coach's month, he made it to Kate's doorstep and knocked.

A light came on, ambient through the frosted glass pane.

The door opened. She yanked him through the door and closed and locked it behind him.

"Look at you." Her eyes glowed and she pushed him back against the door with a hand. "It's unfair."

He dropped his backpack, toed out of his shoes and took her by the hips. "What do you mean?"

She scanned him, gaze drifting downward, from the sweater he'd pulled over his collared shirt, to his gray dress pants. "You'd look good in a paper bag, Liam. But this whole nerdy professor look is just cruel."

Pulling her between his braced legs, he buried his face where her neck met her shoulder. "Sounds like it'll work in my favor."

"So will—"

He flicked his tongue down to her collarbone.

She shifted her weight into him and whimpered. "That." Her breath was soft, with an almost needy hitch. "So will that."

"Mmm, only the beginning, Katie."

Chapter Eighteen

One more glimpse of Liam's tattooed forearms, exposed by his rolled-up sweater and shirtsleeves, and Kate would be headed toward total ruination. She was *weak*, and she couldn't even chalk it up to the hands on the clock over her dining table pointing to after three in the morning.

She settled in the V of his legs. He was hard. And she wanted him too badly to keep up her defenses. "I thought I'd have to argue harder to get you to come here."

He lifted his head from where he was lavishing her collarbone with attention. "Are you serious?"

She shrugged. "You like your rest."

"Kate. The minute I knew seeing you was an option, rest was the last thing on my mind. I needed to celebrate. And you… Everyone else was going home to their partners and families, and I… You're all I h—"

Vulnerability flashed in his gaze. He snapped his mouth shut.

Hers fell open. *You're all I have?* No. He couldn't have meant that.

"I'm all you want?" she supplied.

"Yeah," he agreed quickly. "All I want."

She pressed against him harder. Damn, she could barely think when that glorious ridge rocked against her core. "I'm flattered you wanted to revel in your win with me."

"Felt like a night where anything could happen."

Her sleep camisole ended an inch before her low-riding shorts began, and he teased the warm skin in the exposed space. She shivered. Her hips tilted forward, dragging up his length.

His Adam's apple bobbed. "You trying to figure out how much I'm into this, Kate? How much I want you?"

"Oh, no. I can tell."

"These damn pajamas," he muttered, sweeping her into his arms.

She flung her arms around his neck. "Liam!"

"Problem?" He headed for her bedroom door.

"You surprised me."

"Tell me you don't have plans tomorrow. I've been given the day off. The team has orders to rest. Hard series, as you saw." He nudged the door open with his toe and walked her to the bed, still freshly made from when she left this morning. She'd been waiting out on the chaise for him. A lamp on the right bedside table cast a warm glow over the navy walls. She was going to soak in every second of the low light and Liam's body on her cream sheets.

"Hold on tight," he instructed.

"You can put me—"

He used the arm he'd had under her back to fling the covers wide. He placed her on the bed and tumbled in after her.

"—down."

Strong arms bracketed her body as he loomed over her, a hot look in his eyes. "That work for you?"

Of course not. She was barely wearing anything, and he was fully clothed.

"No street clothes in my clean sheets, sir," she said lightly, stripping him out of his layers and tossing them in a rumpled pile in front of her dresser.

Down to his boxers, he sprawled on the mattress, pulling her against his chest. Their legs tangled. "No need for weak-sauce excuses. If you want me naked, say so."

"I want you naked." She rose to her knees, straddling him. Oh, God, having him between her thighs in a bed was enough to make her stupid. She knew she was. *This* was. The more she let herself get close like this, the more she'd get attached. But she couldn't not. She craved him.

He arched a brow.

Palming her hips, he ran his hands up her sides, stealing the soft fabric of her shirt on the way. A few inches of her stomach peeked between his thumbs.

He sent her a satisfied look.

She skimmed her palm between his pecs, and—damn. The skin over one side of his ribs bore the marks of a rough check to the boards he'd taken in the first period.

"Oh, ouch. You're bruised."

"This is nothing compared to what I'll look like after three more rounds," he said ruefully.

"Mmm, yes, I hope you get terribly beaten up, and then bathe your wounds with champagne from the Stanley Cup."

He laughed. "Bloodthirsty, aren't you?"

She traced a careful finger over the painful-looking splotch. "Are you sure this isn't broken?"

"Very. One—I can breathe without feeling like I'm being stabbed. Two—I carried you in here no problem."

She worried her lip with her teeth and drew her thumb outside the edge of the contusion. "I should get you some ice."

"I don't need ice, Kate. It'll be fine in the morning."

"It'll be a mess."

"I can say this with all certainty—if I get to wake up next to you, the last thing on my mind will be a few aches and pains."

Her cheeks warmed.

"In fact," he continued, his voice gravelly, "I'm hurt *you're* noticing it, given where you're sitting."

He lifted his hips an inch, just enough to thrust his erection against her core.

She gasped.

He slid his own hands higher, taking her camisole up to the underside of her breasts.

"I've been thinking about tasting your nipples again for my entire road trip."

Mmph, she wanted that, too. But only if it wasn't going to hurt him.

"Your health matters more than sex, Liam," she said. But she couldn't resist sliding forward again. The hard pressure shimmied up her spine.

"You say that, but then you move like you're planning to use me until sunrise." His gaze danced. "Mixed messages."

He rocked his pelvis, taking her for a ride up and down his covered length. Her thin shorts were getting more damp by the second. He tugged the center of the delicate, lace-trimmed fabric to the side. His hand brushed her wetness.

"Oh, my God, Liam."

"Better bare?"

She could only nod, a rapid, erratic confirmation.

"You're soaked for me." His fingers stroked again, circling her entrance.

"Uh-huh."

"I love it, Kate."

Flipping her onto her back, he ran a reverent hand through her hair, as it spilled across the pillowslip.

"Goddamn, you're beautiful," he growled, sliding off her top.

Gathering her wrists and pinning them to her pillow on either side of her head, he kissed her deep. He thrust against the apex of her thighs. Slow. Measured.

Capturing her lips with his, he collected her gasps.

She dug her fingers into his tousled waves and tightened her thighs around his hips.

"Unless you want to still be awake at sunrise," she said, her words almost a moan, "you'll need to get rid of your underwear. And my shorts."

"Getting there," he promised. "This isn't working for you?"

Absolutely yes, and absolutely no. "Don't you *want* more?"

He chuckled, low and disbelieving. "I'm so damn hard right now, Katie, I can barely breathe. But I intend to savor you."

Her legs clenched more. "I'm not fragile."

"Yeah, and maybe I like a lighter touch. I get enough rough play on the ice."

Releasing her wrists, he kissed his way down the curve of her neck, between the slopes of her breasts, a tantalizing trail along her skin and toward her navel.

Need raged through her, intense, unquenchable. The best she could do was grasp for whatever remnant of control remained.

Taking her pajama bottoms between his teeth, Liam dragged the thin fabric down. He followed with his thumb, parting her and skimming around her center.

"Yes, *there*—"

He withdrew as quickly as he'd started.

She choked on the emptiness. "*Liam.* Come back."

He slipped her shorts off her ankles, kissing the soft depressions behind the joints.

"Come back where?"

"Argh." She reached for him. "You are the worst. You know what I meant."

"Yeah, I do," he said, sounding as serious as she'd been teasing. He stumbled out of his underwear, put on one of the condoms from his pants pocket and settled between her thighs again.

His thick tip teased her labia.

She pulsed around him. He slid in, slow and decadent.

Clutching his shoulders, she strained toward him.

"That better, Katie? Am I still the worst?"

She whimpered. "Did I say worst?"

Another slow thrust. Bottoming out, he groaned. It felt like every muscle in his body tightened against her.

"You sure did." He licked a line up her neck. Every breath, every sound, soaked into her skin. "Ready to take it back?"

"Yes. *Yes.*"

The pace he set, luxuriant minutes where the weight of his

gaze and every caress of his hands and tender sweep of his mouth declared for this one, long moment she was the very center of his world.

She was an ember floating on the breeze, ready to set anything she touched aflame.

His laugh teased her neck. "The one problem with trying to devastate *you* is I'm about three seconds away from losing it."

"So come."

"Before you? No."

"I'm close, too," she said. The pressure low in her belly climbed toward unbearable.

He gritted his teeth. "Nothing feels better than having you like this."

"Touch me," she begged.

"Anything," he said, sliding a hand between their bodies. He delved a finger over her mound, finding her sensitive nub.

"*There.* Circles, *please*—"

Kate clung to him, a moment, soul-wrenching—

She let herself go, a dam of emotion breaking loose.

Heaving a breath, head swimming, she whispered, "*Liam.*"

His body surged, and he groaned, landing on his forearms. His cool, sweat-dotted forehead rested against her shoulder.

"Katie?" he returned on a breath.

Her heartbeat pounded in her ears. Could he feel it racing? He had to. His chest pressed to hers, and there was no way the thrum wasn't passing from her skin to his. Betraying everything she was feeling.

Hell. He would have heard it in her voice, anyway. All her desire, wrapped up in the two precious syllables of his name.

She wasn't supposed to have feelings.

Maintaining distance, impermanence.

Safety.

This didn't feel unsafe, though.

This felt like exactly where she was supposed to be.

* * *

Kate woke up with Liam snuggled up behind her. Her cynical side had wondered if he'd sneak out at night, but she knew better. Had he planned to leave, he would have told her.

She couldn't see the clock, or the flashy silver watch he'd left on the nightstand, the one capable of keeping more precise time than the Greenwich Royal Observatory, but the sun had risen high enough it was no longer glaring through her window. It had to be after ten.

After ten, and she had two-hundred-ish pounds of nearly naked hockey player tangled in her sheets.

Well, tangled with her, really—one of his arms stretched under her pillow, the other was a band over her ribs, hand splayed over her thin tank top, between her breasts and her navel. So many inches of beautiful skin, and all that intricate ink twining from his wrists up to his shoulders. Without moving, she could only see his left forearm, where a tiger lily and a sunflower softened the few spears of wheat reaching toward a splashy purple lupine. She'd lived in Canada long enough to recognize the nod to the two provinces where he'd grown up. In black, his parents' signatures were scrawled near the inside of his wrist.

For someone who moved on all the time, he'd sure picked a permanent reminder of the people and places he'd come from.

She settled into his warmth, stopping her curiosity from spiraling further. Maybe the orgasms, or his optimism after the big win, were fooling her brain into this lazy, sleep-in perfection.

"No offense to the blue beast, but waking up in your bed beats the spite couch any day," he mused, voice raspy.

"Oh, shoot, did I wake you up?"

"Not really. I came to enough to recognize being in your bed, and being awake and snuggling with you is better than drifting back to sleep," he murmured behind her ear.

Her heart skipped and she turned to face him.

Jesus, his face was too much to handle before her morning

coffee. All this man had to do was blink and she melted for him. She brushed his hair off his forehead. "It has to be after ten."

"Goal achieved, then," he said, mouth a drowsy tilt. "I wanted to keep you in bed for as long as you'd let me. What did you dream about?"

You. "I slept so soundly, I don't remember."

"Terrific. I did my job."

She rolled her eyes for show. "Do you remember your dreams?"

"Sure. Hockey, a bit. And sailing. But on ice? And your dad was there? Didn't make sense."

He rolled onto his back and tucked her into his side.

The indulgence of it all…

She cuddled up to him, giving in. Not every morning had to be productive. He probably needed this after his game last night and the late flight.

"Do you like sailing?" she asked.

"One of my best friends in Desolation Cove had a small sloop. We'd take it out for overnight trips. There were hundreds of little nooks to anchor in, not another human in sight. Over the course of a night, the boat would swing around with the water, free and easy. Still secure as hell, though. Safe from rougher waters."

Her mind spun. Was he trying to allude to something? His feelings? Or how he was hoping *she* would feel? Argh, it was too early to parse analogies.

Especially when all she wanted was to settle into this cocoon and ignore how letting him be her anchor would only end in her drifting far, far from where she wanted to be.

"Did you like living in BC?"

"No."

The air in the room shifted palpably.

She was about to change the subject, but he continued.

"Mom was healing. Dad was struggling to hold things together. And it felt like so much of the financial strain was my fault, even though they insisted on making hockey happen for me. I couldn't get out of the Cove fast enough. And when I did, I felt I was deserting them. The only way I could find any balance between doing what I loved and making sure they were okay was to excel in my entry-level contract."

"That's hard, Liam."

"Life's hard sometimes. Even with more money than most people have access to. No matter how hard I tried, I haven't been able to spend away my mom's pain or buy my dad more years without declining brain function. I can only do what I can to keep them as comfortable as possible. Though I'm not sure the house will ever feel like—"

He swallowed with an audible click.

"Home?" she whispered.

"Sorry, I didn't mean to get so serious this early in the day," he lamented, closing his eyes and sucking in a breath. When he blinked them open, they were a clear, too-bright green.

She wasn't about to ignore his cue to lighten the mood. "It's not early, silly."

"Time doesn't exist today, superstar."

For once, she'd go along with the notion. One day of taking a break with him wouldn't keep her from meeting her enrolment target.

"We need to talk about game three," he said, the corners of his mouth twitching. "I want to spoil you."

She snuggled in. "Lay it on me. What kind of spoiling are we talking about?"

He seemed to be making a habit of it, whenever he wasn't on the road.

"Well…it's not just for you." His butterfly-light touch danced down the bridge of her nose. "God, I love your freckles."

Stalling. Impatience bubbled behind her ribs. She arched a brow.

"Sophie helped," he explained.

"With *what*?"

"Tickets."

She eyed him. "Did you not expect me to be in *your* seats for the Daggers home games? In your jersey, this time."

"The only thing better would be you walking around in it all the time," he rasped.

Oh, my. That was a downright *claim.*

Her pulse skipped. His decadent, possessive smile—she couldn't get enough of it.

Not good, not good, not good.

"All the time…to make the ruse more convincing?" Her racing heartbeat weakened her voice.

He paused and stared. Serious eyes raked over her face.

Cradling her cheek with the care he'd show to an irreplaceable treasure, he said, "Yeah, Kate. The ruse."

He couldn't be gentler.

But also…resigned?

And she hated that. She wanted his cocky expression back.

"What's wrong?" she asked.

He stroked her hair. "This is our last lazy morning for a couple of weeks. Let's make some coffee and enjoy it in bed."

He went to move, but she stopped him with a hand to his chest. "Tell me what you're thinking."

"I don't think you really want to hear it."

"How do you know?"

"You look afraid."

She had to keep herself from rearing back at the word.

Caution was one thing. Sticking to past lessons learned, even. But fear? No, thank you.

Her throat tightened as she blurted, "Why does this have to be our last lazy morning?"

He paused. "I'll be in and out of town. Gone tomorrow. Back Wednesday."

"You could stay here," she offered. "On the days you're playing at home."

His jaw went slack.

"If you want. I don't want to distract you," Kate said.

A part truth. She *didn't* want to get in the way of his on-ice success. But her desire to distract him in other ways was ballooning out of control. The way his gaze heated when she teased him with glimpses of skin and fleeting kisses fueled a previously unknown fantasy.

And the more time she had to revel in their physical pleasure, the less she'd have to worry about wanting an emotional connection, too.

Chapter Nineteen

DENVER UP 2-0 AGAINST FLOUNDERING WINNIPEG SQUAD
Can the Daggers strike another blow to take a stranglehold over the series?
The Denver Star, May 8

Deep bass thrummed through the arena and under the soles of Kate's sneakers. Eleven of Kate's players, plus parents and a few of the kids' siblings, were packed into the box. Any River Otter not wearing Daggers merch was proudly in their own jersey of the same blue. And Kate… Well, she had a blocky, white 44 plastered to her back. Earlier, Connor had given her a hard time about not having "Sullivan" between her shoulders as he'd limped through security with her.

She'd held back from reminding him not to ruin his body over a playoff series. No point in wasting her breath. Being a Sullivan meant it wasn't just a game. They lived it, breathed it. Always left every ounce of effort on the ice.

He hadn't looked too banged up in the first period, though.

And Liam had been on freaking *fire.*

With the second period a few minutes away, most of the kids were full of the catered hot dogs and fries they'd eaten during the intermission. More than one face sported a smear of ketchup. Unlike their parents, who were enjoying the lounge section and high tables of the suite itself, the kids were all sitting—or standing in front of their seats—in the three rows of seating that fronted the box. Kate occupied the highest row at the edge, next to a suite of professional-looking, mostly middle-aged adults. The group kept looking over fondly at Kate's team every time the kids got excited.

"Aunt Kate!" Maude tugged at her sleeve. "Look!"

Her niece pointed at the Jumbotron. The screen read:

Welcome to the Hollow Valley River Otters 10U

"Oh, that's fun," Kate said, as her players went nuts, whooping and shaking the fronts of their jerseys to draw attention to the logo. A camera was broadcasting crowd reactions on the Jumbotron, and panned to their box, recording the happy chaos. "We'll have to thank Natalie."

Maude flashed her a mischievous grin. "Or Liam."

The screen shifted.

Love to Coach Kate from #44

Oh, he didn't.

The kids' whoops turned to whistles and ooohs.

As if Natalie—or Liam himself—had given the camera operator notes on where Kate was seated, the meters-tall image focused on her rapidly heating face. Her pink cheeks were on view for twenty-thousand fans. *Cool, cool, cool.*

"Wave, Aunt Kate," Maude admonished, waving both her arms like she was trying to flag down a rescue plane.

"Oh, good grief. *Maude*," she said. The show had to go on, though. She blew a kiss in the general direction of where the camera had to be located.

The entire damn arena cheered.

Once the noise died down, Kate settled in her seat. She'd never hear the end of this.

Though the part of her not turning beet red was thoroughly charmed. *Argh.*

The Daggers skated onto the ice and the noise picked up in the arena again.

Kate clapped along, relieved the attention was back on the people who deserved it.

A body slid into the seat next to her.

Kate glanced to the side and returned Florence Johnson's welcoming smile. The journalist wore a blue Daggers' cap and a denim jacket over a team T-shirt. "Hey! You made it."

"Told you I would. Thanks for the invite. After this, plus a visit to one of your practices, I'll be able to finish my article." Florence cocked an eyebrow. "So… You're the 'Coach Kate' who earned the big cheer from the crowd, I take it?"

"Guilty."

"Or lucky." The woman's brown eyes sparkled.

"That, too."

As they watched the play, Florence asked Kate a few questions about her teaching plans for the summer. Her brief explanation turned into a longer conversation on coaching philosophy and sowing the seeds of leadership in young players.

"How much of it is connected to Maude?" Florence asked, nodding her head toward Maude, who was right up against the front divider with Shayla.

"A fair amount. Carrying the Sullivan name, especially with her father—my brother—gone, is heavy on a pair of young shoulders. Things have changed, so she'll be taken more seriously than I was when I was trying to make hockey my career, but I still want to make sure she never misses a chance she deserves. But it's about girls like her friend there, just as much. Shayla saw Maude playing hockey and wanted to join in, but she lacked the confidence to join a team of mostly boys. Between my beginner skating class and a 3-on-3 team with as many girls as boys, she's been taking huge strides. Too many girls don't get the chance to play young, and then never feel confident enough to try."

"You want them to reach their potential."

"Of course. And along the way, I want to make sure they don't drown in the flood of boys trying to make it to the NHL."

"A flood of white kids, too," Florence said quietly.

"Yes. That's true," she said. "I'll be honest, one thing I wanted to avoid for the school was to have Connor fund a big chunk of it, like he wanted to do. The academy's success needs to come from me and from the product I'm offering. But I did accept his annual commitment to fund scholarship spaces, and we've committed at least half of them to go to kids from racialized communities each semester."

Florence nodded. "I bet if you mentioned it to my brother, he'd contribute."

"That would be generous."

They watched for a few more minutes, enjoying the kids' theatrical reactions to missed shots and odd-man rushes.

When the whistle blew, Florence said, "I wanted to wait to tell you until after we'd had the chance to talk, but I have good news for you. Sounds like the *Star* is interested in the article."

Kate's jaw dropped. "That's…all of Denver. And beyond."

The reach it would bring for the school… *Holy crap.* She had five-year and ten-year goals for the school—expanding the age range and the skills the academy offered, hiring more teachers, becoming a fixture in the Hollow Valley hockey community—but she was trying not to look too far beyond her fall ice time yet. Opportunities like this made it hard not to get excited. She couldn't wait to tell Liam.

Hopefully, the Daggers would hold on to their lead, and he'd want to celebrate her news as much as a notch in the playoff win column.

The Daggers lost in overtime. Kate ushered a gaggle of disappointed River Otters out into the hall, waving goodbye to them and their families. Liam had asked Kate to stay at his place after the game, so Maude was getting a ride home with Pavneet and Shayla.

She was sad for the Daggers, of course. But with Florence's lead on the *Denver Star* article, she couldn't hold back her grin. Then again, with the loss, Liam might not be up for sharing in her happiness. She'd give him space, if he needed it.

She made her way to the elevator. Halfway down the long hallway, she ran into Natalie and Scone coming from the other direction.

"Smiling about the Jumbotron message, still?" her friend asked, giving Scone a silent command to sit.

"Not exactly—guess what?" She explained Florence's good news.

Natalie squeed.

Kate squeed.

They squeed together, then peered around to make sure no one had caught their middle-school-esque reaction.

"Shut the front door! Kate, you are doing the thing!"

"I am." She grinned again. "God, it feels good. Though I'm going to have to thank Liam. He's gotten us extra attention. Enrolments have been climbing."

"Oh, you got attention, all right," Natalie said with a smirk. "The television broadcast thanks you for his sappy declaration of love."

She blinked at her friend. "It wasn't just in the arena?"

"Nope. And social media's eating it up." Natalie rubbed her hands together. "Making my job so *easy* today. Even with the loss."

Nerves bolted up her spine. "And there's no Bad Luck Kate chatter?"

"Most of the guys manage to have partners and balance their careers. No one's blaming you for anything, Kate. Not this time."

Another miracle.

"Some things in life are hard, but maybe this isn't one of them," Natalie said. "Where are you meeting Liam?"

"How do you know I'm meeting him?"

"Couldn't think of another reason why Maude would be leaving with Shayla."

Kate made a face.

Natalie rolled her eyes. "Please. If I had a man like him waiting for me tonight, I'd be running to meet up with him." Scone narrowed his doggy eyes. "Fine, walking calmly so as not to elevate my heart rate. But still."

Kate would have claimed the dog hadn't understood Natalie, but he seemed to have a bigger vocabulary than average. He'd probably picked up on "running."

"We're meeting downstairs. And then going to his condo."

"Oh *really.*"

"How is this a surprise?"

"It's not. But have you been there yet?"

"No."

"So it's a big deal." Natalie nudged Kate with her elbow and then led the way to the elevator, and into the bowels of the arena. They were about twenty feet from the hallway to the dry locker room when they spotted two familiar faces.

Connor and Liam strode toward Natalie and her. Both had damp hair. Liam's was starting to dry, tightening from finger-combed waves into mussed curls. He must have forgotten his usual styling product.

Maybe she'd get the chance to run her hands through the clean strands.

Liam's blank expression brightened when he saw her.

"Guess what!" Natalie called. "One of us might have her hockey academy featured in the *Denver Star.*"

"What? Love, that's great." Liam swept Kate up in a hug and spun her around. "*Huge.* Makes up for the loss tonight."

"You can't be serious."

"Sure, I am." He set her down and cupped her cheeks. His gaze was earnest. "For one—we're still up two-one in the series, and we nearly had them. Bad bounce got us. It happens. And more importantly, you deserve as much fanfare as I do."

A yawn punctuated his insistence.

"We can postpone," she said. "You're tired."

"No chance. I can't wait to get you to my place."

Unmistakable suggestion colored his tone.

Her brother coughed, interrupting. He was rubbing his right

hip with his left hand. A disgruntled crease marked the space between his eyebrows. "Who's writing the article, Kate?"

She explained her meeting with Florence, then said, "Maybe it'll catch the eye of a couple more Hollow Valley businesses." She'd canvassed the town for sponsorships, of course, and had a small number, but news coverage like this might convince some holdouts. "I want them to see how integral a part of the town's hockey community I plan to be. Of the town *itself*."

Liam squeezed her shoulders. A strained gleam edged his smile. Hopefully he wasn't faking how much he wanted her to come over.

Connor frowned.

"What?" she said.

He let go of his hip and jammed his hand into his hair. "I've been trying to increase my donation for over a year."

"I know," she said gently. "And I needed to try doing it myself, first. And I'm succeeding, Conn."

"I know you are," he said. "And I'm damn proud of you. I also want to make things easier for you."

"And offering to pay for it all implies you don't actually believe I can establish my place here on my own terms."

A mix of regret and pain twisted his mouth.

Aha, finally. She'd put forward the same argument a few times, but he'd never seemed to get it.

"Pssst, Sullivans—this isn't the place for this," Natalie reminded them. "I need to go check in with Jonesy before he takes off. Can I trust you two not to bring the ceiling down if I leave?"

"Of course." Kate sighed as her friend saluted them playfully and walked away. She hadn't intended to get into it with her brother at all, let alone somewhere anyone could walk by. "Conn, can we be happy about this, please? And sad about the loss if you need to. And for God's sake, go rest and get ice on your hip before you grimace your way into being a headline."

"I'm fine."

"*Rest, ice, compression, elevation!*" she chanted, mimicking using pom poms with every word. "Rice! Rice! Rice!"

He scowled harder, though he aimed it at Liam. "Does she ride you like this?"

"Oh, she rides me like—"

"Liam!" Kate shrieked. She reached up and slapped a hand over his mouth.

"Jesus Christ, man," Connor said.

Liam lifted a shoulder and said something that sounded like "you asked," but it was against Kate's palm. He licked it for good measure.

She yanked it back. "Ew!"

"Don't be late for practice tomorrow morning," her brother snapped.

"It's optional. I'm going to rest," Liam said. "Like you should."

Connor turned on a heel, then swore and clutched his hip.

Kate's breath caught.

Liam examined them both. "And by rest, I mean letting your sister—"

"*Liam!*"

"Share my coffeemaker. Geez, Kate, what did you think I was going to say?"

The wink he gave her assured her he was thinking the exact thing she'd meant to interrupt.

He put an arm around her and leaned to her ear. "I might be tired, but I'm still in the mood to celebrate. With you very much on top."

Chapter Twenty

Liam swung the front door to his condo open for Kate to enter, then followed behind. His stomach was heavy, like he was winding up to take a penalty shot. Had she felt this on edge when she'd invited him into her home?

"My humble abode," he said.

She glanced up at him with an encouraging smile. "Can't wait."

The light in the entryway was the sole source of illumination, casting her freckles with a cinnamon glow. The light dissipated into the open-concept space. He'd bought the place furnished. It was nice enough—a top-of-the-line kitchen with a marble counter shot through with green, the color reminding him of the reef out front of his parents' house at low tide. The living room, with clean lines and a focus on the floor-to-ceiling windows with a view of a park across the street and city buildings beyond.

Now it seemed…blank.

Kate might not have filled her place with all her own furniture yet, but she'd spread her charm around with knickknacks and small touches. Even though she hadn't been planning on occupying her dad's pool house indefinitely, she'd still made it home.

Nothing about Liam's place suggested anything close to homey.

He'd been through enough staged apartments to know what a pared-down living space looked like.

Spare. Colorless. Ready to have someone put their own spin on it, except he'd never bothered.

He shouldn't like her small, lively space more than his bigger, more functional one. He'd never needed his apartment to feel like home before, and he'd be a fool to consider it as a possibility.

So long as he never made a place home, it could never be taken away.

He flicked on the switch for the dangling pot lights over the island, his gut churning, knowing she'd find the apartment underwhelming. Why it mattered, he wasn't sure. They weren't planning on moving in together or anything.

Except something about him craved her approval. He wasn't going to get it with gray walls and charcoal couches, even if they were the softest velvet he'd ever felt.

Not when Kate loved spiteful teal chaises and mirrors with photos taped to the edges.

She loved the joy and life and memories made in a space, not the space itself. And Liam could no more give her that than he could decorate a living room to actually look *lived in*.

All he could give her was a few more minutes of pleasure. And damn, he planned to do that well.

She toed out of her sneakers and took his hand, her gaze darting around. She dropped her bag on the floor. The sides gaped open, revealing those tortuously tiny pajamas and a sweater. "Show me around."

"Not much to see." He rubbed the back of his neck and waved his hand, palm up, in a sweeping motion from the fridge, past the glass table he'd never eaten at, to the windows and the view. The squirrels in the tree on the other side of the glass were more moved in than he was. "There's this, the bedroom, a bit of storage in the laundry room…"

"I'm not here to judge your decor choices, Liam. Not when I'm living in the equivalent of my dad's basement." Her lips twisted and she squeezed his hand. "You didn't want to settle in at all? Even if it was for seven or eight months? I mean…you went to the trouble of buying a penthouse."

"And I enjoy the view whenever I'm here."

The only view he wanted right now was *her*.

Christ. He'd been fighting off an erection since the moment he first spotted her in the concourse, wearing his jersey. He never wanted her to take it off. She turned and let go of his hand, then walked between the couches and over to the window. With his number 44—and his last name—on her back, he was liable to lose control before they'd even begun.

It was a *mine* in clothing form.

Call him territorial, possessive, over-the-line—whatever. He loved the idea of everyone thinking of her as *his*.

Talk about stupid. She couldn't be his so long as he couldn't be *hers*.

She scanned the windows with serious eyes.

"Can anyone see us?"

"No. I had privacy film installed."

"Smart man."

"I've been known to have a good idea from time to time." He tucked in behind her. "Including inviting you over."

Circling a finger and thumb around each of her wrists, he lifted them until her hands were pressed to the glass.

She inhaled sharply.

It had taken him all of a day of kissing Kate to learn touching her neck made her shiver. He ducked his head, tilting to press a soft line from the back of her ear and along her silky skin.

She moaned.

Oh, hell, yes, even better than a shiver.

"My favorite view of the day was looking up at your suite and seeing you cheering with your team." He parted his lips, tonguing a trail and then scraping his teeth next to her royal blue collar.

She arched against him, baring more of her neck. Her fingers splayed wider on the window.

He swore. "Katie..."

Her tight, round ass swayed from one side to the other, turning him to steel.

He spread his own hands over hers, just his fingertips touching the window as they overlapped her own.

"You scored for me and everything," she purred.

"Glad you noticed," he said.

"I can't take my eyes off you while you're on the ice. Watching you skate—especially watching you bury the puck—turns me on."

"Oh, yeah?"

She nodded. Her ponytail brushed his cheek, tickling right above his playoffs beard. "You're gifted."

"In more ways than one," he said.

Her laugh tinkled through the room.

"Oh, I'm not joking, Sullivan," he said.

She had leggings on, thank God. Made it all the easier to slide a hand along her hip, over her mound to cup her sex, with only a couple of thin layers of fabric between his palm and heaven. She gasped and wobbled, and he held her to his chest with his other arm. But she kept her hands on the window, and holy hell, was it hot to have his fingers between her legs, making her leggings go from damp to downright wet. She squirmed, a needy noise at the back of her throat.

"Damn, Liam."

"Want me to not joke some more?"

Maybe he'd get down on his knees and taste her while she took in the Denver skyline.

"Yes." She dragged her teeth over her lower lip. "Your fingers. *Inside* my pants."

Ah, the express way.

He didn't plan to rush with her. But if she wanted to take the edge off, he'd never say no.

He circled his fingers over soaked fabric.

A sweet cry escaped her, and her hands drifted toward her breasts.

He tsked, and slipped his hands off her to take her wrists again. "Hands here, Katie. Don't move them."

"But—"

"You can touch your breasts all you want when I have you on my bed with my face between your thighs. Hell—I'll beg you to keep my jersey on while you play. But right now, your orgasm is mine and mine alone."

She shifted, as if her breasts were uncomfortable. "Li…"

"This is why I have two hands." Sliding a palm under her T-shirt, he cupped the soft mound through the smooth cup of her bra. Not lined. Her nipple pebbled against his thumb, and he teased a slow circle over her aroused flesh.

Uh-oh, he was going to do himself in right alongside her. Gritting his teeth and breathing in a thread of calm, he delved his other hand below the crossover waist of her leggings and under the thin layer of microfiber.

Soft. *Slick.*

He buried two fingers to the first knuckle. The heel of his palm pressed against the spot he knew made her melt. He'd only made her come apart a handful of times, but the feel of her shattering under his touch would be seared on his soul until his last breath.

All he needed to do was slide a little deeper, twist and press *just like that*, and—

"Liiii..."

Oh yeah. That's what he wanted to hear.

She was a beautiful mess in his arms, and the one thing holding him together from losing it was the ability to ignore his own blissful agony.

He was *not* going to lose it until she was writhing on his sheets and he was bottomed out inside her.

He wasn't done making her scream his name in the living room yet, though. The image of being on his knees for her was dancing around in his head. He had to make it a reality.

Cradling her to his chest, he eased her away from the window and onto the open end of the sectional.

Confusion clouded her dazed, sated expression. She fell back against the cushions, lips parted like they were promising a night of long, slow pleasure.

He knelt and tugged her hips toward the edge of the seat. Easing her leggings off, he mouthed a teasing trail up the inside of one of her thighs.

"Wh-what are you doing?"

"Celebrating, Katie. Celebrating." He lowered his head and kissed her all the way to oblivion.

Kate was wrecked, her brain stumbling over how exactly they got to his room. He might have carried her? Her clothes were somewhere on the floor in the living room. His were probably in the hallway. She was pretty sure she'd stripped him while he leaned against the wall.

She'd definitely gotten on her knees.

His thigh muscles had turned to granite as he'd fought to stay standing.

And him moving in her…impossible to forget. Every second was blue-sky clear but disjointed in the incoherent mess of her mind.

Uncountable minutes, jumbling the ascendant before and the sated after, anchored by his arms.

"You're staying, right?"

Liam's question came out in a more vulnerable tone than Kate expected. Uncertainty marked his brow.

"You need to ask?" She burrowed further under the covers of his palatial bed, more deeply into the circle of his arms. His embrace was secure enough that they could have dropped out of a plane and he'd keep her safe from impact.

She wore a threadbare, gray T-shirt he'd lent her, marked with a faded logo of the CHL team he'd played for. She wasn't going to tell him she'd brought her own pajamas in her oversize tote bag. Admitting how irresistible it was to sleep in his clothing was a bridge too far. "The toothbrush and spare sweater I packed in my tote bag don't speak for me?"

"You might have changed your mind."

"You ruined me twice in your living room in less than twenty minutes, followed by carrying me in here for a third orgasm. Why would I want to leave?"

"Because staying overnight isn't about coming, Katie. Not when you're wearing something of mine to sleep in. We both know full well you have shorts and a camisole in your Mary Poppins carpet bag."

She stared at him.

"It opened when you dropped it in the hall. Your jammies peeked out."

When she'd started this up with Liam, she hadn't expected him to be so emotionally…open. Calling a spade a spade wasn't part of their deal, no matter how much they'd agreed to enjoy each other until he moved on to Kate-free pastures.

"Your shirt looked soft. I'm a sucker for comfort."

He tucked her closer. "This is better than comfortable."

She swallowed and shifted to get even closer. *Do not get used to this.*

"What's your favorite breakfast?" he asked.

"Froot Loops," she said quickly.

"Kate," he chided. "I'm serious."

"I am, too," she defended. "The only time we got sugary cereal as kids was on holidays, and if we were lucky, my mom would buy us one of the multipacks of individual boxes of cereal. Which was ridiculous, because with the way my brothers and I ate during hockey season, we could go through a Costco-sized box in one sitting. But there was something decadent about the individual packs. I'd get up early to claim the two Froot Loops, leaving my brothers to fight it out over Frosted Flakes and Corn Pops. My mom would always take the Rice Krispies."

"And your dad?"

"On the road too often to be part of the routine."

"Hmm."

"No need to analyze it. Long in the past, now."

"If you say so." He brushed the hair off her forehead with gentle fingers. His gaze was equally tender. "I'll have to get you cereal for next time. Tomorrow, though, we could do omelets or eggs Benedict."

"Is there a good place nearby?"

"Yeah, my kitchen table. Just because I never eat there, doesn't mean I don't intend to make you breakfast."

The simple offer made her heart catch in her throat.

"What?" he asked carefully. "Don't trust my cooking?"

"No one's made me breakfast in a long time," she said. "Vince, uh, wasn't much of a chef. And after my mom died, we were on our own for breakfast a lot of the time."

Liam studied her, clear concern on his face.

"Look, I don't want to imply my dad was a crappy father. Was he the most attentive? Not when it came to non-hockey-related issues. He spent time with us on the ice. And yeah, that meant more time with my brothers than me, because of their loftier ambitions, but whatever. And in terms of cooking us breakfast, we were teenagers by then. Toby was already in Detroit. Connor was off billeting. It was just Jake and me. Jake tried, but I was the better cook, so it made more sense for me to make the food and him to clean up. Occasionally, if Dad was home on a Sunday, he'd make pancakes. Never tried to replicate my mom's crepes, though. They were like, wafer-thin. God, they were delicious."

"I read once how taste memory is almost as strong as scent memory, given how connected taste and scent are in the brain," he mused.

And because she was feeling softer than usual, and being in the shadowy light and the soothing sense of safety, her mouth kept running. "I miss my mom so much. And Toby. *Fuck.* I wish they both could see how amazing Maude is, on and off the ice."

And for her mom to see how, with a couple decades difference, Maude was going to be able to go places that hadn't existed for Kate. She had to believe her mom would have been proud of the academy, of everything Kate had done with her life.

"I miss my dad, too," he murmured into her hair.

The ache in his voice made her chest catch. "Liam… That's… It makes so much sense."

"It's not the same, though."

"It's still grief. Missing someone, or the way they were." And what they'd never be. "Losing the support system you depended on. And everything a person brings to a family, and to a home."

"Yeah." His agreement was barely a whisper.

Damn, she hadn't meant to push him to the edge. "And I've heard about the dominance of taste and scent memory, too. What's your favorite?"

His breath hitched. "The Hollow Valley arena smells exactly the same as the rink in Saskatchewan where I learned to skate."

"Ohhh, tiny Liam on skates."

"Not *too* tiny. I was seven. Not an infant like you."

She laughed. "Are there pictures?"

"A few places. My parents' mantel. A bin in their garage. Probably at the arena itself. I donated some money for a renovation a few years ago and they insisted on putting up a display case about me."

"Because you're a big deal, Liam Caldwell."

He let out a scoffing *psshh*. "The hockey league was like family when Dad and I were missing a big part of ours."

"When your mom was deployed?"

"Yeah." He kissed her forehead. "But when she came back injured, and then we moved… It was never the same. It's why I admire what you're doing with your school so much. You're creating that sense of family for kids. When I've helped, even for a few minutes, I've felt how special it is. Been a while since I've been an integral part of a hockey family, but I know what it looks like when I see it."

She tightened her arm around his waist and pressed her lips

to the hollow of his throat. This man might very well be the end of her heart.

Been a while since I've been an integral part of a hockey family.

There was one right at his fingertips. Most professional hockey clubs were built on camaraderie. Connor always talked about his teammates being his brothers. Of course, not every player fit seamlessly—some people weren't built for those kinds of relationships—but Liam wasn't unpleasant or prickly or bad for team chemistry. The guys seemed to like him.

And if he was able to see how special those kinds of bonds could be and still insisted on distance, on leaving, he had to be running on purpose.

"Do you think you'll look for that kind of community with one of your own teams at some point?" she asked carefully.

She wanted him to feel connected, for his health, his *soul*...

"It hasn't been a priority for a long time," he answered, a creak in his voice suggesting it wasn't a *whole* answer.

Could it be now? With me?

She didn't want to contemplate the *what if* possibilities of being with Liam Caldwell. If she did, she'd be choosing to ride an emotional roller coaster without a lap bar.

"But if I *was* looking..." He shook his head and sighed. His thumb stroked an absent pattern along her back.

Her gut nagged at her to pry. *Screw it.* "Keep going."

"With what?"

"*If you were looking.* You cut yourself off."

He groaned and let go, sliding his arms from around her and rolling onto his back. He rubbed his face with both palms. "We don't do this, Kate. Sticking flashlights into each other's dark corners. Looking through the cobwebs and shadows. It's not part of what we have."

"Right," she said, taking one of his hands and lacing their

fingers. "You don't need to spill your guts. Especially not before tomorrow's game."

He'd rejected the Daggers' offer. Chosen to leave. So long as he didn't want to meld into the world where Kate was rooted, she needed to protect her heart. She couldn't make a future with someone who ran at the first sign of depth.

Chapter Twenty-One

Liam: do you have your mom's crepe recipe?

Captain Sullen: WTF Caldwell

Captain Sullen: It's eight. And our morning off.

Liam: As if you weren't awake

Captain Sullen: Not the point. And no, I don't have the recipe

Captain Sullen: Might have been from our granny's old Good Housekeeping recipe book

Liam: Was that so hard?

Captain Sullen: Yes

Liam: See you at the 1:00 meeting, sunshine

Liam was unsurprised Connor was up already, but he hadn't expected to be awake before eight himself. Especially not texting his captain with one hand, on the hunt for a decades-old recipe. After a game—and after some rather spectacular post-game activities—he was usually good for 9:00 or 10:00 a.m., at least. *Especially* when he was still cuddled up with the woman responsible for the sated hum in his limbs. He'd been lying here awake for an hour already. Kate, sprawled across his chest, made for a perfect lure to keep him in bed all day. Her slow, rhythmic breathing reminded him of waking up to the waves on the shore of a beach.

Staring at the pretty curves of her face—her pert nose, the line of her jaw, her plump lips—was the work of hours. The last thing he wanted was to wake her. She needed the sleep as much as he did. But his brain was spinning from the questions she'd asked him last night. From his almost-responses, too.

But if I was looking...

Damn it.

He'd been too close to finishing.

If I was looking for community, I'd start here. With you.

Or worse: *You make me want to look.*

No. Why would he open himself to losing something so vital again? He needed that crepe recipe. Something to keep his thoughts from circling.

He savored the weight of her against his chest for a few more seconds and then disentangled her limbs from his, one slow movement at a time.

He was halfway off the bed when she murmured, "Where're you going?"

"Bathroom," he whispered, kissing her forehead. "Go back to sleep, love."

"Mmm." She burrowed under the covers. He tucked them around her chin for good measure.

Dark lashes lay on freckled cheeks. He wanted to kiss every fleck.

Tearing himself away before he lost his will and crawled back in, he went to the bathroom, grabbed sweats and a T-shirt from his dresser and then padded to the kitchen with his phone in hand for research.

He found a veritable inventory of recipes online, more than one from the source Connor had mentioned. Skimming through a few of them, they seemed simple.

Hmmm. He was flicking between two browser windows, waffling on the recommended kind of flour, when a text notification popped up.

Captain Sullen: The lemon syrup is what really made it

Before he could start searching for the second recipe, another text alert appeared, this one of an image. He opened it and took in the handwritten index card. The unfamiliar script detailed what looked like a lemon-flavored simple syrup.

Helpful of his captain. Unexpected, too.

He typed a reply: Thanks, Sully. I owe you.

Captain Sullen: You do. Now my dad thinks I'm making him crepes for breakfast.

Liam: You couldn't tell him I was the one who'd asked?

Captain Sullen: Christ, no. I don't want to compound his worry you're actually serious about my sister.

Liam paused. I *am* serious about your sister.

A couple of weeks ago, he would have sent that message as a cover.

Now…it was too close to the truth.

He was up early during the damn playoffs, not because he was obsessing over last night's loss, or the game tape he needed to watch with his team this afternoon, but because the woman in his bed had talked about her mom's recipe like her heart was still breaking.

Because she'd pushed him too close to facing the cracks in his own heart.

Captain Sullen: Don't forget the whipped cream.

Liam: Buckwheat or white flour?

Captain Sullen: White

Liam: You're a good man.

His captain didn't reply.

Might as well bring some more amusement to the man's morning. Connor might pretend to be annoyed by these kinds of shenanigans, but Liam knew the captain loved seeing his sister happy.

Liam: You wouldn't happen to be nearby with a can of whipping cream and some lemons, would you?

Connor replied with a middle finger emoji.

Liam laughed. He hadn't been serious. He could source what he needed at a place nearby. He didn't expect Kate would be waking up anytime soon. She'd been sleeping like the dead when he glanced at her after emerging from his en suite. Just in case, he jotted her a note about running to get coffee and left it on the counter.

He threw on a hoodie and jammed his feet into soccer slides, and then made his way to the coffee shop around the corner. It was a good thing he patronized the shop well, because it only took a little flirting and a twenty in the tip jar to convince his favorite barista to sell him a mostly full canister of whipped cream and one of the lemons they kept in stock in case someone wanted a slice for their tea. He ordered a masala chai, too. He'd been planning on making her a latte with his Keurig, but he couldn't do the milk art at home the same way as the talented barista.

Supplies in hand, he returned to his condo, where he stored the whipped cream in the fridge and got to making the syrup and then the crepes.

God, they were finicky. Rotating his wrist to make a circle out of the batter was trickier than chipping the puck toward the net.

Four misshapen clumps of half-cooked batter crowded a paper towel on the counter.

His heart rate picked up. If he didn't figure this out soon, all he'd have to show for his efforts was a decent lemon syrup, whipping cream, two rapidly cooling drinks and a brain still doing its best to make him face Kate's questions.

Kate rolled over, sure this bed was the equivalent of living in a cloud. Liam's ultrasoft, feather duvet was beyond indulgent.

She was still in the T-shirt he'd lent her last night, and the cotton was so worn in she could barely sense it on her skin. *He,* however, was nowhere to be found.

Had he not wanted to wake up together?

Shit. Of course he hadn't. After the turn their conversation had taken last night, it was surprising he hadn't come up with an excuse to ask her to leave right then.

The bed was cavernous without him, and the sense of being an impostor slunk along her limbs.

She sat up, clutching the duvet to her chest. Unlike the main area of his condo, his bedroom looked lived-in enough. On the plain, pale wood dresser sat a framed picture of him, about a decade younger. In the shot, he crouched with one arm around a woman in a wheelchair, her green eyes identical to Liam's, and a seated man who had the rest of Liam's face. Going off his father's looks, Liam Caldwell was going to be a handsome devil when he was in his fifties. And with the Winnipeg jersey Liam was wearing over a dress shirt and tie, she assumed it was a picture from when he'd been drafted.

The only other personalization was a blown-up and framed photograph of an inlet in what looked like the Pacific Northwest, hung over the headboard. Too specific a shot to be stock art. Had he taken it himself?

A squishy armchair, made for one but big enough for two, squatted in a corner beside the dresser. A zip-up hoodie was draped on one of the brown leather arms.

She climbed from the luxuriant froth of the duvet, grabbed the hoodie and shrugged into it. Her oversize purse, with her spare clothes in it, was in the main entry. At least his hoodie went two-thirds of the way down her thighs.

He'd still know she wasn't wearing underwear.

She took a quick, sharp breath. All right. Would it be awkward this morning? Maybe. But she could go get her stuff and make a quick exit. She opened the bedroom door. A familiar smell wafted into her nostrils. Sweetness, tangy citrus, almost like a baked good, but not quite.

She rushed into the kitchen, then halted, grabbing the counter to steady herself.

Liam stood at the stove, his eyebrows knitting in concentration like they did during practice drills. He tipped a frying pan in a careful circle. Pale yellow batter spread and sizzled.

Excitement caught in her throat. "*Liam.* Are you making..."

He glanced at her and placed the pan on the burner. Holding out his free arm, he beckoned her into his half embrace.

She went, staring numbly at the thin crepe in progress.

His lips brushed against her forehead. "Morning, sleepyhead. Hungry?"

With a skilled flick, he turned the crepe.

"How did you..."

He tilted his head toward the counter and an unsightly stack of half mangled attempts. "Practice. Luckily, I made extra batter. And *way* too much syrup."

The small pot caught her eye. She gasped. Her hands flew to her mouth.

He cocked a brow. "You okay, superstar?"

No. She was not. She was more liquid than the sunflower-bright syrup. "It's...lemon. How did you know?"

He lifted the crepe onto a small, golden-edged stack on a plain, white plate. His mouth grazed her hairline again. "Turns out your brother is more resourceful and romantic than I gave him credit for."

"Connor?"

"The very same."

"You thought of it, though."

"A good surprise, I hope." He poured another dollop of batter in the center of the pan and swirled it around.

"I've never been able to get that right," she lamented. "And you figured it out in what, thirty minutes?"

"It's all in the wrist."

His hand drifted from her hip toward the center of her belly, and then down. He stopped just before he got anywhere good and twirled a circle as precise as his work with the pan.

She gasped, leaning against him. "Excuse me, sir. Those are your fingers, not your wrist."

"And yet. Still magic."

"Not right now," she said. "We need to eat, first."

"And then?"

"You tell me."

His lips curved along the shell of her ear. "You know I won't send you home wanting, Kate."

Chapter Twenty-Two

A NEW CHAMPION FOR GIRLS IN HOCKEY
Kate Sullivan brings decades of experience to a new skills school in Hollow Valley
Florence Johnson, Guest Columnist
Denver Star, May 11

Two days after Kate stayed over at Liam's, he was headed for the airport for what would hopefully be the Daggers' last trip to Winnipeg. He would always be fond of the prairie city, even though the team had traded him to Chicago a year and a half into his contract because they'd been desperate for a goalie. During the playoffs, though, no room existed for nostalgia. The shorter, the better, when seven-game series were involved.

He'd left plenty early for his flight as usual. Instead of getting to the airport with time to spare, though, he turned in the direction of the Hollow Valley arena, first. And once there, as if dragged by a magnetic force, his feet took him to Rink Two.

"Liam!" Maude broke away from her class and skated to the boards. "Come skate our quick feet drill with us!"

He motioned to his suit. "Sorry, Maude. I can't race right now. I'm on my way to the airport."

She cocked her head. "The airport is in Denver. Why did you come to Hollow Valley, first?"

"Your aunt is here, kiddo. Not in Denver. And she's my good luck charm."

"And you're going to win game five, so there won't be a game six," Maude said gleefully. "Though I *would* like to sit in a box again. *If* there's a game six."

Kate glided up, leaving her college-age employees in charge of the drill. "If there is a game six, I think your mom's planning to take you to sit in Uncle Connor's seats."

Maude's face brightened, then fell. "I want to go to another game. But I don't want you to lose tomorrow."

"A win tomorrow would mean at least two more games at home in the next round." He leaned in. "In the *conference final.* Even better hockey."

Kate tapped the top of her niece's helmet with a gloved hand. "And with that best-case scenario out in the universe, *you* need to get back to your place in line."

Maude waved a vigorous goodbye. "Score lots, Liam!"

He shot the kid a grin and saluted her.

Kate leaned her forearms on the boards and blinked at him. "I was not expecting to see you."

"Wasn't done seeing *you*," he explained.

"I was going to call you tonight," she said. "I'm only nine away from my enrolment target for my first July class. And Florence Johnson's article came out this morning. Did you see it?"

"Saw it, posted it to my socials, sent it to my mom. You *are* a champion, Kate Sullivan."

God, he wanted to push her closer to her target.

Even if it meant her becoming *more* of a permanent fixture in Hollow Valley, when he'd be somewhere else next year. And a couple years later, somewhere else again.

With all the kids facing away from him, he took a quick video of them power skating down the ice.

"What are you doing?" she asked.

"Some quick promo for you." He posted the video with the caption: A reminder of where it all begins. He tagged Kate's school. Then, he flipped his phone around to show her the finished product.

"You didn't have to do that," she said.

"It's a small thing, Katie," he said. "Tell Maude—when you make your enrolment target, we'll go out for ice cream."

"That would be a considerable jump," Kate said.

"Anything is possible. Make you a bet—if you make it, I'll wear your jersey on our sundae date."

"Where on earth would you get one of mine in your size?"

He shrugged. "I'll have to figure it out, I guess."

Her eyes narrowed. "I thought the ice cream was contingent on making the target."

"Ice cream is contingent on how desperate I'll be to see you after I come home from my road trip."

Her eyes widened. "Home?"

"Uh, sure." He swallowed. Damn it, he didn't want to mislead her. "Temporarily, anyway."

He kissed the hell out of her, one last moment to keep him company while he crashed alone in a hotel bed.

"Bye, superstar. See you in a few days for ice cream."

DENVER DAGGERS: A WIN TONIGHT WOULD END THE SERIES
And in the nick of time for their struggling captain?
Denver Star, May 12

Kate stared at the score on the TV behind the bar. Natalie, who rarely traveled with the team, perched on the other side. Scone was sitting under the lip of the bar, his usual routine.

"Well..." Kate made a face at the numbers. Five-two. The Daggers had been handed their ass. Her brother, specifically. "I've seen Conn play better games."

Natalie sighed. "He'll be disappointed. He's looked tired ever since he took that hit in the last round."

"Or injured," Sophie groused, ducking under the counter flap. "He insists he's not, but I think he's lying."

"Soph, shhh," Kate said. "Someone might hear."

"Every second commentator is talking about it, Kate. It's not news."

"No, but everyone here knows you have access to the truth."

Sophie waved her off. "As if Connor's been confiding in me."

Natalie studied their friend. "You want him to."

Sophie bristled. "No, I want him to be healthy."

Kate and Natalie shared a look.

"Stop it," Sophie said. "And look at you." She tapped the 44 on Kate's back. "A non-Sullivan jersey at Sullivan's. Sacrilege."

"And here I thought it would be lucky."

Liam had seemed off tonight. Had she distracted him too much?

Sophie loaded a tray with drinks and hustled off to the corner of the bar.

"Someone has to lose," Natalie mused, eyes on the TV over Kate's shoulder. "And Winnipeg was the better team tonight. Plus, this gives us the chance to win the series in front of a home crowd."

Home.

It'd been echoing in Kate's head since the minute Liam so casually dropped it at the rink before he left.

He hadn't been talking about the home-away dynamic of a hockey game.

But he'd qualified it.

Was he lying to himself? Or was she getting her hopes up for no reason? Detonating her life again, like she'd done with Vince, wasn't an option.

But when Liam was throwing around words like *home*…

"Should I ask him to stay?" she blurted.

Natalie blinked and sipped from the straw of the soda water Kate had served her in a pint glass. "Um, sorry?"

Her stomach curled in on itself. "Oh, God. Nothing."

"No, what do you mean by *stay*? Do you mean Liam?" Natalie asked.

"I'm sorry. You work for the Daggers. I'm putting you in an awkward place by even asking."

"I'm your friend first." Natalie's head tilted. "*Haven't you* asked him to stay?"

"That wasn't our deal."

"What do you mean, *deal*? Since when is a relationship a deal?"

Oh, crap.

"Since—" She shook her head. "I just mean—when we started dating, we knew he'd be leaving."

Natalie's face was soft. "Oh, honey…"

"Nothing I can do about it now."

"Isn't there? Couldn't you tell him how you feel?"

"Your romantic side is too damn dangerous, my dear," Kate said.

Kate's phone buzzed in her pocket. She checked it.

Love of My Life: Not the game we wanted.

I'm sorry, she replied, adding a sad emoji.

Love of My Life: Will you be off by the time I get to the hotel?

Kate: Yes. But if not, I can take a break. It's slowing down.

Love of My Life: Because of the loss?

Ouch. She didn't want to pile on his guilt, but he'd read through any dishonesty.

Kate: Partly.

Love of My Life: Damn. Sorry.

Kate: You are not singlehandedly responsible for the success of your team, Liam Caldwell. And definitely not for the drinking habits of the Hollow Valley regulars.

He sent her a kiss emoji.

She tapped out one last message.

You'll get them next game, and then Sullivan's will be packed. I'll need a foot massage at the end of my shift.

Love of My Life: You know I'm good for it.

Natalie cleared her throat.

Kate startled.

"Is that who I think it is?" her friend asked.

"Yes."

Natalie traced a finger through the condensation on her glass. "He must be texting you right after getting out of the shower."

"Maybe," Kate said.

"No, seriously. You're his first call, Kate."

"I'm not his first anything," she said.

Confusion scrunched Natalie's features. "You *don't* want to give this an actual shot?"

"What's the point? I'm not following him, Nat. Everything that matters to me is in Hollow Valley."

Except Liam.

"Oka-ay," Natalie drew out. "Maybe you do need to ask him to stay."

"I can't. He…he needs to leave." *Or chooses to run.* "We have finite days together—an immutable fact."

"Everyone does, Kate. But it makes me sad you know exactly when the end will come. He seems good for you. Brightens up your world. And that ass." Natalie winked.

"*Ma'am.* He is your coworker."

Natalie deflated. "Yeah. They all are."

Something in her friend's tone tweaked Kate's suspicions. "And is that a problem?"

"What? With Liam? No, of course not. He's pretty, but he's not *my* pretty."

"And who is?" Kate prodded.

Natalie turned scarlet. "No one."

Kate leaned in. "Are you having a secret, scandalous affair with someone from work, Natalie Jane?"

"Of course not!"

"Well. Now I'm intrigued. And anytime you pry about Liam, I can do the same with you."

Her friend shot her a pleading look. Scone barked, one of his alerts Natalie's pulse was high. Natalie reached under the bar, probably to put a hand on his head. "Kate, please, don't."

Sophie scooted up beside Natalie, on the customer side of the bar.

"Don't what?" she asked in a theatrical whisper.

Natalie's eyes went wide with panic.

"Nat doesn't want me to fall in love with another hockey player and leave town," Kate said smoothly.

Sophie scoffed. "I seriously doubt the second part, but I fear the first is a long-lost cause."

Same, Soph. Same. Kate sighed and chucked a lemon wedge at her friend, who caught it right before it beaned her in the forehead.

"He's already texted her since the game ended," Natalie said, nudging Sophie with an elbow.

"And he called you earlier today *and* last night after he landed? That's more communication than you ever got from Vince."

"As if my failed marriage makes a good metric."

"It does as a bargain basement limit. One never to approach again. But Liam seems to know what he's doing," Sophie said.

"Let's hope he does," Kate said.

Because she sure didn't anymore.

Chapter Twenty-Three

The sun was barely up the morning after the Daggers lost game six at home, but Liam and Kate were out for a run, catching a few last moments together before Liam had to leave for the airport.

He sucked in a breath of fresh mountain air and sneaked a glance at Kate's flushed face.

Her gaze darted his way. "Ye-e-es?"

"Anyone ever tell you you're beautiful?"

Her small laugh warmed him more than the physical exertion. "Pretty sure you did twice last night."

"I had to cheer myself up after the loss, love," he said.

Her smile froze.

"Ye-e-es..." he echoed.

"Calling me 'love' without an audience?" She sped up a little, pushing it on the hill.

He matched her speed. "Habit, I guess? I'll stop."

"You don't have to." She ducked her head. "I know you don't mean it."

"Except..."

A sharp pair of eyes pinned him, slowing his gait.

Right. Time to keep his suspicions about his feelings to himself.

He didn't need the distraction. The Daggers were tied 3-3, and tomorrow's game would decide whether their season was done, or they moved on to the conference final. This run was supposed to be relaxing, set him up for his travel day to Winnipeg, not leave him in a tangle over the confusing, captivating woman jogging next to him.

At least the neighborhood was soothing. If nights with Kate didn't already make the drive out of the city worth it, the peace of the small community would. Her street was still quiet. Only the engine of the occasional commuter interrupted the rhythm of their footfalls on the sidewalk.

They were making their way up the hill to where the road ended and branched into one of the many trails surrounding the houses.

He pointed at a FOR SALE sign in front of a massive, chalet-style house. The decorative wood exterior and angled roofs reminded him of the places he'd rented for a couple of All-Star weekends he'd spent in Whistler earlier on in his career. Or, he supposed, they were similar to homes in Aspen, being in Colorado. "New sign, isn't it?"

A corner of her mouth turned up. "Yeah. The house is *gorgeous* inside. Vince and I toured it when we were originally looking to buy here. He didn't like it, though. Didn't want to be too close to my family, which is why we chose a place in Denver." She smoothed her ponytail. "Red flag, right? Anyway, I'm surprised it's on the market again so soon. The kitchen is to die for. And the fireplaces… If I had the money, I'd buy it for myself in a second. Even though I'd be rattling around in it alone."

Or with me.

Damn, it was too easy to picture snuggling under a plush blanket together in front of what had to be a wood-burning fireplace, based on the chimney. Or planting her hands on the glass of those expansive windows and making love to her in front of a view of the mountains.

But if he had it all, if Kate and this house and this town were his home, how quickly would it be taken away?

"Where would you put the spite couch?" he joked, pushing past the roughness in his throat.

"Honestly?" She stared straight ahead.

"Of course."

"I think I'd leave it behind. No need to bring crappy energy with me."

"Brilliant plan," he said. "Plus, it deserves to be retired, for all we've put it through. Raise its number to the roof and fade off into couch obscurity."

She cleared her throat. "This time with you has helped me process."

"Same." He caught her wrist and gently pulled her to a stop.

Her eyes flashed gold with curiosity. "Something on your mind?"

"Fly to Winnipeg to watch game seven. I want you there when we win."

Taking both his hands, she tilted her head. Her eyes were all rich honey apology. "You know I would if I could. I'd take off work, buy a last-minute ticket—"

"I'll buy your ticket. Don't dig into your savings for me."

"My kids have two games this weekend. And there's no one to step in and coach." She cupped his cheeks. "I'm so sorry."

He forced a smile, needing her to know he understood. "It's going to be a winning weekend."

The niggling in his gut, telling him it wouldn't be the same to win without her there, refused to leave.

DAGGERS WIN GAME SEVEN IN A NAIL-BITER
And after scoring the game winner, Caldwell's currency is rising. Rumors of teams interested in signing him rise to five.
Denver Star, May 18

The morning before the Daggers were flying out to start the conference final in Los Angeles, Kate woke up nestled in Liam's bed. The warm cocoon of cotton, soap-scented skin and hard muscle made her want to stay in this exact spot for as long as possible.

She had a long day ahead of her—planning with Sophie, followed by two afternoon classes—but she wasn't going to rush away these languid moments.

Who knew how many more of them she'd get? Tomorrow he'd be on the road for two games, which meant four nights away. Beyond that, it could be anywhere between two more games or five… Another series, or not. And the more Liam shone from game to game, the more he'd be worth come free agency.

The farther he'd run.

"You awake, love?" he asked in a sleepy mumble.

Feeling all swoopy whenever he called her "love" was as futile as expecting him to stay, but she couldn't bring herself to ask him to stop. "How did you know?"

"The minute you wake up, your mind starts going, Kate Sullivan. I can hear it whirring." He lifted a mischievous eyebrow. "Will Sophie be annoyed if I make you late for your meeting?"

"Depends on why."

Green irises flashing, he rolled her to her back, pushed up the worn CHL team T-shirt she'd now claimed as hers and pressed a kiss between her breasts. "Think of it as a choose-your-own-adventure. Higher, or lower?"

"Mmm, I think…lower."

His kiss landed right above her navel. "Excellent choice."

Her phone buzzed on the nightstand. She ignored it.

"Still lower?" he murmured against her belly.

"Oh, yes."

Another buzz. Probably her brother. He could wait.

Liam tasted his way down to the edge of her underwear and caught the microfiber between his teeth.

Buzzzzzzzzz.

Her panties thwapped back in place.

"Why don't you check it," he said, kissing over her mound. "It might be an emergency."

"I doubt it." But it was killing the mood, so she grabbed her phone to at least silence it.

The notifications were all from Sophie.

Princess Sophia: We did it.

Princess Sophia: The magic number.

Princess Sophia: We're in the game.

Elation shot off like a champagne cork in her chest.

"Oh, my God, Liam!" She levered to sitting, making him shift to an elbow.

He cocked his head. "Something better than oral?"

Her heart was going double time. "Yes!"

His face fell.

"I mean, no. Well, sort of..."

He groaned, flopped on his back and slung his arm over his eyes. "My ego can't take a hit like this before coffee, Katie."

"No, it's different." She scooted his arm up and grinned at him. "I did it. Well, we did. We hit our enrolment target. Our fall ice time is secure."

She could stay. Start growing her roots deep enough in Hollow Valley soil to never be yanked out.

"Oh, wow, beautiful. That *is* better than oral," he exclaimed, bear-hugging her and peppering her face with kisses.

"No, it's not. Nothing is better than the way you get me off," she teased.

"Say less." His solemn smugness was the most adorable thing. "Seriously, though. I knew you could do it. And this calls for a celebration."

He slid back down her body.

"I thought you were going to take me out for ice cream."

"Oh, I will, after we get home from beating LA twice. But first, I'm going to finish what I started."

She settled against the pillows and clutched the sheets. Liam Caldwell certainly knew how to follow through.

SPRING THREE-ON-THREE SESSION ENDS THIS WEEKEND AT HOLLOW VALLEY ARENA
River Otters to play Eagles in repeat 10U match
Hollow Valley Courier, May 24

On Saturday, after two straight Dagger losses to LA on their road trip, Kate was hoping for the opposite result for the River Otters' final game of the spring season.

The kids were wired for sound, warming up in their end of the rink. She shook her head, amused by the five players in a row on the blue line, bobbing on their knees in reverse butterflies, stretching their groins.

"That's new," Sophie commented. She stood behind the players' bench with Kate, bundled in a thick flannel jacket and clutching a travel mug.

"They saw Connor and Liam doing it before the game we watched at the Dagger Den. Apparently, it's now required."

Sophie covered her mouth and giggled.

"I know. Peak hero worship."

When Kate got the signal from the ref, she called her players in for a pregame chat, then sent out her starting line. "Let's go, Otters!"

She wanted this win for them badly. It would mean they'd won more than they'd lost, and getting over the .500 mark would be a big accomplishment for this group.

After a minute of play, the whistle blew when one of Kate's players, and one of their opponents, managed to get tangled up with Shayla, who was playing goal today.

"Change! Tiimonen, Redfox, you're up!"

The pair hopped off the bench.

Sophie squeezed Kate's shoulder. "I'm going to go sit with

Pavneet and Anneli. Revel for a moment in being done morning practices until September. Want to come over to Pav's place tonight? We're setting the kids up with a movie and making dragon bowls."

A *yes* flitted on the tip of her tongue, but she hesitated. "I, uh, haven't talked to Liam yet. He's going to call me when he gets home."

Sophie nodded. "You have plans, then. No worries."

Not exactly. But with their remaining nights together creeping toward single digits, the thought of passing up a night in his bed made something far too close to panic rise in her throat.

God help her, she'd gone from him being an idea to being one of the pivot points of her life.

"Ugh, I promised myself I wouldn't let this happen."

"What, spending quality time with a man you enjoy being around?"

Kate let the question hang as she tapped a couple of players on the back and called for the next line.

"I'll go," Sophie said. "You need to focus. But know there isn't anything wrong with making space for someone in your life. At first, I didn't think he could be that for you, but now…maybe."

Which only proved Kate hadn't been honest enough with her best friend about her suspicion that Liam's fear of settling down ran deeper than he was willing to admit to anyone, even to himself.

"Speaking of…" Sophie pointed toward the stands on the other side of the rink as she exited the bench.

Four broad forms, clad in travel-day suits, were slipping past hockey parents and grouchy, tagalong siblings. One was on crutches.

Oh, no. Connor had finally admitted his hip was aggravated. Was he going to be able to play in game three tomorrow? He'd waited years to get back in Stanley Cup contention.

Her dad and brother found seats with Liam on the bottom row

of the bleachers. Rika Tiimonen nodded at the trio and continued to where Anneli sat with a toddler in her lap.

Liam and Connor cupped their hands around their mouths.

"Otters, Otters, Otters, oy oy oy!"

"Go, Maudie!"

Lord, those boys could make a ruckus if they put their mind to it. Her dad let out a whistle and clapped, nearly as loud.

Liam lifted a hand in a wave. Excitement rushed in. He was here, hours before she'd expected to get to see him. She ached for a hug—to hug *him*, after the Daggers' loss last night.

The men kept up the cheering throughout the game, encouraging Shayla when she let in a couple of goals, whooping and applauding when Maude scored. Tiimonen's daughter, Kesia, put one in, too, tying it up.

With five minutes to go in the third, Kate's players were starting to lag, missing passes and losing foot speed.

She called a time-out.

"Come on in, Otters! Have a drink!"

She leaned her arms on the boards and widened her smile. The players on the ice crowded around her, and the ones on the bench leaned in to hear.

"What's the plan, Coach?" Kesia asked.

"To give you all a chance to have a drink. And to tell you how proud I am, and how much I love seeing your creativity on the ice. I see you all keeping your heads up and trying to talk to each other. With five minutes left, everyone's going to get one more chance to be out on the ice. You all know what to do. Get the puck and get to the net. Quick transitions. Stay with your checks when you're defending. Let's finish like winners, no matter what."

She sent out Sammy and Ivy Redfox. The siblings flashed around the ice, seemingly buoyed by the time-out.

Kate called for a change, then a minute later, one more.

Maude was vibrating, impatient for her turn. With a little

more than a minute to go, the play got whistled down. Kate called her niece and Kesia. "Defensive end. Let's go!"

Maude won the face-off. Kesia carried it in, passed it back to Maude, who took a shot.

The puck skidded toward the net. Kate held her breath. Her heart pulsed in her windpipe.

These kids had worked so hard and—

It missed.

Her stomach wobbled.

All six players were behind the net, battling.

"Defense back!"

Kesia scrambled around the corner, carrying the puck with her.

The rest of the team stood at the bench, cheering.

She jammed at the goalie's pads.

The goal horn sounded.

"Yeaaaaaah!" Kate hollered, pumping her fist.

The River Otters erupted, only to be outdone in volume by their parents and families in the crowd. The celebrating trio on the ice were so excited, Kate had to call out a reminder to play out their last twelve seconds.

Her heart was so damn full.

Ten minutes later, they'd done an end-of-season handshake line, the three stars—including Maude, for scoring first—had been announced and had their chance to skate a circle with their sticks raised, and she'd awarded the Otters' player-of-the-game otter hat to Shayla, for her first win in goal.

"Finishing above five hundred was our target for the season, and guess what—you met it! I'm so proud of you."

"Ot-*ters*. Ot-*ters*," they chanted, filing toward the dressing room.

As Kate brought up the rear, with Maude in front of her, she braced her hands on her niece's shoulders. "Your goal was *out-standing*, kiddo. Really got the team going."

Maude turned, smile as wide as the rink. "Thanks. Shayla should play goal *all* the time."

"If she wants to." She happened to agree. After seeing Shayla in goal today, she was going to talk to Pavneet about putting her daughter in a goaltending clinic. Something Kate was going to be able to run, having secured her fall ice time.

"I can't *wait* for winter," Maude gushed.

Kate chuckled. "Let's get through summer first."

"And the Daggers winning the Stanley Cup!"

"I know they want to."

Starting with the hot-as-hell forward waiting at the corner with a small duffel bag over his shoulder. Liam held out his hand for the kids to high-five on the way past. They clustered around him, faces bright and shoulders square.

"Hey, Otters," he greeted. "What a way to end your season!"

The kids all started talking at once, recounting their favorite parts of the game.

He grinned at Kate over their heads.

She returned it with a wink.

Wisely, he let their chatter run its course, nodding along and making eye contact with each kid.

"And tomorrow, you'll win, too, Liam," Maude asserted.

Liam shot her a pair of finger guns. "I like your optimism, Maude. I think we can win, too. Even though it takes a lot to get to the finals, and even more to get those last four Ws. For the two Stanley Cup rings I've earned, I have eleven seasons where I came up empty."

Sammy Redfox frowned. "Losing sucks. We won today, but we lost a lot this season."

"It's okay to have big feelings about those losses. I gotta tell you, when I went to bed after losing last night's game, I was sad," Liam said, catching Kate's eye.

They'd talked late into the night, given Liam had been wound up after playing and annoyed he'd had to spend one more night in a hotel, though traveling during the day today instead of in the middle of the night last night was the better option, especially during the playoffs.

The sheer admiration on the kids' faces was adorable. They stared at him, eager to soak in his wisdom. They needed to get out of the way for the next game's teams, though. "All right, Otters, one last bit of advice from Caldwell, here, and then it's time to change."

"Phew, Coach Kate, no pressure," he cracked. "I loved watching you all play today. All *season,* for that matter. Winning feels awesome. Soak it in. I encourage you all to think of one area you'd like to get even better at, and to make a measurable goal. Like, not 'I want to improve my stick handling,' but 'I will weave around five pylons without losing the puck.' The more specific you can be, the more you'll know you're improving."

Most of them nodded. A chorus of thanks surrounded him.

"And, because I hear you made the goal you set at the beginning of the season, I have a surprise for you in the common area, after you get dressed. It's a sweet one."

After another round of high fives, the kids shuffled off to the change room.

Kate stopped in front of Liam and linked hands with him. The small contact centered her.

"You were gone all of four days. Why did I miss you so much?" she murmured.

"I'm irresistible," he said, grinning in satisfaction.

"Also, you're doing my job for me." She stroked his beard-roughened cheek. It approached downright unruly. Jesus, it was sexy. "Thank you for encouraging them."

"When I was their age, a rink like this was my home. It's something I haven't, uh, haven't experienced the same way since. And it's something to cherish, Kate. If I can add to it in a small way, it's a privilege."

It could be your home if you stayed.

She buried the thought under a smile. "They don't know how lucky they are to have you mentor them. What surprise do you have for them?"

"You'll see." He brushed the few strands of hair escaping her ponytail off her cheek and tucked them behind her ear. "Sorry I was late. I stopped at Rika's on the way so he could drop his stuff off."

"You gave him a ride?"

"Yeah, we knew we were both coming to the same place. Your brother and your dad used their car service, but I'd left mine at the airport." He glanced over his shoulder, to where Connor was talking to Sophie. By the way she was gesticulating and he had his palms up like he was in the middle of a bank robbery, their sister-in-law was giving him the gears about playing injured.

"Is he on tomorrow's roster?" Kate asked quietly.

"Not sure," Liam rolled his neck and winced.

"Are *you* okay? No new bumps or bruises?"

"Yeah, I'm fine, love." He rubbed her shoulder.

"I didn't expect you to be here," she said. "And especially not with some mysterious surprise. I thought we were meeting up later."

"I decided both was better."

"You have a game to worry about!"

"Coming today was the perfect break. Two losses in a row is tough on the psyche. I know it sounds oversimplified, but if they can win, so can I."

"It's still hard to believe you'd want to spend your precious off-hours watching kids play hockey, given none of them are yours."

He lifted a chiding brow, and lowered his lips to her cheek, right by her ear. "*They* aren't mine, Kate. But you are."

Her soul swelled, buoyed by the suggestion of being his so fully. Even for a moment. Would it really hurt to pretend they could belong to each other and she could still keep her heart guarded?

Yes, yes it would.

Deep inside, she craved being his.

Calling him *hers*, too.

Gaze soft, he caressed her cheek with a warm, wide palm. “Stay here for a couple of minutes before you come into the common area. I have one more thing to do before you bring the kids in.”

“Fine. But I’m wildly curious,” she said.

“Good.”

She took a few minutes to round up the team from the dressing rooms before leading them through the doors across from the concession.

A long table stretched the length in front of the trophy case. Gallon pails of ice cream, a half dozen flavors, filled one end. Her dad stood behind it, scoop in hand. A sundae shop’s worth of toppings scattered the rest of the table. Bottles of syrup, and bowl after bowl of sprinkles, cherries, chopped pineapple, halved bananas, tiny marshmallows, and a rainbow of popping pearls.

Liam and Estelle stood to the side, giving the kids free rein of the table. And Liam was wearing a very distinct maroon and gold jersey.

“What did you do?” Kate asked Liam. As much as his face was a showstopper, as always, she couldn’t take her eyes off the blocky, golden M on his chest.

He’d made their sundae date happen and had worn her college jersey. This man was going to be the death of her.

She closed the distance between them and ran her finger along the crest. “Where did you get this?”

“We had a bet, Kate. Ice cream after you made your enrolment target.” He held his arms out and spun, a classic “check out what I’m wearing” pose to show off SULLIVAN and the number eleven.

"I thought we'd hit up the shop on Hollow Valley Avenue, not this. And not roping my dad into it."

"Happy to help, Kate! Not every day my granddaughter gets to be a star of the game."

She shook her head. Since when was Tal Sullivan *cheerful* the day after a loss?

"Where did you get that jersey?" she asked Liam.

"From the university website," he said cautiously, as if *she* was missing something.

"Did you have it custom made? How did you do it so quickly? We only found out about the enrolment on Monday."

"I knew you'd make your target, and sooner than you expected. I ordered this when we made the bet, Kate. Two weeks ago. Rush delivery, and the crew at the Dagger Den merch store gave me a hand with the personalization. Wasn't that tricky."

Tricky, no, but *thoughtful*?

Her heart didn't know what to do with itself.

"You didn't have to…"

He smirked. "It lets the world know I'm taken. Speaking of, my girlfriend's father looks like he needs help serving ice cream."

Her breath hitched, and she threw her arms around Liam's broad shoulders. Her face pressed against the logo she'd been so proud to wear. Her hands caught along the last name that had been equal parts a blessing and a weight throughout her life.

"Hey." His arms were a strong loop holding her to his chest. "You okay?"

"You're too much sometimes, Liam Caldwell."

"Look." His expression sobered. "We both know I'm leaving. I can't give you forever. But while I am here, I can treat you like you deserve. And you deserve the world, superstar."

Except she didn't want the world. Just a home, with him in it.

The one thing she couldn't have.

Chapter Twenty-Four

ONE LAST CHANCE FOR THE DAGGERS' SEASON
Down 3-2 to a healthier Los Angeles team—and down Connor Sullivan to a labral tear—can Liam Caldwell and Oskar Larsen fill their captain's skates?
Denver Star, May 31

Five minutes remained in the third period, and Los Angeles had a one-goal lead.

The clock ticked down. Their chance to even the game was disappearing with each descending second.

A hand clamped on Liam's shoulder, belonging to the stone statue who'd been hovering behind his end of the bench all game.

"We need your magic, Caldwell."

"Yes, Coach."

One last shift.

Every damn part of him was sweating. From nerves, not exertion.

When Coach called for his line, Liam launched off the bench, snagging the loose puck and sending it to a charging Oskar Larsen. Lars pitched it to Tiimonen, planting the Daggers in the offensive zone. Brian Boyle and an LA defenseman were battling it out in front of the goalie, creating a screen.

They'd practiced this, cycling without Connor—

The puck was on Liam's stick, and he slapped it toward the net.

The light went off.

Euphoria shot through him. His teammates swarmed him in a happy melee, even Boyle.

The relief of a tie score. They still had a chance. They—

The LA coach called a time-out.

His stomach jerked.

Lars, who'd let go of Liam, swore.

Liam echoed it.

The coach was deep in conversation with the referee. *A coach's challenge.*

Lars, one of the alternate captains tasked with on-ice discussions in Connor's absence, went over to the ref, discussing the play in his typical, still-morning-lake manner.

Liam returned to the bench.

Coach Sullivan's demeanor was the opposite of Lars' calm one. He waved his tablet in agitation. "Goalie interference? Bullshit! Boyle got shoved into the crease."

Liam's jaw clenched.

"You had Smitty's number, Caldwell," Coach bit out. "It was a beauty."

A beauty that might not count.

Compared to the middle of the season, scoring was effortless again, when the circumstances were right. But he couldn't control his damn teammates, and Boyle pushed the limits—and the line of the crease—too often.

The ref took his place at center ice. "Due to goaltender interference, the ruling on the ice is overruled. No goal."

The air left Liam's lungs like it had been sucked out by a vacuum.

It only took a second for the classic "ref you suck" to reach the rafters.

The play continued, despite the incensed crowd's chorus.

Don't let the call derail you.

Liam caught his breath. He could aim glove-side or try for the top left corner. The LA goalie was weaker there—

The whistle blew.

The other ref called Boyle, who'd stayed on the ice after the disallowed goal, for tripping.

Coach Sullivan started shouting again.

Liam rarely went out on the power play, and sitting on the bench for this long was going to kill him.

He patted Jonesy, one of their best penalty killers, on the numbers. "You got this, man."

Come on. I want to get out there...

Forty-five seconds remained after the penalty expired.

His skates hit the ice and he bolted toward the blue line, catching a pass from Tiimonen. There was enough traffic in front of the net, and he took a shot.

A fucking brilliant one, but somehow, the goalie stood on his head to save it.

His heart pounded in his ears, louder than the music and the cheers.

Lars won the face-off, got it to Jonesy—

Another miss.

Rebound.

To Liam… Wind up…

The horn sounded.

Numbness descended over his limbs and buzzed in his ears, dulling the disappointed hush of the crowd.

That was it.

His last moments as a Dagger, lost to a disallowed goal and a saved puck and three seconds too few to shoot again.

Lars glided over, his expression solemn. They stood side by side, gripping their sticks with the blades on the ice, watching the Los Angeles players dogpile their goalie.

Nothing, *nothing* in this sport was as much of a knife to the heart as being on the outside of a team who'd just won a playoff series.

Well, except for watching another team win in the final round.

And the Daggers wouldn't be making it that far.

Lars glanced sideways at Liam. "Been a pleasure playing with you."

"You, too, Oskar."

"I wanted more than this," the Norwegian confessed.

"Same. It feels unfinished."

More than usual. He'd lost before, in the third round, no less. Today, it wasn't hollow. The ache was bottomless, throbbing through his gut. It lingered through the handshakes, the raised sticks to the crowd, Coach Sullivan's brief words once the team was back in the dressing room.

A minute later, microphones were jammed in his face, questions coming over each other.

"Liam, thoughts on the disallowed goal?"

"…free agency coming up, any comments on the rumors?"

"…impact of losing your linemate in the last game after it took you months to gel?"

Goddamn it, there were too many voices. He couldn't keep up with them.

Swallowing, he scrambled to focus on anything relevant.

"It's been a privilege to play with this team. We wanted to go farther, no question."

"Given the Daggers' playoff run, are you regretting turning down the contract offer?" The question came from one of the local sports radio guys.

I'm regretting I won't wake up with Kate in my bed a few weeks from now.

Or a bed they bought together, in a house—a home—they bought together…

He gritted his teeth. "My situation isn't a guarded secret, but Jesus, it's not the day for that."

"He's always had one foot out the door," Boyle sniped from Lars's other side.

Seriously? With phones and recorders on?

"Leave it, Brian," Liam said with a glare.

"I'll give you a quote," Boyle said.

"No, you won't," Lars said, steering a half-dressed Boyle toward the showers.

Shit. Coach, as well as the PR team, was going to have their heads.

"Emotions are high after a loss as significant as this one," Liam explained. "And the ruling on the goal wasn't the one we wanted."

"And do next year's pastures look greener?" the sports radio reporter persisted.

Liam stared, not intending to start turning the rumor mill. "Let us say goodbye to this season, eh?"

As gutting as it was to take off his gear for the last time as a Dagger, he at least knew the routine.

Saying goodbye to Kate?

He knew he *had* to do it. But he didn't have a clue how.

An hour after the final whistle, Kate waited for Liam in a hallway near the dry lockers. Most everyone else had cleared out. She leaned against the painted concrete. Her heart weighed heavy. They'd tried so damn hard, especially the suit-clad man moving toward her. Had Liam Caldwell ever *trudged* in the time she'd known him?

"Hey," he murmured, stopping near her. "You waited."

"Of course. You said you'd want to do something tonight, no matter what." She stood and wrapped her arms around him.

His palm was wide on the back of her head, and the notch of his collarbone exposed by his loosened tie and undone button was the perfect place to nuzzle. She soaked in the clean scent of his soap.

And for one short moment, holding him, trying to fix an unfixable feeling, everything was how it should be. Not the loss, obviously, but trying to support him through it.

Except it isn't.

The longer they pretended this *was* okay, the more he accepted her support, the harder it would be on both of them in a day or a week or a month or however long it took them to officially pull the plug.

But she couldn't let him go. Not yet. Even if they only had this last night.

He kissed the top of her head, inhaling deeply.

"I'm so sorry," she said.

"Me, too," he mumbled into her hair.

"Should we get out of here?"

He paused for a second. "Maybe it's better I be alone tonight."

Her heart pitched wildly. "Are you sure? We have tomorrow to be alone. Or the next day, or the one after. Like you told the reporters—today's not the day for talking about the future."

"I wasn't about to bare my soul for the press, Katie."

"Bare your soul for me."

His expression shuttered and he stepped back. "Like I said, I need to be alone."

He might not mean— "For tonight, or forever?" she asked.

He cupped her cheek, stroking a thumb from the corner of her mouth to the edge of her jaw. Something he'd done before, always with promise in his eyes. Not now. Today, the green was flat, regretful. Resigned.

"Katie…"

Forever, then. She lifted her chin. "So this is when you run."

"No, this is when I do what I said I would do. You have your ice time for the fall and will be a foundational part of the lives of the kids you love and the town you've made your home. And I will go to wherever I can best protect my family—"

"Are you really protecting them? Or are you too scared to stick around?"

A red flush crept from his shirt collar into his cheeks. "Scared? Big talk from someone who's managed to replace *one* piece of furniture since her divorce. You didn't want to fall for me any more than I did for you. And that's after *one* loss. I've lost over and over and *over.* It just won't *end.* My mom will be in pain for the rest of her life. My dad is *disappearing.* My home—"

He rocked back another step.

She reached out, but he moved his arm away.

Her neck got hot. "You think I've only lost once? What, did you forget I lost my mom? And my *brother.*"

He flinched. "Of course not, but—"

"'But' nothing. I've lost a parent slowly and a sibling in a flash. And I didn't let it stop me from loving the rest of the people who matter to me. From wanting to share my life with them."

"And I want you to have that. Tenfold."

So why don't you want to share it with me?

She opened her mouth but couldn't get the words out.

"Our arrangement worked, Kate." He was infuriatingly blank. "We got what we wanted. And now it's done."

This wasn't what she wanted. Not his footsteps, echoing as he walked away. Not her heart, cracked and bruised on the cement floor.

Not the feeling that he knew, truly knew, how to show up for a partner in so many different ways, like making her mom's crepes and spending time with her team and showing up on her doorstep at two in the morning and just *listening.* But when it really mattered, this pivot point where he could have made a different decision, he chose to leave. Chose being afraid alone over taking a risk together.

And she could be hurt or angry or sad or all of it, all together, swamping her from all sides. She was allowed to feel. But he'd told her. The whole time he'd been treating her like someone he could love, *he'd told her he wouldn't.*

She only had herself to blame.

Chapter Twenty-Five

Liam dragged himself through the doors of the Hollow Valley Arena the next morning. He'd barely slept, despite having played three periods of gut-wrenching hockey less than twelve hours ago. One last task to check off for the Daggers—locker clean-out day—and he'd be back to Denver to pack up his clothes before hopping on the latest flight he'd been able to book to Vancouver. The day would be jammed, even without the season-end checklist. His agent would be breathing down his neck about his next steps, and he'd already received an email confirmation from his Realtor of the condo listing getting posted today.

He slunk through the common area, keeping his head down. Surely, Kate would steer clear of the rink today. She wouldn't want anything to do with him.

Running. As if. He didn't *run.*

He chose to leave.

He—

"Liam!" A woman's voice stopped him in his tracks.

He took a breath. Not Natalie or Sophie, ready to take up arms for their friend, and definitely not Kate.

Estelle.

Who must not have heard about the breakup, because she wrapped him in her spindly-but-strong arms.

She didn't say a word.

He hugged her back, taking the replacement for his own mom's or grandmother's arms for the time being. "I'll miss you."

She released him and patted him on the cheek. After three playoff rounds of not shaving, he was rivaling the lumberjack mascot of the Desolation Cove minor hockey league.

"The beard's out of control," he said, purposefully taking her affection as a reminder of his facial hair, *not* as the comfort he knew she'd intended. "Better go deal with it before I leave today."

"Keep it to a trim," Estelle said. "Kate likes it. I heard Natalie teasing her about it the other day."

His throat was thick. "Estelle, about Kate. We…" He dropped his gaze to his sneakers. "I mean, I'm leaving—"

"And I won't hear any goodbyes from you," she said. "I'm on an 'until we meet again' basis only."

"Yes, ma'am." He gave her another hug. "Take care of yourself. And…her."

She sent him on his way with a stern, knowing look.

He never loved locker clear-out day. Check-ins with the medical team, the coaching staff, one last chat with the media, all while processing how they lost a game they could have won.

He was nearing the end of his required list, when he ran into Connor in the locker room.

His captain was on crutches, and he was favoring one side.

Liam didn't bother telling him how the team had missed him last night. Connor had eyes. He'd been watching from the press box.

Connor tucked the workout clothes he'd been folding into a bag and grimaced at Liam. "I'm betting your medical clearance with the team doctors went better than mine."

"I'm so damn sorry, man," Liam said.

"No one ever said this career was anything but fleeting."

"Are you done? For good?"

"Depends on how the surgery goes."

Surgery. Shit.

Liam's gut bottomed. Kate had lost a brother after a surgical procedure. How would she and the rest of her family handle Connor going under the knife?

"Soon?" he asked.

"Yeah, within the next week or so."

Huh. Soon enough for Liam to stick around to help Kate through it. His parents would understand if he delayed his visit in order to support her.

And offer her what, two or three more temporary weeks?

It didn't matter what word he used to describe his choices. Kate's accusation of him running. His justification of it as leaving. Either way, he'd been doing it since he was a teenager, and he was a damn expert.

She would be better off if he was long gone.

"That's the worst," Liam said.

Connor's head hung. His full weight was on his crutches as he slumped forward.

Liam reached out to squeeze his shoulder. "Let me know if there's anything I can do."

Aside from being the man your sister deserves.

Surprisingly, his captain didn't slough off the comfort. "Are you willing to stay and take over the captaincy while I'm healing for six months?"

Liam shook his head.

"Yeah, didn't think so." Connor's mouth was grim. "Did you already have your chat with the coaching staff?"

He nodded. "Had to apologize for the near-skirmish with Boyle last night. Not the foot I wanted to leave on. I played nice with the press during my last interview this morning, though."

"Did Coach go hard on you over your scoring slump?"

"A bit. Until I brought up how being around the River Otters dealt me some much-needed perspective. We get paid to play a game. One with love and passion and community at the heart of it."

And he'd be leaving two of those three things behind.

A damn roundhouse kick to the solar plexus, one he hadn't braced for.

"He's a sucker for Kate."

So am I.

Connor's throat bobbed, and he raked a hand through his already messy hair. "You talk about community, but you're sure eager to walk away from it. If you lose the one person you've let in in a hell of a long time, you'll regret it."

"Didn't think a dressing down from you was a part of my schedule today." He gritted his teeth and started tossing things from his locker at random into his bag.

His phone rang. His mom. He answered with a terse, "Yeah?"

"Oh, honey," she said, all empathy.

His bubble of hot frustration deflated. "Crap, sorry, Mom. Good to hear from you."

"You don't need to put on a happy face, Liam. I know yesterday was the worst."

He hissed out a breath. The on-ice loss throbbed, a constant reminder he'd have to wait a year for another shot at the greatest trophy.

The emptiness, though—the gutting hollow—was Kate and Kate alone.

"It'll fade," he insisted.

A brutal lie, but whatever.

"I'm glad you'll be coming for a summer visit. I want to hug my son."

His eyes stung. "Mmm-hmm. I'll email you my flight information."

"While you're here," she continued, "we're going to need your help moving."

His bag slipped from his fingers, landing on the wooden seat with a thunk. "I'm sorry, what?"

"Moving, honey. It's time."

Knees shaking, he moved his bag and sat. "You *and* Dad?"

"We want to be together."

"But the house…"

"I love it, I do. But the constant parade of nurses, the fear of him wandering away—it's too much. We need to simplify."

"But I promised him he wouldn't have to leave our home."

Liam's voice cracked. "The last place we have where he was *him.* It's…it's all we have left."

"Sweetheart. I'm not saying memories don't matter. At some point, our memories of him will be all we have left. And we both know how brutal it is to see memories fade. But a house doesn't hold those memories together. We do. My home isn't a building, Liam. It's the people I love, for as long as I can hold them in my arms, and beyond. Your *dad* is my home."

Something too close to a sob cracked in his throat. He covered his face with a hand, avoiding Connor's concerned glance.

"Mom, I…"

"You need a home, too, Liam. Who's yours?"

Kate.

"I can't… I mean, I don't—didn't—" He swore. "I love you, Mom. I'll send you that flight information."

"Thank you. And please, think about what I said."

You need a home, too.

He'd more than think about it.

After another *I love you*, he said goodbye and jammed his phone in his pocket.

"You okay?" his captain asked.

"No."

Connor exhaled. "Me neither."

He finished emptying his locker as Connor did the same.

The last thing he got to was the photocopied picture of Kate and him. He'd have sworn Jonesy had papered over his locker with the copies a lifetime ago. He started to peel the picture off, then stopped.

"Leaving it for posterity?"

"Something like that," he answered Connor. The memory of her sweet lips pressed to his in the tunnel washed over him, and a laugh escaped.

Kate's brother lifted an eyebrow.

"I didn't know she was going to kiss me," he admitted.

Connor clenched the handle of his right crutch. "Were you in love with her, then? That night?"

Liam had no desire to acquaint himself with that blocky fist, but what was the point in lying anymore? "I barely knew her then, man."

"And now?"

She's my everything.

And she didn't know it. He needed her to know it.

He needed to *show* her.

Slinging his bag over his shoulder, he backed up a step and pulled his phone out again. "I have a few details to iron out."

A call to his agent and changing his flight home…

No. Changing where and who he was *calling* home.

"Don't forget about my sister," his captain warned.

"I would never. I promise."

He couldn't keep the one he'd made to his dad any longer, but this one—it'd be for a lifetime.

Chapter Twenty-Six

"Can you pass me those sticks, Dad?" Kate, who'd been taking inventory in her school's storage room at the arena for the past few hours, pointed at a corner behind one of the many shelves.

He handed over the half dozen pint-size sticks with a sigh. He'd joined her about an hour ago, and the help was speeding things up, but they wouldn't be out of here until after dark.

The longer she spent here, the less time she'd have at home alone, replaying Liam's parting words in her mind.

Cursing, she dropped the sticks in the correct storage container with a clang. As if she needed to be by herself in the pool house to be swamped by Liam's declaration.

And now, it's done.

And now, it's done.

God*damn it.*

She grimaced, and focused on her dad, who'd been deflating over the course of their task. The inevitable low came once all the adrenaline of the playoffs wore off and the busyness of locker clean-out day subsided.

"I'm surprised you want to help me tonight, given how much talking you had to do today with all your end-of-season player evals," she said.

"It was more positive than negative," he said. "The playoff run gave my coaching staff a lot to work with, in terms of feedback."

Not all positive, though. "Connor told me about his surgery."

Even if she hadn't already been feeling like a walking, exposed nerve, her brother explaining the extent of his procedure would have sent her to her knees.

"He's…he's not Toby." She didn't bother to try to keep her voice from shaking. "And we have to be strong for him. He'll be okay. He has to be. But…"

Two seconds later, she was in the center of a burly bear hug.

"You and I can be scared together, Katherine. And then we can keep our smiles on for Connor."

A dry laugh escaped. "Smile? You?"

His genuine bark of laughter was a two-second reprieve from reality.

He hugged her tighter. "Very funny, Katherine."

"We need to keep laughing, I think."

Even if it felt like Liam had stripped the joy from her life as he'd walked away.

"We will," Tal promised. "You feeling steadier now?"

Not inside. But at least her legs weren't shaking anymore.

She nodded, and he returned to counting the small cones she had stored on a metal rack.

"Said goodbye to Liam." Regret broke through his usual Resting Grump Face. "Thought the playoff run might be enough to get him to extend his contract."

Just like her dad to be more comfortable talking about Liam leaving the team than leaving *Kate.*

"He needs to move on." She nearly choked getting it out.

He arched a brow.

"I'm not going to push him, Dad. His priorities matter."

And in another world, with a different set of circumstances, maybe she could have been one of those priorities.

"So that's the end of that?" he asked.

"Yeah."

He frowned. "Still too raw after your divorce to find something new, then."

Liam's asinine point about her furniture choices poked her. She shoved it aside.

"No. Vince is in my past. And I learned from my mistakes with him. Even in the beginning of my marriage, I was making compromises about my own future to make room for Vince. I picked a college based on where he got drafted. I held off on starting my academy because I knew we wouldn't be guaranteed to stay in one place until he'd retired. And I wanted to do those things. Part of being in a relationship is building a life together, making compromises sometimes to make it work. But he was never willing to make those same compromises for me."

Tal shook his head. "Seemed like Caldwell was in your corner."

"He was. He showed up for the things that matter to me, even in the midst of an attempted Cup run."

Which was why she'd ended up fooled.

"So why's he leaving?"

A lump formed in her throat. She swallowed, trying—and failing—to get it to dissolve. "He and I have very different ideas on what it means to build a home with someone."

Her dad chuckled.

"Thanks, Dad," she sniped. "Appreciate the humor."

He shook his head. "It's not a *funny ha ha* laugh, Kate. You're in a tough bind. Coming off a failed relationship isn't easy, and you found yourself with another one. But then again, we're all complicated, aren't we? No such thing as an easy person."

"No, but it would have been easier if I hadn't been relegated to the sidelines from a young age."

Silence hung between them. He stared at her, blinking in shock. "You were the star of your team, all the way through college. How is that the sidelines?"

"I had to fight way harder than my brothers to get to that place, and you know it. If it was between a chance for Toby, Connor or Jake and a chance for me, they won out. And the four of us—and Mom—were always working our lives around yours. First, when you were playing, and then when you were coaching. Hell, Mom downright *told me* that's what a wife does for her husband when he's in pro sports. So forgive me for taking a while to break that pattern and to insist on a life where I don't feel I'm losing myself year by year. Mom's way isn't the only way to be a hockey player's partner—"

His face turned stormy. *"Katherine."*

She held up a hand. "We all know that criticizing her now that she isn't here to defend herself feels awful, but it's true. It's *hard* to be mad with a dead person. Especially when I loved her so much." Another lump filled her throat. "And I love you, too. But still, I'm mad at you. Because as much as you wanted us to succeed, you weren't there to see us doing it half the time."

"Road trips are part of the job."

"It wasn't the physical distance!" She set her clipboard down and leaned against one of the shelves. "After Mom died, you disappeared, even when you were home. And then after Toby? You've been a *shell.* I know you've been trying. Family dinners and you coming to Maude's games and the fundraisers... Putting a roof over my head again. But sometimes, I need the words. To talk to you. Like..."

"Like we're doing now?" he said ruefully.

"Yes," she whispered. The slump of his shoulders was more than she could take. It was like the shelves lining the narrow storage space were collapsing in on her.

"You're right, Kate. I did the best I could at the time, but sometimes, it fell far short. And I don't want you to lose yourself again, honey. You're the damn light of my life."

She didn't bother to keep the shock from her face.

"I don't say it enough, I know. And don't get me wrong, I love your brothers just as much. I didn't tell Toby enough, and now I can't. I should say it more to Connor and Jake."

She nodded.

"Not being able to go back and fix the obvious mistakes is the rough thing about life," he continued. "All I can do now is work to make sure I'm not still making you feel like you're forever trying to catch up to your brothers. Am I?"

She shook her head.

He paused. "You know, Kate, those games I watch aren't just Maude's. They're yours, too. You're a hell of a coach, Kate."

Oh. *Oh.* "I have a hell of an example."

He lifted a shoulder. "I want you to see the difference you make and to be proud of your success. You're *not* on the sidelines. You're in the thick of the play." His mouth flattened. "At work, anyway."

"Why the qualifier?" she asked.

"You picked a man who you knew was leaving. Weren't you giving yourself an out, so you wouldn't get hurt?"

She blinked in surprise. Had she done that? It was…almost exactly what she'd accused Liam of doing. It *couldn't* be true for her, too. Sure, she'd jumped all over the chance at a fake relationship. To build her school and use media attention for her own benefit for once. To have fun with a man who turned out to be caring and attentive and romantic. And with Liam's staunch opposition to emotional strings, it should have been the perfect guarantee against getting—

—hurt.

Oh, dear.

Their plan had worked.

Except she *was* hurting, and he was, too.

Why hadn't he felt safe enough to fight for something real with her? For that home he so clearly yearned for? Was his pain that incapacitating? Or had she failed in some way?

"Kate?" Her dad's voice was soft. "What's wrong?"

"I got together with Liam for show, Dad. The night I kissed him and fans recorded it—he and I had talked all of twice before. We didn't lie about it to anyone. But we implied we were more serious than we were. And we always intended to break up once the season was over."

Her dad gave her a beleaguered look. "The boy showing up in my yard at 3:00 a.m. is not for show, Mary Katherine."

"It started as one," she hedged.

"But that's not how it's ending."

She nodded.

His expression turned thoughtful. "I don't want you to make a mistake you'll regret in the future."

"What, you're in his fan club now?"

"He's grown on me," he grumbled. "Don't get me wrong—I don't want you to give up all the work you've put into your school to move to Boston or Toronto or whichever team will throw the most money at him. But I don't want you to end up grumpy and alone like me, either."

"Dad…"

"I'm serious. When you lose someone, be it to death or divorce or whatever, it's too easy to stay in an ugly place. Because loving someone, being devoted to another person, *can* mean suffering. One partner will eventually lose the other. Sometimes way too soon."

"You're only adding fuel to Liam's reasoning, Dad."

"I *know* I disappeared when your mother died. And Christ, none of us have been the same since Toby. But then, you and Conn and Jake are braver than I am. So be brave, Kate. You've fought tooth and nail since you were a kid to play hockey, and now to coach and teach and eke out your place in Hollow Valley. And something tells me Liam is worth fighting for, too."

She looked around at the mess she'd made. The jumble of equipment was easy to sort out. Her feelings for Liam, less so.

"Maybe my definition of happiness has been too rigid since my divorce. To protect myself, and to give myself an excuse not to risk my heart again. Accomplishing all the things that are important to me *is* rewarding. But doing it with Liam's support makes it better. I just want to *be* with him, Dad. Might not be how I pictured it, but he's…he's *necessary* to me. You're right. I can't let him go."

"I want that for you, Mary Katherine. Your mother and I may not have been perfect, but goddamn, we loved each other. Added meaning to each other's lives wherever we could." His eyes were starting to glisten.

"How about you let your old dad finish your count and clean up for you? You might catch Liam before he leaves the arena."

"He left hours ago," she said. Estelle had let her know.

She pulled out her phone and sent him a text. Where are you?

Love of My Life: On my way home

Passing her dad the clipboard, she smiled sheepishly. There was no time to lose. "I walked here. Can I borrow your car?"

Kate stood on the sidewalk outside Liam's condo building. The longer she stared at the sign—the one that *hadn't* been here a couple of days ago—the more her stomach roiled.

FURNISHED PENTHOUSE.

FOR SALE.

Not a flashy, eye-catching sign. Small. Classy. Emblazoned with the logo of an exclusive, international real estate firm.

For sale.

Why did the sidewalk feel like quicksand? If she moved, she'd sink lower…

Liam hadn't answered his buzzer when she'd pressed the unmarked button. Or the text she'd sent, the one *after* he'd told her he was on his way home.

Had he meant Desolation Cove? Was he on a plane to British Columbia?

Holy God. He'd left town without even telling her.

She made her way back to her dad's SUV, her return trip to Hollow Valley fueled by scorching fury.

She pulled into the dimly lit driveway, still seething…so much that she almost rear-ended the peridot green BMW parked in the shadow of the lilac bushes.

Her mind spun faster than the belts of the still-running engine.

Why was his car here? Had he left it here before going to the airport?

No. That made no sense. She turned off the engine and sat in silence for a moment.

He's here.

Her hand fumbled on the handle. Why was it so hard to open the car door? Only her dad's earlier encouragement propelled her out of her seat and around the side of the house.

And hope.

Fine. She was still hopeful.

Liam was *here.*

She found him two seconds later, sprawled in one of the pool chairs, staring at the turquoise-lit waters.

Two seconds after that, he was on his feet, striding toward her, his green eyes dark in the ambient light.

"Where did you go?" His voice was mildly panicked. "Your dad said you left the rink over an hour ago."

"Where did *you* go? You texted you were going home. And I went to your place, and you weren't there. But there was a sign there, Liam " Her nose burned, and she sucked in a teary breath. "For sale. Furnished. Are you going to sell the bed we made love in?"

He reeled back. "Katie, I—"

"And then I thought you'd gone *home* home. And you didn't text me back."

He dropped one of his hands to reach in his pocket, then held out his black-screened cell phone. "I drained most of it calling and emailing my agent and Realtor. My mom, too, to explain I'd changed my flight."

"And you didn't have a charger in your car?"

"Well, I might have used the rest of it up a half hour ago, sitting here watching that damn disallowed goal from last night, over and over."

"What happened to going home?"

"I *did*." He jammed his phone back in his pocket.

"Oh, you meant *my* home."

"Sure, but—"

"Whatever. It doesn't matter. You're here."

"And so are you." He kissed her, a few seconds of bliss. It slowed her chaotic thoughts, centering her before she broke away.

"No kissing me to distraction. I thought you were gone. Headed to your parents' without saying goodbye, without me getting to say what I needed to say."

His fingers trailed through her hair, his expression unfathomably tender. "And what did you need to say, superstar?"

"I want you to stay. Don't sell your condo."

He choked on what looked like thin air. "Katie—"

"Look," she cut in. "I know it's not possible for you to keep playing for the Daggers. You're going to take the best deal somewhere else. But if you had a place here still—" Jesus, this wasn't coming out right. She shook out her hands and took a breath. "We could make a home together. For at least *part* of the year. We've both lost too much not to know we won't grieve love again. But isn't it worth it to be by each other's sides *while* we grieve? Or to make sure we pack so much love into our home that when things shift or change, it'll have all been worth it?"

"Katie..." His voice was so low. *Loving.* Why did he have to sound all loving?

"I know, I know. Lining up my school and your career will be hard. But sometimes, people make unorthodox arrangements work. Especially since we don't have kids yet."

There he was, choking again. "Yet?"

She waved a hand. "Not the point."

"Or very much the point—"

She cut his disbelief off with a tiny kiss, a sweet brush as she rose on her toes and leaned close to his ear. "I love you."

His hands landed on her hips, gripping, holding her on her toes. *"Katie."*

"I do. I love you, Liam." He wasn't letting go, so she rested her cheek on his chest and looped her arms around him. The thin material of his polo shirt was a little chilly from the night air spilling off the mountains. She splayed her hands on his back. "Oh, my God, your trap muscles are unfair. Mmmph. The rest of the world will have to live without knowing how good this feels."

"Katie, are you punch-drunk?"

"A little. I went from being wildly pissed off at you to more relieved than I've ever been in my life, and it's left me in this weird space where it feels like anything can happen. And I want it to, Liam. I don't want to hold you back. And I don't want to give up what I've worked for. But I *do* want to be with you. When you go, I don't want this to end. We can get creative. Especially if you keep your condo and have somewhere to come back to in the summers—"

"Hey. My love. Take a breath."

He released his grip on her hips, and she lowered onto her heels. It put her right in line with his serious, shaken gaze.

"Liam?"

"I didn't know you wanted all that."

She nodded. "I'm sorry I didn't have enough courage to tell you earlier. And it'll depend on where you sign—"

"About my contract—"

"It doesn't matter. Wherever it is, we'll figure it out. If you're in Denver for the offseason, we can manage. And maybe you'll sign somewhere in the Western Conference and will play here enough."

He stroked her cheek, exasperation crossing his face. "Hey. What happened to taking a breath?"

"My mind's going too fast."

"Let's slow it down a bit, yeah? Starting with something important." A breath shuddered from his chest. "I'm not taking my condo off the market. I don't want to live in Denver."

Chapter Twenty-Seven

Liam finally managed to get a full sentence in edgewise. The one he thought she'd want to hear. *I don't want to live in Denver.*

So why did Kate look like he'd cracked a panel of plexiglass over her head? Those precious honey eyes reddened and her throat bobbed. He reached for her, but she held up a hand.

No, then.

Confusion swirled behind his sternum. Didn't she *want* him closer? Wasn't it better for him to be in Hollow Valley?

"I thought you'd be happy…"

"By the definitive proof that you're leaving?" Her arms were tight around her chest, like she was trying not to cave in on herself. "I just told you I *love you*, for God's sake."

He tilted her chin up with a finger and connected with her wet gaze. "Kate. Love. I'm not leaving. I'm not planning to buy something out of state. I want to live *here*."

She glanced from the main house to her current pad. "At my dad's?"

He guffawed. "Not unless you really want me to. I meant a home of my own in Hollow Valley. Ideally, in the near future, of *our* own."

"Ours." A brilliant smile lit her face.

"Yeah." He closed the space separating them. "You and me. Another thing I didn't get the chance to get out—I love you, too."

"You…you were so scared, though."

"I still am," he admitted. "But with you, I can put it aside. Katie, you ground my existence. You're my home now, and no matter what life throws my way, so long as you're by my side, I'll be unshakable."

Cradling her cheeks with his hands, he pressed his lips to hers, a kiss laden with relief and promise.

When he broke the kiss, her eyes were glassy in the ambient

light of the pool. Yup, every damn day he was blessed to have with her, he'd spend some of his time kissing the sense out of Kate Sullivan.

One of her hands splayed on his chest. "Why did you change your flight? Aren't you going to visit your parents?"

"I will, but I'm going to wait a few weeks. I want to be here for you when Connor has his surgery. I can't imagine it will be easy, and everyone else in your family will be processing their own feelings. I want to make sure you have someone who can put you first. My mom thinks it's a good idea, if you're worried about her and my dad."

"*Oh.*" Her fingers tightened, catching his shirt. I didn't expect…"

"I know. I haven't given you a reason to fully count on me. And I'm going to change that. Walk with me," he said.

"Where?"

"I have something I want to show you."

He held out a hand, and she threaded her fingers through his.

He led her out to the street. His destination was three blocks away, about as far up the mountain as the street went. The hush over the street was almost reverential. Something about the last threads of dusk demanded silence. And he was okay with the quiet. He'd made more than one big decision today, and even though he was excited to recount the details, he didn't mind rolling them out slowly.

He pulled her to a stop when they got to an aggregate driveway. "Were you serious about liking this property?"

Her eyes darted from one side of the expansive structure to the other, the one she'd gushed over on their run a couple of weeks ago. He hadn't been able to get it out of his mind. Wood construction and palatial windows. Thickets of evergreens, purple-tipped catmint and lavender broke up the lawn. Hopefully, she'd find it perfect for turning it into a home. His favorite feature was the extra bedrooms, for whatever family they created down the way.

"I love this one. Especially if you'd be here in the offseason," she murmured. "And I could arrange my teaching schedule to have stretches of time where I could travel to you, too."

His heart was bursting. He wanted to make this woman happy every single moment of her life. For as long as she wanted to walk hand in hand, he was going to grab hold and not let go. But as much as he'd made the right decisions for *him* today, he wasn't going to barrel forward unilaterally when it came to anything concerning both of them.

"Only if you're good with having me as a neighbor," he said.

She spun, bracing her hands on her hips. "Hold on. *Neighbor?* You implied you wanted me *with you.* You said *ours. No* take backsies."

"I don't want to pressure you."

"I want every second I can get with you, Liam Caldwell. I want to wake up and see your unfairly pretty face staring back at me and be bowled over all over again."

He laughed. "Let's tour this place together. Make sure we both like it before putting in an offer."

An eagerness crossed her face, but she bit her lip. "I need to contribute to it, too."

"Of course. We'll figure it out. I'm not going to make big decisions without you. Except, well, I made one—"

"Yeah, putting your condo on the market isn't *small.*"

"It's not about the condo," he said. "That's the smallest thing."

She ringed her arms around him. "I'm glad sharing *I love you* ranks higher."

"The highest." He kissed the crook of her neck—the sweet skin there was irresistible. "Me signing with the Daggers for what'll likely be the rest of my career doesn't hold a candle to you telling me you love me."

She stilled. "I—what now?"

"Oh, I think you heard me, superstar."

"I hope I did." Leaning back, she unwound her arms from

around him and pressed his cheeks between her palms. "Liam. You didn't. *How?* I was with my dad an hour and a half ago, and he didn't say a word. And the Daggers wouldn't have given you top dollar."

"I asked them to leave your dad out of negotiations. I wanted to tell you myself. And no, they couldn't offer me what I might have gotten elsewhere. But my contracts have been an excuse, Kate. So long as I was pretending it was about the money, I could always leave before I got attached to a place. Before I had to admit to myself how empty my life was before I had this. Before I had *you*."

One of her hands covered her open mouth.

"I want to belong to this team. In this town. And to each other. You're fast becoming the center of my world, Katie."

"Same," she whispered. "When I'm with you, I don't have to choose between everything I've built already and everything you and I will build. Or actually, I *do* choose. The life I've built *and* for you to be mine."

Rising on her toes, she pressed her lips to his.

He groaned and sank into her sweetness.

Warm with a hint of the chai she loved.

Plush and too delicious for words.

With one hand cupped under her ponytail and the other at her waist, keeping her from lowering her heels back to the concrete. He slowed his tongue, his lips, savoring the decadence of not having to rush.

They had a lifetime for this.

"Back where we started," he murmured. "Turns out, we were saved by a kiss."

* * * * *